Tennessee's
Coal Creek War

Another Fight for Freedom

By Chris Cawood

Magnolia Hill Press
Kingston, Tennessee

Photos from August 27, 1892, edition of *Harper's Weekly* and from souvenir booklet of Company C of Nashville, Tennessee, with credit to W. E. Singleton of Knoxville, Tennessee.

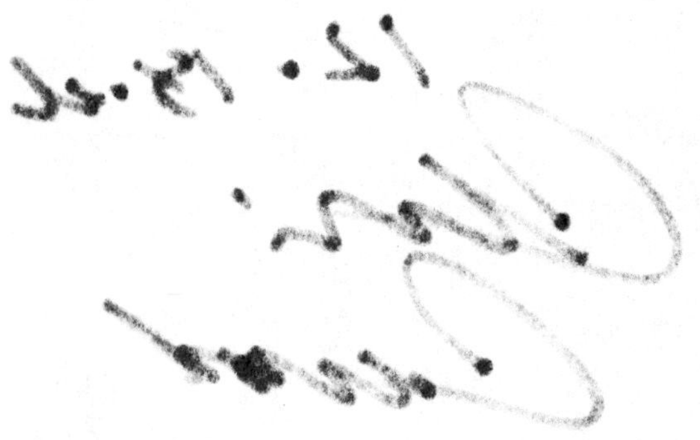

Cover design by Usha Rao, Oklahoma City, Oklahoma.

Printed in United States of America

Library of Congress Catalog Card Number: 95-76607

ISBN 0-9642231-0-4

5 4 3

Dedication

This book is dedicated to the miners of the 1890's, their hearty and talented wives and daughters, and to their kinspeople of this generation.

The sound of the miners' picks and shovels echoes through the ages into the ears of all those who seek freedom and justice.

April 1891

After the last snow had fled the slag piles but before the first iris or dogwood bloomed, the Boyds packed their wagon and turned their backs to Briceville. The winter of discontent melted into the spring of irony.

Bernice, the white sow, led the procession, followed by eight month-old piglets. Then Betsy Boyd's twin four-year-old sisters with their little sticks. They were in charge of keeping Bernice on the road headed toward Coal Creek from Briceville.

Betsy, at seventeen, was the oldest of the five Boyd children. She walked between her sisters and Nellie, the mule, who was pulling the wagon filled with all of the meager earthly possessions of the Boyds.

Pots rattled against the sides at every bump in the pock-marked road that was layered with coal dust and ash. The seven hens in wire cages cackled and fanned their wings with the back and forth sway. The wooden chairs, bedsteads, and dresser creaked as wood post rubbed against wood post.

Grandma Dolan sat in a chair in the rear of the wagon, teeth clinched against the chill, a blanket clutched about her. At eighty-five, she vowed this would be her last move—except to the graveyard.

Tethered to the rear of the wagon was the small cow with the prominent hip bones followed by her two-week-old calf.

Betsy's two brothers trailed behind, picking up anything that dropped off the wagon. They took turns batting pieces of slate rock with wooden stakes toward the creek the road followed.

Rain the night before had turned every hole in the road into a black, oily pit. The white sow approached a large one. The twins ran toward her, trying to guide her around. Bernice looked back and then stepped into the slime. Her hind feet slid beneath her, and she sat there, her backside covered with the filthy water.

"Get out, Bernice, you're gettin' dirty," little Belle Boyd yelled at the hog. The sow peered back over her shoulder, stepped out of the hole, shook herself, and lay down in the middle of the road just beyond the slime pit. The eight young pigs seized their chance and attacked their mother's belly, each finding a teat for its hungry mouth.

"Whoa, whoa!" Daniel Boyd spoke sternly to Nellie and pulled back on the reins. Nellie snorted and stopped. Daniel tied the reins down, pulled his hat lower on his head, and took a long draw on his pipe. His wife sat beside him at the front of the wagon. Betsy walked back to the side and looked up to her father as the other children gathered beside her.

"Can't you make her go on, Papa? We'll be late getting to Uncle Will's."

Daniel Boyd looked first at the sow and the feeding frenzy of the pigs then down at his daughter. "There's three things in life you can't speed up, Betsy: A man makin' whiskey, a woman birthin' a child, or a sow feedin' her young." He grinned and looked at his wife. She pulled her bonnet tighter around her head.

She leaned toward him. "You shouldn't be talking that way in front of your daughters. They hear enough rough talk around the other miners without hearing it out of their own father's mouth," she whispered to her husband.

"They're likely to hear sterner and coarser talk than that from the miners before the year's out. What with the Tennessee Mine locking us out, there's going to be a lot of mouths to feed and no man in the family working.

"We're lucky. We have a sow and pigs, seven hens, a cow and a calf. Brother Will's going to let us stay with him until we get a place of our own. We can make it through the winter."

"And, Papa, don't forget we have this," Betsy said and swung the leather pouch in front of her. "We still have the coal company's scrip."

"They're not worth a damn," he said and spat. "I told you to get shut of those. I don't want to hear the tinkling of those brass tokens again. They won't let us work the mine; they throw us out of our home—I'm sure as hell not spending their tokens at their store."

His wife nudged him with her elbow. "Please watch your language, Dear."

"It's gonna get bad, Sal. I just heard today they're expecting them to send convicts in to work the Tennessee Mine. There'll be trouble. Just mark my words." His wife shook her head.

When the young pigs were finished feeding, Daniel Boyd snapped the lines over the mule's back, and the procession renewed its journey toward Coal Creek and beyond to Will Boyd's. There the family would spend its spring and summer as farmers, preparing for the rough winter ahead.

Indeed, the Boyds were not alone on their trek. The closing of the Tennessee Mine at Briceville had left a hundred and twenty-five men without work. A hundred of those men and their families lived in company provided housing along Coal Creek. The houses weren't much. Just unpainted clapboard on rough wood framing, squatting out over the creek. One and two story buildings with two, three, and four families per dwelling.

Now, the Boyds, among the hundred families that were scattering in all directions, sought help from family to make it through the tough times. The animals would help. They had always kept the farm animals on a little lot next to their company house. It was Sally's and the children's project. Now it was paying off.

The tattered band of miners ahead and behind them included those who hauled all their goods in wheelbarrows or on their backs. Several had horses or mules. Most didn't. It was the price they paid for having become so dependent on the coal companies.

It had become a closed society and economy. The men worked ten and twelve hours per day for the company. The company paid them two and a half cents per bushel of coal mined—fifty cents per ton. In the winter, they bought the coal back for heating their hovels at the rate of six cents per bushel or two dollars a ton.

They were paid once a month in company scrip—brass tokens or paper certificates. Their rent for the company houses was taken out first and then any balance on their store accounts. Prices at the company store in Briceville or Coal Creek were up to twenty per cent higher than other stores. The token scrip was accepted at other non-company stores but discounted because of the trouble in redeeming it. A pair of shoes cost two dollars at the company store but just a dollar and a half at another store.

The miners had no choice. They had bitten into the system, and now it was biting back. They owned little except their work tools—picks and shovels—and the clothes on their backs.

The verdant hills of spring on the edge of the Cumberland Mountains of East Tennessee masked the honeycombed black seams of coal lying beneath and the mine tunnels that followed the minerals. Like moles they had brought the black mineral to the surface. The industrial revolution was being fueled with the coal of Tennessee, Kentucky, and West Virginia. And the coal was being mined by the wiry, hard-muscled men who knew no other occupation.

Twenty or more mines augered deeply into the mountains of the Briceville-Coal Creek area. They had quaint and hopeful names—Shamrock, Thistle, Rose, Empire, and Betterchance—but the story was the same everywhere. The miners had to accept the terms of the owners or they didn't work.

In December of the previous year, the miners at the Tennessee Mine had asked for two things that were guaranteed to them by state law. They wanted to be paid in real money instead of scrip. And to insure that they were being paid properly, they would hire one of their own men to be with the company man who weighed the coal, to serve as a "check weighman."

By law they were entitled to it. But the law was scoffed at

by the mining companies. They refused, saying the miners should have "implicit faith and trust" in the company to treat them right. The miners didn't have that amount of trust, so it had come to this. They were without jobs, homes, and food.

Eugene Merrill stood on the porch of his store in Briceville and looked out at the pitiful sight of the miners stringing out toward Coal Creek on their exodus from the company housing. Just up the dusty road, hammers banged, nailing boards across the doors of miners' homes to insure that no one sneaked back in.

Barefoot children chased their dogs back and forth across the road, not realizing their predicament. Mothers and fathers with bundles tied to their backs led their mules or sat forlornly in wagons.

Merrill sat down on the bench on the porch and joined two men who were beyond their mining years. They whittled on cedar sticks while he mulled. He felt responsible. He was the organizer. Knights of Labor and now the United Mine Workers—he belonged to both. It was the miners' only salvation as he saw it. Solidarity.

But now, second thoughts troubled him. Were the miners strong enough to withstand this lockout by the company? Could the miners hold out as long as the company could go without mining its coal? Convicts?

The dreaded word crossed his mind. Would they actually bring in convicts to work the Tennessee Mine? If they did it at the Tennessee Mine, it meant they could do it anywhere. Already they were working convicts in southeast Tennessee. But that was a good hundred miles away.

Then there was the Knoxville Iron coal mine at Coal Creek. They had worked convicts for the past fifteen years. The situation was tolerated but not condoned by the free miners. They wouldn't stand for a spread of that to the Tennessee Mine, would they?

"Reckon they's gonna be a heap of hungry and cold children this winter," one whittler said without looking up.

"Right smart number, it appears," the other one replied, again without raising his head.

Merrill had been a miner himself. He organized the other miners and was placed on the black list of all the mines in the area. It was the story of his life.

Born in October, 1849, in France, as Jean Rousseau, he had moved as a child with his mother and father to New Orleans. When his father died and his mother remarried, his step-father adopted him and renamed him Eugene Merrill. He was thankful for that. He wasn't sure how his French name would have gone over in the Tennessee mountain country.

From New Orleans, he had moved with his parents to Illinois, where he first worked in the coal fields. Always the organizer, he ran into trouble there and moved on to Tennessee to start a new job, a new life, and his old labor organizing occupation.

They could fire him from his coal miner's job, but they couldn't run him out of the county. He borrowed money and opened the store that competed with company stores. His was the only one where the miners could get full value for their scrip and still get good prices. Merrill didn't make much, but he got by.

Now, at forty-one, he was watching many of his good customers walking away in despair. Their livelihood was gone and so was part of his. If these hundred and twenty-five miners could be forced out of their jobs, there would be no security for the other thousand miners in the county.

Governor John P. Buchanan stood and poured himself his first shot of bourbon for the day. He looked at his watch. It was an hour until his noon appointment with Superintendent of Prisons E. P. Wade. He walked to the window of his office on the first floor of the Capitol Building in Nashville and looked out at the shanty-town of derelict buildings that ringed the hill.

There were only a few men and women ambling by. The legislature was not in session and it was early in the day. There was little business for the saloons and bawdy houses. During the legislative session, when the railroaders and industrialists were in town, the area would be alive with lights and music all night. Now it was quiet. He could stand some quiet.

Overseeing a state government that was just now recovering from the "War for Southern Independence," as he termed it, had grayed the hair and thickened the girth of the Confederate veteran. He had won a two-year term in 1890 on the strength of a farmers' and labor coalition. It was tenuous. He knew he could be a one-termer. He would fight on though, as General Nathan Bedford Forrest had taught him. He was in control. He took another drink. Yes, he was in control.

Superintendent Wade was announced, and he came in carrying a thick book. He shook the governor's hand, sat down, and opened the volume.

"It's the prisoner lessees, Governor. They have found another place to work a hundred or so of them."

"What is that to me?" Buchanan asked, and stroked his thick mustache.

"They want to put them in the mine at Briceville. To break the union—the miners who won't work because of the contract dispute."

"Do we work them in mines in other places?"

"Yes, nearly a thousand in all. But we haven't put any into Anderson County since those went into the Knoxville Iron mine in seventy-seven. They're mainly in southeast Tennessee. Inman and Tracy City."

"Did I carry Anderson County in the election?"

"Yes."

The governor stood and walked behind Wade. "What does the contract say? Are we obligated to let them go any place? I hate this system. Leasing out convicts. It's slavery, with us as the masters and the lessees as the overseers."

"The contract says anywhere in the state at any lawful occupation that they've been worked at before. We're making money off them. The system is more than paying for itself. It's sixteen hundred prisoners that we don't have to feed, clothe, house, and provide guards for. Without it, we would need a big tax increase."

"Oh. I love this system." The governor grinned. "If the miners ask, tell them I had no choice. We're bound by the contract. I was against it when I was in the legislature, but I have to uphold the law since I'm governor."

"All right, Governor. I'll give the go ahead to move convicts to Briceville."

"Wait, E.P. Stall them. Maybe the problem will go away. Time cures a lot of ills."

The superintendent left the office and the governor's secretary laid a letter on his desk for his review and signature. Buchanan looked it over and beamed. "This is good, Clare. This is the perfect wording to persuade Mrs. Davis to allow the great state of Tennessee to be honored as the final resting place for her husband, the late President of the Confederate States of America. Send it off to her immediately." The governor signed the letter with a great flourish.

The Boyd family made the seven-mile trek from Briceville to Uncle Will's near Coal Creek in less than a half day, despite their frequent stops to point Bernice and the pigs in the right direction. They had followed the narrow valley between Vowell Mountain and Walden Ridge to the Wye near Coal Creek where the railroad forked to service the mines on both sides of the mountain.

Across the railroad, they entered the little town of Coal Creek where curious storekeepers and residents lined the streets and eyed the rag-tag band of unemployed miners and their families with sympathy and concern.

The storeowners and shopkeepers depended on the miners' money. No one but the coal companies would make a profit if they brought in convicts. The convicts wouldn't buy anything or go anywhere outside of the stockade.

Business came to a stop as the sad parade made its way through town. Some turned toward Clinton to the south and others toward Careyville to the north.

The Boyds didn't have far to go. Will Boyd owned a hundred-acre farm just a little east of the town. Only half of it was tillable, running from one ridgetop to another. Will had a wife and three sons of his own. Now with Daniel and his brood, there would be thirteen mouths to feed, twenty-six feet to shoe, and thirteen bodies to bed down.

The men and boys were busy at it as soon as they unloaded the wagon. Will had already brought in a wagon load of rough lumber and slats from the sawmill. They would add a room or two onto the log house. Everybody would work and they would all get through. That was the plan.

Daniel allowed that Will was the smart one in the family. He had gone to farming while the other boys went to mining. One brother had already been killed in the mines when a piece of slate roofing fell on him. Another brother was mining in Illinois. Will had never set foot in a mine. He said he couldn't stand the dark, dank, close quarters. He had to be in the sunlight and open air.

The women busied themselves inside while the male Boyds carried beams and boards and began the building process. Sally and Betsy took the lead in arranging their wagon load of belongings around the two open rooms of the house. Will's wife, Ollie, was in the kitchen off one of the great rooms boiling potatoes and making cornbread on the coal stove. It was the only modern convenience that they owned. They didn't have to depend on the fireplaces for all their cooking.

Grandma Dolan sat in a rocking chair near the still-going fireplace and stared at the burning wood. Her hands made the motions of knitting a non-existent shawl.

Ollie came out of the kitchen and joined Sally and Betsy. "Come here, Betsy. I haven't got to take a close look at you since you got here. We've been so busy."

Betsy walked over and stood in front of her aunt.

"My, my, you are pretty, girl. How old are you?"

Betsy blushed and dropped her head. "Seventeen."

"Seventeen? Oh, my. I'd been married two years by the time I was seventeen. I'd already had Luther. You are pretty, child. Look at those blue eyes and that thick hair. It's nice the way you wear it pulled back. We're going to have to find you a man. The marrying kind. One that has a job or a big farm."

Sally flinched at the words—a job or a big farm. Was Ollie

telling her that Daniel was the wrong kind to have married? He didn't have either a job or a big farm.

"But you're too skinny. We're going to have to put some meat on those bones. Men don't like skinny women. They think they're sick. Can't hold up their end of the work."

Betsy backed up a step. "I don't want to get married, Aunt Ollie . . . not yet, anyway. I want to be a teacher. I want to go to college."

Ollie Boyd looked at Sally and then back at Betsy. "Go to college? There's no women's college around here. How much schooling have you had?"

Betsy smiled. "I've finished nine years. All that they had. I got perfect marks. I'm going to be something. I've heard that the state university at Knoxville might start taking women. I'm going to be one of the first."

Aunt Ollie shook her head. "You'll need more than that to get into a university. Nine years won't do it. And you'll need money too. It costs a lot to go to a college."

Grandma Dolan, still knitting with imaginary yarn and needles, spoke from her seat near the fireplace. "Leave her be, Ollie. Everyone should dream. Some come to pass. Some don't. But they never come true if you don't dream 'em first.

"For a hundred years, all us Cotters have been able to read and write. Men and women. We're all Methodists too. When I was ten, my grandmother told me about Bishop Asbury spending three nights at our house a long time before. That's when reading and writing took hold in the Cotter family.

"Now, the Dolans, that's another story. My husband, bless his departed soul, never cared anything about reading and writing. I married him. He had a job and a farm, but I had to account for all the figuring and reading.

"Leave Betsy be. There's plenty of time for marrying. 'Marry in haste, repent at leisure.' I think Ben Franklin said that. You have to begin your learning and get most of it whilst you're young. Marriage and children will sap the energy out of you."

Ollie sat down. "Yes, you have to dream. But I find myself working more than dreaming. There's hardly time for anything else."

She was silent for a minute. They all were. "Except quilting. They're having a quilting down at the Drummonds tomorrow. Jake Drummond is turning twenty-one and his mother is inviting us all down to do a quilt for Jake. There'll be some cider and maybe even a cake.

"Betsy, you need to go. Jake Drummond is a handsome young man . . . and he can read and write too."

Grandma Dolan nodded. "You'd better go, Betsy. There's not many educated men around here. Just because you ride the horse, don't mean you have to buy him."

"Do I have to take anything?" Betsy asked.

"Just a piece of cloth to make into part of the quilt. Maybe from an old dress," Ollie said.

Grandma Dolan looked over at her granddaughter. "Be careful where you cut it from." She patted her chest. "You could be giving him your heart, or . . ." she patted her lap, "something else."

That night Betsy took some shears and cut a piece of cloth from the back of a worn out burgundy dress.

Jake Drummond had mined coal since he turned seventeen. But now he hadn't worked since December when a roof fall had broken an ankle. He counted himself lucky though. Another miner had been killed in the same accident. He had labored at four different mines in his four years. Fraterville, Thistle, Shamrock, and Tennessee. It was at the Tennessee Mine that he last worked and was injured.

His father was killed in the mines ten years before. It was a familiar story in coal mining families. Fathers and brothers worked until they were killed or got too old. If they survived, they could look forward to sitting around, coughing and hacking their last years away, struggling for every breath. His brother, Richard, two years older than Jake, had mined for seven years. The closing of the Tennessee meant that neither of them had a job.

A quilting served as a backdrop for celebration, society, and industry. Church and quiltings were the places where young ladies and gentlemen were introduced properly. The younger and older women quilted while the young men would run about playing games and, with their boisterous talk and exaggerated movements, try to get the attention of the young ladies. Many a quilting had led to the introduction of a young lady to her future husband. The young man whose birthday it was would end up with the quilt made by the working together of the mothers, aunts, and young women who had cast an eye on him.

Sally, Ollie, and Betsy represented the Boyd household at the Drummond quilting for Jake.

Mrs. Drummond stood near the door and introduced every visitor to Jake as they came in. "Jake, you know Ollie Boyd. This is her niece, Betsy, and Betsy's mother, Sally Boyd."

Jake shook the hand of Sally and bowed slightly. Then he looked at Betsy and held out his hand.

Betsy held her hand out. She knew it was cold. She felt the blood retreat from it as soon as she had seen Jake Drummond.

He was not bent like the old miners and the way her own father looked. He stood erect—the tallest in the room. His dark hair swept back with a part in the middle. Clean shaven, his face was like carved ivory. His prominent cheek bones served as altars upon which lay piercing blue eyes.

She knew he was a miner. His skin was not tanned like a farmer or outdoorsman. He was like all the young miners in that way. She had seen the effects that the coal dust had on the older miners. Despite the daily washing, miners' skin exposure to years of coal dust eventually gave them a mottled complexion, raccoon eyes, and gaunt features.

Jake Drummond was young—not bent, blackened, or broken—yet. She knew it would only be a matter of time until he would be the same. The mines did it to them all.

When he took her hand, she felt the strength of a man who had gripped a pick and shovel in the mines but also the tenderness of one who could have set a fallen baby bluebird back into its nest.

"Betsy Boyd. Boyd? Did you have a brother, uncle, or father who worked at the Tennessee Mine?"

He still held her hand. Her tongue would not work. "My fa . . . fa . . . my father worked at the mine."

"Daniel?"

"Yes."

He still did not turn loose of her hand. He smiled. His teeth were even and white. "Daniel Boyd. Yes! He's funny. Always good for a joke. A laugh. He never told me he had a daughter like you."

She finally was able to withdraw her hand. "Like what?"

"Like you."

Jake's mother interrupted and led Betsy, her mother, and aunt to the middle of the room where the women had begun working at the quilt frame. Betsy looked back toward Jake Drummond. What had come over her? What had made an educated young woman sound like she couldn't speak more than five words? And tongue-tied at that.

Jake Drummond walked to the corner of the room where a cluster of young men stood talking and leaning against the wall. He took one by the shoulder and leaned toward his ear. "See that girl with the blue dress? Betsy Boyd. I'm going to marry her."

"What makes you think she'd have the likes of you?" the other youth said, and they all laughed.

Betsy took out the piece of cloth she had brought for the quilt and looked over her shoulder to Jake Drummond. "I wish I had listened to Grandma Dolan," she whispered to herself.

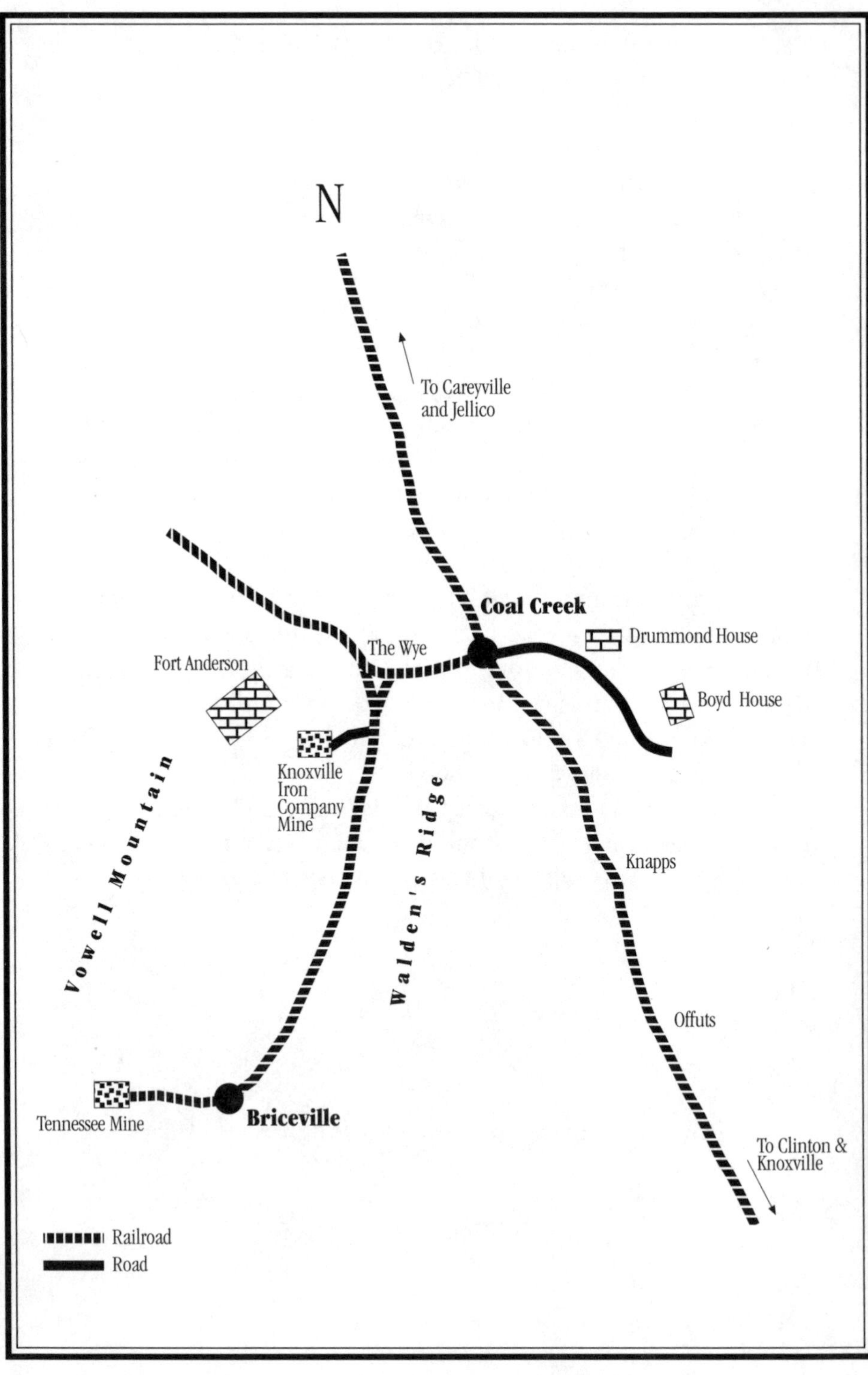
N
To Careyville
and Jellico
Coal Creek
Drummond House
The Wye
Fort Anderson
Boyd House
Knoxville
Iron
Company
Mine
Vowell Mountain
Walden's Ridge
Knapps
Offuts
Tennessee Mine
Briceville
To Clinton &
Knoxville
Railroad
Road

June

Jake Drummond loved horses. His older brother, Dick, swore that he must have been half Indian to ride bare back as well as he did.

Jake would grab Charmer, his big black mare, by the mane and swing his long legs over her back as she took to a gallop. No bridle, no saddle. Just him and Charmer racing off to town at Coal Creek or on through the valley to Briceville. It was the pure feeling of freedom that he loved. It was exactly the opposite of the confining prison of mining.

Lately, he had been riding more toward the Boyd's farm house near the Clinch River than in the direction of Coal Creek. Jake had also become a regular at the Coal Creek Methodist Church. He would find himself sitting on the same pew with Betsy, her mother, and twin sisters, Belle and Estelle. He had never been so religious in his life. Every Sunday for a month now, he had gone home with the Boyds for dinner after Sunday morning worship. He would ride Charmer while the Boyd women rode their wagon pulled by the faithful Nellie.

Today, though, he was on a different mission with Charmer. It was time to go back to work. He needed a job. He rode with a bridle in Charmer's mouth so that he could tie the reins to a hitching post when he was visiting the mines. He started at Coal Creek and worked his way to each mine on his way toward Briceville.

He stopped and inquired at four of them. He by-passed the Knoxville Iron Company mine. He wouldn't work in a mine that used convicts. Some free miners did. But neither Jake Drummond, his brother Dick, nor their deceased father had ever set foot on the grounds of the Knoxville Iron Company's mine.

He passed the mine superintendent's house. The Chumbley place was one of the best around. It had nine rooms and was painted a brilliant white—almost daring the coal dust to mar it. A stone wall set it off from the road, and a garden and orchard adorned the side and back yards. He nodded his head. The house was like a pearl sitting forlornly lost in a bowl of dried India ink.

The words were the same at each of the mines he visited. "We'd like to work you, Jake. But we're overloaded with miners. What with the Tennessee shutting down, there's an abundance of men wanting jobs. I hear there's work in Illinois."

He knew of men who had already left for Illinois, Kentucky, and West Virginia. He had considered doing the same himself back in April. But that was before Betsy Boyd. He'd find work here, now. Or he'd farm. He wasn't leaving these coal-filled mountains or Betsy.

He kicked his heels lightly into Charmer and spurred her on down the road. Just around the next curve was Briceville where a cluster of mines supported the store owners. The railroad ended just beyond Briceville near the Tennessee mine. If anything, Briceville, though smaller, was a bit rougher than Coal Creek. It was more isolated—blocked in by mountains on three sides. Hardly ever did a deputy sheriff from Clinton come as far as Briceville. It was too far and too hard to get there. The law in Briceville came down to who had the fastest gun or the biggest fist.

Liquor was not legal in Coal Creek. But in Briceville, unemployed miners made a living brewing corn liquor in stills that dotted the mountain sides. There was a house or two where brightly clothed women with painted lips and rouged cheeks would sit on the porches and wave at miners who had just been paid, inviting them into their parlors. They didn't take scrip.

Jake doffed his hat to a quartet of these women. He smiled, but he didn't stop. Eugene Merrill's store was just ahead.

In a back stock room, Eugene Merrill and a dozen miners sat on wooden nail kegs, facing each other and engaging in heated debate.

Merrill stood and gestured toward the lone window. "You can't give in to Mr. Jenkins and the Tennessee owners now. If you do, you might as well just sell them your souls. Because they'll own them just like they'll own your bodies and minds. We have to stand together."

The miners looked at each other. "Frenchy, that's easy for you to say. You own a store. We don't have jobs. We can get by this summer with the help of family. But come winter, there's going to be a heap of suffering," one of the miners said while the others nodded.

"Your credit's good at my store," Merrill said. "I'll just carry you on a tab until times get better. And they'll get better before winter. Mr. Jenkins is going to need his coal out of the Tennessee when the orders for winter start coming in. He can't leave it shut."

There was a knock on the door to the stock room. Merrill opened the door just enough to see who was on the other side. "Come on in, Jake. We've room for another miner."

Jake Drummond entered the room, took off his hat, and nodded his head at the other miners. Some acknowledged him and some didn't.

"Y'all know Jake Drummond, don't you? This poor boy and his brother are trying to support a widowed mother. This boy and boys like some of you have are what you're standing for. You want them to have it better, don't you? If we give in now, the owners know they can do it over and over again. The next generation of coal miners won't be any better off than we are."

Another of the miners looked Merrill in the eye. "Gene, we don't want your credit. We want to work and pay our way. And, sure, we want our sons to have it better than us. But if we can't feed them this winter, there won't be any future for any of us."

"Yeah, Gene, and what if Mr. Jenkins brings in them

convicts to mine the coal? What do we do then? I remember back in seventy-seven when they put them at the Knoxville Iron Company mine. We shot off a little powder, but they've been there for fifteen years," said another of the seated miners.

Merrill looked at Jake, the youngest miner in the room. "What do you say, Jake? What do you think we should do?"

Jake sat silent for a minute. He hadn't been at the mine at the final lockout. He was home nursing his broken ankle. He was angry at first. He wanted to take his father's revolver from the Civil War and hunt down some mine owners. Anger had given way to fear that he would have no job, and then to a determination that he would make it. He had a future. He thought of Betsy Boyd.

"We've got to stay firm. We can't let the owners see a crack in our resolve. I read some. I know some of you do too. You remember what they said before the Revolutionary War when they were signing the Declaration of Independence? 'We must all hang together, or we shall all hang separately.' That's how I feel. If they see they can do this at one mine, then they'll know that they can do it at all of them. This is not 1877, this is 1891. We can't let them get away with this."

Eugene Merrill smiled. He couldn't have said it better himself. He looked from eye to eye of the other miners who sat in silence and nodded his head approvingly.

Betsy Boyd clasped her hands behind her back as she continued to stand and wait for Mr. Harding to finish reading the letter she had handed him.

John Harding, the superintendent of Anderson County Schools, was a severe appearing man. Long, bushy sideburns cradled a jowly face that rested beneath a bald crown. He would smack his lips upon finishing each paragraph of the letter and let out a little, "Hurrumph."

Betsy had journeyed the eight miles to Clinton, the county seat, on Nellie in hopes of finding Mr. Harding. She needed a job, and she hoped the letter of recommendation from her teacher would be enough.

Her Aunt Ollie had insisted on her being "ladylike" and riding Nellie side-saddled from the Boyds' farm to Clinton. Out of sight of the house, Betsy had swung her legs around and straddled the old mule and dug her heels in. "Giddy-yup" she had bellowed. Nellie's best "giddy-up" was a fast walk that jostled the bones of the rider.

Mr. Harding took his glasses off and looked up at Betsy who was still standing at the front of his desk. "This is very good, Miss Boyd. Mr. Burroughs says you were his best student. Matter of fact, that you were his brightest one in twenty years of teaching. How old are you?"

Betsy tried to look her oldest. She had tied her long hair up into a bun on the top of her head. She stood erect and answered. "Eighteen, sir. Or at least I will be when the school term starts in October."

"Do you have transportation?"

Betsy thought of Nellie and hoped her father and mother would let her use the mule. "Yes, sir."

"Hurrumph." He opened a ledger book and looked at some numbers. "Miss Boyd, you need a high school diploma if you want to be a permanent teacher. Can you come to Clinton and do that?"

"Sir, I need the temporary job worse than I need my diploma right now. My father's a miner and is out of work. I have two sisters, two brothers, and a grandmother, besides my father and mother. I need to do something to help. I couldn't afford to come to Clinton and board and go to school this year."

"Hurrumph. Twenty dollars a month. Five months. October through February. You'll teach the lower four grades. Mr. Burroughs will teach the upper five."

Betsy's heart began to pound. She had a job. She would actually get paid to teach boys and girls to read and write and to use numbers. She could help her family. Her nine years of schooling had already paid off.

"Oh, thank you, Mr. Harding. Thank you. Thank you. You won't be sorry you hired Betsy Boyd. I can assure you of that." She continued on and on. All the while Mr. Harding was busy writing on a piece of paper which he put with the letter from Mr. Burroughs and sealed in another envelope.

"Miss Boyd, I ask you to do one thing. I want you to take this envelope and carry it to a Professor Brimer at the university in Knoxville. Mr. Burroughs said you were a talented student. I believe him to be correct. You need to further your education and live up to the talent that God has given you. Take this to Professor Brimer. He may be able to assist you in preparing for college. He's a friend of mine."

Betsy took the envelope from Mr. Harding's grasp, but her smile quickly turned somber. "I can't go to Knoxville, Mr. Harding. I don't have that kind of transportation. I live near Coal Creek. It's over thirty miles."

Mr. Harding stood. "Ride the train, my dear."

Betsy looked at the floor. "I don't have the fare."

Mr. Harding reached into his pocket and took out a silver dollar. "Here, Miss Boyd. This is my investment in education."

Betsy hesitated. "I can't take that as a gift, Mr. Harding. I'll only take it if you'll let me pay you back out of my first earnings."

Mr. Harding smiled. "It's a deal. But you must see Professor Brimer within the week."

At the Palace Hotel dining room in Knoxville there was a meeting of men wearing suits and smoking cigars. The Palace took up a half block at the corner of Reservoir and State streets. It was the newest hotel. Electric lights, a telephone, an elevator, and steam baths attracted elite travelers who would pay three dollars a night for the best suite.

The meeting this group of men was having concerned the Tennessee Mine and the miners. E. P. Wade, the superintendent of prisons, sat beside B. A. Jenkins, superintendent of the Tennessee Mine. On the other side was John Morrow of the Tennessee Coal, Iron, and Railroad Company.

Wade represented the state which had the convicts. Morrow

was the general lessee of the convicts and had placed them in Inman, Tracy City, Oliver Springs, and at the Knoxville Iron Company coal mine in Coal Creek. Now, Jenkins and his co-horts at the Tennessee Mine wanted approval to work convicts at Briceville.

"What did the governor say?" Morrow asked the prison superintendent.

Wade shrugged his shoulders. "He doesn't like it, but you have the right to work them anyplace you choose."

Morrow turned to Jenkins and his companions. "How many do you want?"

"Forty will do to start. We'll have to train them and build a stockade. The miners might see the light and come back to work. If not, we'll need another hundred."

The three shook hands. The waiter brought dessert. Strawberries and cream over white cake.

Governor John P. Buchanan

June 30, 1891

Betsy left early for the train depot at Coal Creek on Tuesday, the last day of June. The two mile walk took nearly a half hour. The train was on time and the ride to Knoxville took another hour. She had studied her little map that Mr. Harding had given her showing the location of the university in Knoxville in relation to the train depot. She would have to walk another two miles.

But to Betsy Boyd, the walks were like strolls in the meadow. She had a job promised by Mr. Harding and an opportunity to talk with Professor Brimer at the university. She carried the envelope with Mr. Burroughs' recommendation and the note that Mr. Harding had written. It was almost more than she could do to keep from tearing it open and reading what he had written. What was he telling Professor Brimer about her? And why?

Although she had traveled to Knoxville with her mother at least once a year, she had never been down Cumberland Avenue to the university. There were several buildings. Mostly, they were clustered around the top of a hill.

She asked and was told that Professor Brimer had an office in the basement of the science building. When she arrived, the door was open, but another lady was talking with the man inside.

Betsy was not sure this was Professor Brimer. She expected someone about the same age as Mr. Harding. This man was younger, probably thirty at the most. He was rather short for a man, no taller than Betsy herself. He had a mustache and short sideburns. His suit coat was off, but he still wore a vest over a brightly starched white shirt. But she noticed most that there was laughter in his voice.

The older lady came through the doorway holding several file folders and smiling. She nodded at Betsy.

Betsy knocked lightly on the door facing.

"Come in."

Betsy stepped through to where the gentleman stood behind a table stacked with pile after pile of papers. "Are you Professor Brimer?"

"Robert Brimer. And who might you be?" he asked while still shuffling papers from one pile to the other. His glance conveyed the smile that was in his voice.

"Betsy Boyd from Coal Creek. Mr. Harding in Clinton asked me to come see you and give you this," she said and held the envelope toward the professor.

He came around the table and took the envelope. "Please, sit down." He offered her a chair and went behind his own desk which was as cluttered as the table. He tore the envelope open, read Mr. Burroughs' letter, and then the one from Mr. Harding. He smiled broadly. "Henry is a character."

"Henry?"

He looked up. "Mr. Harding. We've been friends for years. He's a man ahead of his times. He says the same about me."

He leaned back in his chair, put his hands behind his head, and surveyed Betsy Boyd for a full minute. Betsy fidgeted and looked again at the cluttered room.

"I'm a history professor, Miss Boyd. I'm also a lawyer. All this clutter is a project I'm putting together on President Andrew Johnson."

"History?" Betsy asked. "Why are you in the basement of the science building?"

He stood up and smiled at Betsy. "You are very observant, Miss Boyd. I am here because I am an irritation to the administration. I am a burr under their saddles." He picked up the letter from Henry Harding and shook it lightly. "Henry knows that. I'm pushing for the enrollment of women at the university on a full time and equal basis as men. Henry thinks you should be that first woman. He says you need a high school diploma but that you are very bright and seem to have initiative." He paused and looked back at Betsy. "Do you have initiative, Miss Boyd?"

Betsy thought for a moment. She couldn't remember hearing the word spoken before in her presence. She didn't want to act uneducated. He seemed to be using it in a positive manner. He combined it with "bright" so it must be a good word. "Yes, Professor Brimer. I have initiative or I wouldn't be here."

He nodded his head. "I'd say so."

He showed her to a table in the corner where a large black machine sat. "You know what that is, Miss Boyd?"

This time she knew she couldn't fake it. She laid her hands on the cold metal and looked at the flat pieces that were just big enough for her fingertips. They sat on levers which moved with a bit of pressure. She noticed that the flattened surfaces had letters of the alphabet printed on them. "No. I don't have one of these at home."

Professor Brimer laughed. "Neither do I, Miss Boyd. It's a typewriter. You press the buttons and it prints letters on a sheet of paper. Sit down and try it." He placed paper in the machine and rolled it up. "See, each key—they call those levers with the finger places *keys*—has a letter of the alphabet, a numeral, or a punctuation mark printed on it. When you push it down with a finger, the lever forces another piece of metal up that strikes the paper. With the help of an inked ribbon, it imprints that letter on the paper. Try it."

"I don't want to waste the paper, Professor Brimer."

"Don't worry. I have plenty of paper. Make your name."

Betsy looked at the row of keys, found the one with the B, and pushed it with her index finger. It barely moved.

"Don't be afraid of breaking it, Miss Boyd. Push it with more force."

She did. Then she found each of the other letters in her name and pushed the keys for them. When she had pressed all five, she looked at the paper and smiled. "It has my name,

Professor Brimer. But the *b* is lower case. It should be an upper case."

Professor Brimer pointed to another lever. "If you hold this and press the key, it makes the letter print upper case." He leaned over her and pressed the *B* while holding the lever. "See that?"

Betsy's smile widened. "It's like magic. How does it do that?"

Professor Brimer pulled one of the metal key strikes up. "See, each of the ends of these levers has both the upper case of the letter and the lower case. The other lever I pushed adjusted the point at which the lever strikes the paper. That's what makes it upper case or lower case. It's not magic, but it's pretty ingenious."

He reached over and took a book from beside the typewriter. "This is a manual that tells all about how to work the typewriter. Do you think you could learn to use it?"

Betsy looked at the machine and then at the book. She knew there must be at least fifty keys and levers on the machine. There was a roller and a ribbon. She was good at tying bows and other rope knots, but she had never used any kind of equipment like the typewriter.

"Has anyone else around here learned to use it?"

"Yes, there're a couple of ladies upstairs who use the same kind of machine."

Betsy looked back at the machine and then opened the book. "If they learned to use it, then I can too," she said and looked straight into Professor Brimer's eyes.

"Good. I need all of these papers that I have written placed in type with this machine."

Betsy looked at all the stacks of papers on the table and on Professor Brimer's desk. She felt her stomach roll and the palms of her hands break out with perspiration. "Today?" she asked.

Robert Brimer doubled over in laughter while Betsy sat looking first at the big metal typewriter and then at Professor Brimer. Finally, he straightened back up and swept his hand through his hair. "No, Miss Boyd. Not today. But I would like you to make a good dent in them between now and the time you start teaching in October."

Betsy lowered her head. Then she looked up. "I would like to help you, Professor Brimer. But I have no way of coming over here. My family has no money. My father is a miner—one of those they won't let work."

Professor Brimer walked to his desk. "Never mind the transportation. A friend of mine does legal work for the railroad. I'll get you a pass. And I'll pay you two dollars a day. You'll work three days a week—Monday, Wednesday, and Friday. How's that?"

Betsy was already figuring in her head. She would make nearly twenty-five dollars a month. She could help her family through the winter if she saved her dollars. She looked back at the machine—if she could learn to use the black monster.

"How will that help me get into the university? I don't mean to be ungrateful. But I want to go to college. How will this help me?"

Professor Brimer sat on the edge of his desk. "Just wait. I want you to start on Monday. I'll show you then what I have in mind for you about getting into the university. Is it a deal?"

He stood and held out his hand. Betsy rose from her chair and shook his hand. "A deal."

"I'll see you Monday as soon as you can get here from the train. Your pass will be waiting for you at the depot in Coal Creek on Monday morning.

"And by the way, Miss Boyd, don't pay a lot of attention to what other people here at the university say about me. They think I'm eccentric. Of course, I am. I'm going to get you into the university. Then my next project is to get women the right to vote."

Betsy put her hand to her mouth and shook her head. "You are amusing, Professor Brimer. Women voting? May I live so long."

"I believe you shall, Miss Boyd."

Coal Creek Miners and Trapper Boy

July 5–6

Sunday, July fifth, found Betsy, her brothers, twin sisters, mother, and aunt in their regular pew at the Coal Creek Methodist Church. Jake Drummond sat on the same row to Betsy's right, but her brothers sat between them. She stole glances at Jake, and he at her.

The day before, Independence Day, they all had traveled to Briceville for a gathering with other miners' families, a picnic, and speech making. The hundred and fifteenth anniversary of the signing of the Declaration of Independence was remembered, despite the miners' present lack of ability to attempt "the pursuit of happiness."

The final festivity of the evening for most of the crowd was the anvil shooting contest. The contestants battled for the championship to see who could project an iron anvil into the air to the greatest height and with precision to where it would fall back to the ground nearest the point from which it was launched. All of this was accomplished with the blasting powder they had previously used in their mining pursuits. Since they had not used their powder for mining lately, the miners from the Tennessee Mine had ample supplies for the contest.

Jake's effort had placed him in the top ten, and Betsy's father came in second. While big cities had their fireworks, the mountain folk made do with what they had. Anvil shoots provided deafening noise with the fun of watching a mass of iron lift from the ground like a prehistoric bird which would crash back to earth because its wings could not bear the weight.

Late that afternoon Betsy and Jake had eased through the crowd and walked alone along the creek bank. For the first time, he had taken her hand into his. Neither had looked at the other when it occurred. It needed to be natural and it was. They found a large rock that protruded out over the water and sat there not saying anything while they watched the shallow stream flow toward the town. Then Betsy had brazenly taken off her shoes and put her feet into the cool water. Her dress slid up past her ankles. Jake stole a peek.

Those quiet, peaceful thoughts filled her this Sunday morning when the preacher began speaking. She looked down at her brothers and then at Jake. Their eyes met and she turned back to listen to the sermon.

Before the preacher had reached the halfway point in his remarks, a miner entered the door at the back and eased from man to man, whispering a message. By the time he reached Jake, ten men had, as quietly as possible, spoken hushed words to wives and children and then left the building. Betsy could see Jake's eyes narrow when the messenger leaned toward his ear. His lips pursed, and his brow wrinkled. The man left.

Jake leaned over to Betsy. "I've got to leave. They're bringing convicts in. They're at the depot."

Out of the miners' huts scattered throughout the hollows around the little town, men and women began streaming to the depot at Coal Creek. Word had spread quicker than the report of a Winchester rifle.

Jake ran the half mile from the church to the train tracks. A large crowd milled about the engine and three cars that stood motionless, waiting to be switched to the Briceville branch track. Steam hissed from a pop valve.

He walked along beside the two passenger cars and saw the

faces of convicts staring out the windows toward a scene they had never viewed before. Their eyes searched for the familiar but found none. They wore the striped garments of prisoners. There was little movement from the convicts as they awaited their destiny of mining coal at Briceville, held captive by the great, hissing iron monster.

The gathering of miners and townspeople clustered into little knots where they spoke in hushed tones except for an occasional outburst and gesturing toward the train. For the most part, the women's faces, framed in dark bonnets, reflected quiet acceptance of the hardship they believed would follow while their men talked and postured.

Jake saw Eugene Merrill, hat pulled low over his forehead, standing on the train platform engaged in lively conversation with a handful of men. Jake ran toward him.

"Mr. Merrill, Mr. Merrill. Are these convicts going to the Tennessee Mine?"

Merrill looked at Jake, then toward the train cars, and then back at Jake. He took his pipe from his mouth. "Yes, Jake. I'm afraid they are. It's the mine owners' Independence Day gift to us."

The train began its slow move onto the Briceville track. It chugged past the platform, stopped, and then backed onto the Briceville spur.

Many of the men and women—some walking, some on horse back, and some in wagons—began to follow along beside the train as it made its way west and through the gap in the mountains. Betsy's father, Daniel Boyd, and Jake's brother, Dick, were among the group walking. Jake held back when he saw Betsy sprinting toward him from the direction of the church.

She stepped up onto the platform and stared after the train. "Where's it going? Why are they following it?" She took his hand.

"There must be fifty convicts in those cars, Betsy. They're giving our jobs to the convicts."

Merrill jumped from the platform and began to chase after the hundred or so who were following the train. He turned and walked backwards, shouting at the ones still at the depot. "There'll be a meeting of miners and all of you who are interested in their well being at my store tonight."

As soon as the train with its cargo of convicts reached Briceville, the men were unloaded and marched toward the now boarded-up company houses previously occupied by the miners. With hammers and iron rods, a great noise was made that rolled over the low hills and along the dirt streets of Briceville like peals of a thundering dirge as the houses fell one by one.

The lumber was taken nearer the Tennessee Mine where a stockade began to spring up on cedar poles. The wood boards that once sheltered miners' families would once again help to house the new miners—the convicts.

Ten guards patrolled among the convicts with shotguns while mine foremen and two prison officials oversaw the building of the stockade. It was placed near the opening of the main shaft of the Tennessee Mine. Poles twenty feet high formed the perimeter of the trapezoid built like a frontier fort. When completed, it would be four hundred fifty feet long on the west side, four hundred eighteen on the east side, a hundred fifty on the south, and a hundred fifteen on the north.

The procession that had followed the train to Briceville from Coal Creek watched with eager but saddened eyes as the destruction and construction proceeded.

Merrill's store would not hold the gathering of miners that came to Briceville on Sunday night. Out of the shadow of the two-storied hulking building, they moved to a clearing near the railroad tracks at Thistle Switch. The cacophony of night insect songs was drowned out by the murmuring voices of despondent, yet defiant, miners.

Torches were lit. The men stood to hear Merrill who had organized many of them through the Knights of Labor. They knew his background. His friends could call him "Frenchy." He took great pride in his French heritage. His grandfather had fought with Napoleon.

Merrill was educated and could speak as fluently and

eloquently as most politicians and orators who traveled the country. He had listened to William Jennings Bryan postulate on free silver and the rights of the common man. He had read Jefferson, Whitman, and Thoreau. Also, he had dug coal in two states and breathed in the bituminous air that made him one of these people—the miners of Coal Creek and Briceville—and he could speak their language.

He stood in the back of a wagon. Shadows played across his strong-featured face from the flickering light of the torches.

"Gene, I counted forty of them convicts. But why're they buildin' such a big stockade for forty? Will there be more?" a distant voice shouted.

"What are we goin' to do? They're takin' our jobs. Them convicts ain't going to benefit no one but the owners," another voice cried out from the darkness.

Merrill held up his hands until a quiet enveloped them. Again, the song of crickets, cicadas, and frogs along the creek could be heard. "You're right. You are right. They're not building that stockade for forty convicts. There's more on the way."

A great rustle of voices filtered through the layers of men as each turned to his neighbor to utter his shock or to spit a curse at the mine owners. Someone near the wagon raised a pistol and shot toward the sky. The mule hitched to the wagon lurched at the sound but then was steadied. Quiet was restored.

"Go to your neighbor. Go to your store keeper. Go to your farmer friend. Tell them our plight! We need to stick together. If it's the Tennessee Mine this week, it could by the Shamrock next, or Fraterville, or the Thistle. Every miner's job is in jeopardy. We must have economic power and political power through numbers.

"Every person in this valley, every person in this county, every person in Tennessee has a stake in this. We can't buy the shopkeepers' goods if we have no money. We can't trade with the farmer if we have no jobs. We can't pay our poll tax with scrip.

"Go and tell them. We'll meet again on Thursday at Coal Creek. We need more than a hundred. We need the valley."

A miner near the wagon raised his shotgun. "I say we go kill us a few mine owners. I'm not for all this talkin' and meetin'. I'm for showing them we hain't forgot how to use these guns since the war." He pulled the trigger and sprayed buckshot overhead. A couple of other shots followed from the back of the crowd.

"No, no, absolutely not!" Merrill shouted. "This is not the time for guns and death. This is a time for solidarity and power of numbers—not bullets."

"That's right. Give us a chance to work this out peaceably," someone else in the crowd shouted.

Jake stood next to his brother. "I'm for shooting it out now," Dick Drummond said, and took his revolver from his belt. "Aren't you, Jake?"

"No, Dick. I don't want to kill somebody. Or be killed myself. I want to work so that I can ask Betsy to marry me."

Dick Drummond spat a stream of tobacco juice toward Jake's shoes. "That's all I've heard out of you for the last three months. That Betsy Boyd is going to turn you into a farmer. I should get you drunk and take you to one of these houses down here where the wild women are. You'd forget all about sweet Betsy after you got some of that."

Jake pushed past his brother and headed back up the road toward Coal Creek. He backed Merrill's idea, but he knew better than try to reason with his older brother after he had gotten liquored up.

A crowd still lingered around the depot at Coal Creek the next morning when Betsy made her way to the platform to catch the train to Knoxville. There was curiosity as to when more convicts would be arriving. Rumors abounded. They would be on the next train, someone said. Next week, according to others.

Now, more than ever, Betsy knew she needed the summer job that Professor Brimer had given her. She held a bag that contained two biscuits and a piece of ham, a carrot, and an early summer apple. That would be her meal while at work. She also carried the typewriter manual that she had studied over the past few days. It looked impossible. She hoped this would not be her first and last day at work.

"This is Jim Powell, Miss Boyd," Robert Brimer stated as soon as Betsy entered his office. "He's a co-conspirator in attempting to allow women into the university. He's also principal of Knoxville High School. You are now enrolled in Knoxville High School, Miss Boyd. In the tenth grade." Brimer smiled at Betsy and then at Jim Powell.

Powell handed Betsy three books. "You'll have to study on your own, Miss Boyd. I'll test you at the appropriate time. I'll come here once a week to help you with any difficulties. By the end of September, if you do well, you will have completed your tenth grade."

Betsy looked at the books, then at Mr. Powell. "I can't pay for these books, Mr. Powell. I have no money."

"Nonsense, Miss Boyd. This is my investment in our little project. Bob, here, and I are quite good schemers. You may be the first female scholar enrolled at the university if we have our way. Your hard study and good grades will be pay enough for Bob and me."

Tennessee State Capitol

Bastille Day

Mornings came early for Betsy Boyd. She had promised her father and mother that her share of the chores would still be done despite the fact she had taken the job with Professor Brimer.

There were two cows to milk, a breakfast for thirteen to cook, and assorted other duties every morning, and she took her turn. It was the only way she had persuaded her parents to allow her the three days a week to go to Knoxville.

Now, at the end of the first week of the month, she did one of the things she loved—the prickly job of picking blackberries before the sun rose. Dew still covered the grass and the wild vines that shielded one side of the stream a quarter mile from the house. The sun hung below the ridge distant in the east. Its appearance above the rim would be her signal to end picking, go to breakfast and then to the train depot.

Berry picking gave her quiet time for thinking while she carefully filled her two-gallon bucket with the ripe fruit. She loved dawns almost as much as sunsets. Everything was fresh. A new day was like a new creation—full of hope and promise.

Her spirits had not been dashed by the obdurate typewriter at Professor Brimer's office. In just a day, she began to feel that she could master the beast even though her production had been less than three pages of print that suffered from the lack of proper upper case letters and commas. She would be accomplished at a machine that no one in Coal Creek had even seen.

The books that Mr. Powell had given her had occupied her for the past two nights. She protected them from the other children and hazards of the house as though they were sprinkled with gold dust. They were her keys to a high school diploma and entry to the university. She had lain on her pallet in the loft with the coal oil lamp burning, reading the new pages, which to her were more precious than a catalogue of fine clothes and wares.

And Jake Drummond. She shook her head and smiled. A briar pierced her finger. She frowned and looked to see if there was blood. No blood, little harm. Jake. Jake. What would she do with the bold cowboy miner who would come galloping down the dusty road presently on Charmer, tie her to a post, and run into the kitchen to join Betsy and her family for breakfast?

He always brought something. A dozen eggs. Two pounds of bacon. A bag of sugar. Anything to show he was not a freeloader. He wanted to appear a man of substance in her eyes, she knew. Jake and her father would sit side by side at the table and tell mining stories. And laugh. And laugh.

He was like her father in that. Bad times had not dampened his spirit. Not yet. But this was summer. How would the winter be?

Grandma Dolan sat at her usual place before the fireplace when Betsy returned. Only smoldering wood coals burned slowly beneath a blanket of white ashes in the great stone opening where the winter's fire had flamed.

The Boyds were proud they had never allowed the fire to go completely out. It burned year around— either in hearty flames of fall and winter or in a smoldering reminder of late spring and summer. The fire was a hundred years old or better, they said. It had been carried from their grandfather's home in Virginia to their father's home in Kentucky. And now it rested cozily in the valley of East Tennessee near the Clinch River.

Betsy thought her aunt and uncle silly to keep such a tradition. How can a fire be a hundred years old? It's a burning up of fuel through a chemical reaction. Why keep it smoldering during the summer and waste precious wood? It was not the same fire of a hundred years before, was it? How could it be?

But then Grandma Dolan had told her to never mind—it was a good tradition, even though it was the Boyds'. "Fire is like life, child. It doesn't begin or end. It is just passed on through our bodies. We are the fuel for life like those wood chunks are the fuel for the fire. Some of us are aflame, and some just a smoldering."

Betsy looked at her grandmother whom she loved dearly. "And when the fuel is burned up?" she asked herself.

"Life is passed on, generation to generation. God takes care of the spirits," Grandma had replied one time.

Betsy believed that she already had inherited part of the frontier spirit of her grandmother—the independence, the toughness, the will. She could ride a horse as well as most men. She could beat anyone in most games of skill. She could say "No" to a man like Jake Drummond if she wanted to—or "Yes" if she dared.

"There's another meeting tonight," Jake said, in between mouthsful of biscuit and butter.

"Yep. It's brewing. The men don't want to wait for that stockade to get built before taking some action. Merrill will have a time holding them back once they get to thinking about it," Daniel Boyd said.

"He's recommending a committee of men be formed to make it more official. To give some leadership from throughout the coal mining area. There'll be someone on it from Coal Creek, Briceville, and over the mountain—someone from the Empire, Franklin, or Betterchance mines," Jake added.

"I smell trouble," Grandma Dolan said from her end of the table.

"What does trouble smell like?" Daniel asked and smiled.

"Like a polecat dead for a week under the house in a corner where you can't reach him," she said. "Pass the biscuits."

Everyone else began shuffling from the table while Grandma Dolan finished her biscuit. "Hope I didn't spoil your appetite, but that's the kind of trouble I'm smelling."

Meetings sprung up with the rapidity of summer mushrooms in a damp forest bed every day of the week. Rumor ran headlong into rumor. Guns were cleaned, Civil War muskets and revolvers taken down from hidden places, and torches made from rags, oil, and stakes in preparation for a confrontation all the miners believed to be inevitable.

The forty convicts were pressed hard to complete the stockade at Briceville. The shotgun-toting guards nodded at any stragglers and occasionally swung the leather strap in the air that could otherwise find the bare body of any convict who tried to escape or held back on his work ethic.

Eugene Merrill asked for help from the United Mine Workers. The union had an officer in Jellico—a black man by the name of William R. Riley—who had been successful in organizing. They would send him down as soon as they could get word to him.

Merrill thought on it. Some of the white miners still did not take well to black miners although there were over a hundred who regularly dug coal in Anderson County. It was time to put all that aside. White and black, miner and farmer, landlord and tenant—all had to stand together in this struggle against the greed of the owners.

Meeting after meeting, Merrill and the other leaders persuaded the hundreds of miners and followers to wait another day. Then July Fourteenth arrived. He was reminded by another committee member of his own heritage.

"Isn't this Bastille Day?" one of them asked him early that morning. "Don't you celebrate that like we do our July Fourth Independence Day, Frenchy?"

Yes. He looked at the calendar on his wall. This day was being celebrated as the hundredth anniversary of the storming of the Bastille—the hated prison where political malcontents were taken and declared crazy. Actually, Merrill knew it was the hundred and second anniversary of the event, but the French were always late in celebrating everything anyway.

"This would be a good day to take the stockade, Frenchy. We could strike a blow for our independence and freedom on one of your favorite days."

Merrill thought about it. They were bound to do it. He might as well see that it came off as peaceably as possible. The symbolism would be there, if the ones in power could see. They would free the convicts, temporarily, because they were pawns in the hands of the oppressors. The stockade was the Bastille. What it held was less significant than what it stood for—the worst of man's greed and control playing on the souls of the common man.

The meeting began in early afternoon on the Fourteenth in a grove a mile from Merrill's store. Three hundred miners, joined by another two hundred locals, along with a smattering of wives and children sat on blankets or stood to listen to the speakers. Pickets were posted around the area to insure there would be no company spies.

Betsy Boyd stood beside Jake Drummond. She would have to go to Knoxville the next day, but this Tuesday she was free to see for herself what the miners were planning. Her father had not forbidden her to come, but he had warned her that she would be exposed to some rough talk that was not fit for a lady's ears.

Merrill allowed everyone to have his say. A miner would come forward, wave his rifle in the air, say a sentence or two and then blend back into the crowd. It went on and on. The other committee men spoke. The alternatives were weighed. Bloodshed was possible if they stormed the stockade, but their livelihoods were threatened if they didn't. William Riley spoke on behalf of the UMW. He could not advocate breaking the law. He understood the local miners' position. They had the same problem in Kentucky and sent a delegation to the legislative session to redress the problem. He had known slavery first hand.

It became more and more heated. The miners turned toward the option of freeing the convicts. Fear was distant. Flasks of whiskey were passed around. Tempers flared.

"I'm tired of the mine owners. I'm tired of their demands. I'm tired of their stores. And I'm damn tired of working for their scrip," one miner shouted from the back of the wagon they were using as a speaker's platform. He turned his pockets inside out, retrieving a few brass scrip tokens. He threw them to the ground. "Throw all yours away too. We're not taking scrip anymore."

His example was met with a multitude who did the same thing. Scrip tokens rained onto the ground making a sparkling dust.

"That's silly," Betsy said to Jake. "Give me your kerchief. There's no sense in wasting perfectly good scrip. The company couldn't be happier than knowing that we weren't going to redeem tokens that were worked hard for." Unnoticed, she passed through the crowd, pausing to stoop and pick up the brass tokens as she went. By the time she returned to where Jake was standing, the kerchief bulged with her bounty of scrip.

When the sun began to set, Daniel Boyd found Betsy and told her to go home. He would be there shortly. And, if not, he would be there in the morning. Tell her mother not to worry. He looked at Jake. "You go with her. There's no telling what could happen here later."

He looked back at Betsy. "You take Nellie. I'll walk when it's time. Jake'll go with you."

Jake found his mare and Betsy her mule. Side by side they rode from Briceville down the snaking lane toward Coal Creek. They took their time, stopping to let Charmer and Nellie drink from the stream and to walk out into the cool water themselves with bare toes oozing into the mud and silt from the mountains.

By the time the two reached the Boyds' farm house, it was dark, the katydids were serenading them, and the moon, full in all its splendor, peeked a luminous eye above the ridge.

Jake tied Charmer to a post near the house and then led Nellie, with Betsy aboard, to the barn. Betsy alighted, took the reins from Jake, and put Nellie into her stall. She scooped a gallon of dried corn into the mule's trough and tossed over an armful of pungent clover flecked hay.

"That should do her until the morning," Betsy said and

nodded for Jake to follow her from the dark barn. She turned as soon as she closed the barn door and stared toward the east. "Isn't it beautiful, Jake? I can't think of a thing more beautiful than the rising full moon on a summer's night. Can you?"

He was standing directly behind her, looking over her hair, golden in the reflection of the moon. He thought of something just as beautiful as the moon, if not more so. He was as near as he could be to her without touching. He could almost feel the heat of Betsy's body.

She turned. "Are you listening? Did you ever see anything so beautiful?"

"Yes." He looked down into her eyes, and before she could make any movement to resist or to give in, he put his arms around her, pulled her to him, and kissed her flush on the lips. He lingered there a second while flashes of lightning bolted through his head. He felt her hands push against him as though to shed an unwanted intruder. Then he felt her hands drop to her side and then rise to his back. His hat fell off, making a soft thud when it struck the ground, which brought Jake back to his senses.

He turned loose and stepped back. Betsy put her arms behind her back and looked toward the ground without saying a word.

"I'm sorry, Betsy. I didn't mean to be so forward. When you were talking about the beauty of the moon, I just thought how pretty you looked standing there. I couldn't help it."

She looked up and into Jake's eyes. "I suppose," she said softly. A smile began to play across her lips. "We'd better go on back to the house. They'll be wondering about us." She reached out and took his hand. They walked slowly toward the dimly lit farm house, casting glances back toward the moon that was now full above the rim of the ridge.

"I've got to go back to the meeting. I don't know what they're going to do, but I have to be there. I'm not a shirker. I'll do my part."

"Be careful, Jake. And watch after Pa." She tiptoed up and kissed him on the cheek.

Charmer transported Jake back down the road to Coal Creek

and on toward Briceville at a fast trot while Jake's mind and spirit lingered on the thought of Betsy's kiss. She really cared about him. She had kissed him on the cheek when he left and told him to be careful. Of course, a sister would have done that for any brother. But there was no sister in their first kiss. He longed for this mine trouble to be over so he would have a steady job—a job that would support the likes of Betsy Boyd.

Around a curve near Briceville, Jake pulled Charmer to the left, waded her through the creek, and once again entered the grove where the miners were more restless than ever. The moon, its silver surface shining above, looked down on faces darkened by the shadows of hats pulled low on the brow with the orange flames of torches highlighting only the more prominent features.

The miners sat in small groups, squatting as they had done for so many years in the mines that it was now the most natural way in the world to sit. The small orange dots of lit cigarettes and pipes appeared in the night like lightning bugs stuck to the noses of men searching the ground for answers.

Eugene Merrill and the other men of the committee were making their way around to each little huddled group, whispering the same questions and for the most part getting the same answers.

It was time to move. They would be in control and under control. A show of force. But no violence. Three hundred strong they would walk to the stockade and demand the release of the convicts. The women had already departed. This was dirty business. It could be a deadly business if the guards decided to resist.

It would be foolish for them to attempt to defy the will of so many. Five or ten or even twenty guards would be no match for the miners. They were armed—some with Winchester rifles, some with Colt revolvers, some with shotguns, and some, like Jake, with just the force of their presence. He would be a torch carrier. He hated guns.

Then Jake saw his brother, Dick. He had the revolver that their father had used at Gettysburg. Jake spat. Dick had better not disgrace the Drummond name by doing something stupid.

"Are you ready to go, Jake?" Merrill asked him, stopping in his rounds to the nameless men. "We're going to storm the Bastille and strike a blow for democracy—for the common man." Merrill gave Jake's shoulder a squeeze and passed on.

The huddled groups began to stand and come together in ranks. The leaders lined them up five abreast, making sure that all the ones with guns were in front.

Torches, cigarettes, and pipes were extinguished. They would walk the mile to the stockade at the Tennessee Mine by moonlight, silent and ghostly. The taking of the stockade and release of the convicts would be done by stealth and surprise. They crossed the creek and trod down the dirt road with muted footfalls, resolute in their goal.

Merrill, D. B. Monroe, Matthew Ingraham, George Irish, and Josiah Thomas led the procession. They would be the spokesmen. All were mature, not hot-headed, and knew the stakes. Daniel Boyd kept his hand on his revolver two rows ahead of Jake Drummond. Jake saw his brother several rows ahead holding his pistol to his side.

Cool air funneled down the mountains, making the otherwise hot July night bearable but making Jake feel eerily haunted by fears of confrontation. What if the guards started to shoot? In the darkness what would happen? What would he do? He had no gun. Would he run or cower away like a whipped pup? He remembered his father speaking of the battles in the Civil War when boys years younger than Jake was now became either men or cowards when the first volleys of musketry began.

Jake walked on, concentrating on the back of the head of the miner in front of him. The torch stake he was holding began to slip through his clammy hand. He changed hands on the torch and wiped the damp hand over his face. He was alone with his fear. All the other men did not feel the rolling of their stomachs, the pounding of their hearts, and the pulsating pain in their temples that he felt.

The stockade was incomplete, being only a conglomeration of huts for the convicts and guards and a beginning of a palisade of cedar poles. The eight guards were spread out, six of them already asleep and two on sentry duty when the snaking column of miners first appeared around the bend in the road. The two guards nodded at each other and then pointed toward the parade coming toward them. One ran to the other guards' house and then to the warden's. The lone guard laid down his shotgun and hugged one of the cedar poles when the full import of what he was facing caught up with him.

The warden, pulling on a pair of pants, lurched from his door at the same time as the remaining guards came out of their quarters with shotguns raised toward the sky.

Merrill gave the signal. The marching ranks stopped in place. A hundred torches were lit and another hundred miners' lamps began to glow. The sudden light was almost blinding to the warden, who shielded his eyes with his hand and walked toward the miners. He motioned for the guards to stay behind him.

"What do you want?" he asked. The warden's eyes had adjusted now to where he could see the barrels and wood stocks of innumerable guns. None at the present was pointed toward him.

Merrill and D. B. Monroe stepped forward. "I believe you know, sir. We have come to free the souls of man. A man only has his labor. These men are forbidden to work. They are free men. Yet, you have brought in these convicts to take the bread out of the mouths of these men's children. We have come to remove these stripes, sir," Merrill said. He turned toward the miners and held his right hand into the air. At that, all the miners with guns thrust them upward.

"We shall do it peaceably, sir," Monroe said, "if possible. But we shall surely do it."

The warden turned toward the buildings and then back to Monroe and Merrill. "Give me a minute. I need to tell Mr. Goodwin. He's asleep."

"Certainly," Merrill said. "It would be a good time for him to arise from his slumber."

John Goodwin was the agent for the leasing company that supplied the convicts to the Tennessee Mining Company. His company was the Tennessee Coal, Iron, and Railroad Company which had nearly a thousand convicts leased from the state. He and B. A. Jenkins, the mine superintendent, both were aroused from their sleep and made their way to the meeting. Their eyes widened when they saw the number of miners, silent and in ranks as though for a war engagement.

Merrill, Monroe, and George Irish agreed to talk with the warden, Goodwin, and Jenkins inside the house where Goodwin and Jenkins had been.

"This is all unlawful, Merrill. These convicts are here through the legal authority of the State of Tennessee. If you release these felons, you and each of you will be guilty of a felony yourself," Goodwin said and slammed his fist onto the table.

D. B. Monroe looked at Merrill and Irish and then back to Goodwin. "I guess if we're guilty of a felony and convicted, we can put on that striped clothing and mine coal here." No one laughed.

"We're not going to allow you to take over the valley with convict labor. We have too many children and wives to let them starve," Merrill said.

"All you had to do was sign the contract and you could have worked. You didn't, and we have to get the coal out of the mountain some way. So we're using convict labor. It's legal," Jenkins said.

"We didn't sign the contract because it took away rights given to us by law—we have the right to have a check weighman and the right to be paid in U. S. currency and not scrip," Irish said. "We have an army of miners out there that we can barely restrain from burning down the whole operation here. You'd best give up the convicts without a commotion."

The talk went on for another half hour. The miners' spokesmen did not give in. They agreed not to destroy the stockade or any mine equipment if the convicts were turned over peaceably. They also agreed to march them to Coal Creek where they would put them on a train for Knoxville. The guards, Jenkins, and Goodwin could accompany them. In that manner, they would not be aiding the escape of felons, but only relocating them.

The deal was struck. Within an hour, all the convicts were

taken from their small-roomed huts and lined up for a march to Coal Creek. They would not be mining coal on July Fifteenth.

The miners divided into two segments, putting the convicts, guards, Mr. Jenkins, Mr. Goodwin, and the warden in the middle. At four in the morning, they began the march to Coal Creek. With the miners' lamps and torches burning, both ahead and behind the group of convicts, the strangely lit procession walked in steady steps toward the depot. Only the sound of their steps and the rustling of their clothes intruded on the sounds of the night. In the distance a dog howled.

As they neared the Wye where the gap in the mountain allows passage to Coal Creek, the guards at the Knoxville Iron Company Mine looked on in amazement at the motley group passing before them. The stripes of the convicts' clothing were evident. The Knoxville Iron Company held over a hundred and thirty convicts behind its palisaded stockade walls. They had worked there since 1877.

"We're comin' afta your'n next!" one of the miners yelled toward the stockade. There were shouts of agreement. A roar went up from the ranks to take the stockade of this mine also. It should no longer be tolerated. Make a clean sweep of the valley.

Merrill, Monroe, Irish, and the other leaders finally quieted the hostile yelling and persuaded the miners to go only with the convicts from the Tennessee Mine. They wanted to make a point. And it could be made with this group alone. If the authorities didn't see their point or respond to it properly, there would always be time for the Knoxville Iron Company's mine. One Bastille was enough for this night.

Back in the ranks, Jake Drummond was happy that the leaders had prevailed. He'd had enough excitement for one night. He had not run nor asked out. He was proud to be where he was but didn't want to be a party to bloodshed. Now the authorities would listen. They would remove this blight from the county and let the miners dig the coal as they had for many years. That's all he wanted—steady work and a chance to pursue Betsy Boyd.

The sky to the east began to brighten, rippling clouds of gold like a gilded washboard told of the near sunrise. The torches were put out along with the lamps. The ranks became uneven the closer the miners came to Coal Creek. Women stared from porches and windows of the settlement, watching for their men and glad to see that all was peaceful.

Word spread rapidly. By the time the band of nearly four hundred reached the railroad tracks across from the depot, another crowd of children, old men, and women met them. A cheer went up. Wives ran to meet their husbands. Children were shooed away from the convicts and the guns. Stray dogs ran about, scurrying from one clump of men to another.

Within an hour, a boxcar was readied to haul the group of convicts to Knoxville. It would be attached to the morning train. Once the felons were locked in, the guards, Mr. Goodwin, and Mr. Jenkins would board a passenger coach and accompany them.

Goodwin and Jenkins went to the telegraph in the depot and tried to get a message to E. P. Wade, the state superintendent of prisons, who was in Knoxville. They had no alternative but to go to Knoxville.

In Clinton, Anderson County's seat of government, Sheriff Rufus Rutherford was at his livery stable when a deputy ran to him with the word that the miners had freed the convicts at Briceville.

"Are they running loose?" he asked.

"No, sir. They're at the Coal Creek depot ready to be put on a train to Knoxville."

"Just as well. Let the Knox County sheriff deal with it. I don't have enough deputies to do anything."

"Yes sir."

"Oh. Go and tell the train master at the depot to let the train go straight through without stopping here. I want to get shut of that problem," the sheriff said and went back to harnessing a horse.

When Betsy Boyd neared the depot to catch her train for Wednesday's trip to Knoxville and her job with Professor Brimer at the university, she didn't know whether there had been a train wreck or what great disaster had overtaken the village. The entire population of nearly a thousand must have been standing around the depot. She knew her father and Jake Drummond had not returned from the meeting the past night. For the first time in a month, Jake was not there for breakfast.

Jake saw her before she saw him. He left the ranks of miners and ran to the depot platform.

"We did it, Betsy! We freed the convicts. They're sending them to Knoxville. Maybe there'll be work for us miners now. Your dad and I can go back to digging coal."

Betsy looked at the ragged crew of convicts who were still standing beside the track. "They're going to take them away for good? Just like that? You sure, Jake?"

Jake looked back at the convicts and then at Betsy. "That's the plan. No more convicts. Work for us."

"Sounds too simple to me. Was anybody hurt? Was there any shooting? Where's my father?" She looked over the sea of shadowy faces and finally saw Daniel Boyd. She waved at him and whistled like she was calling a horse.

"That's the beauty of it, Betsy. No one was hurt. Not a shot fired. This was the most peaceful law breaking these men have ever been involved in. I'm going to have to go and get Charmer. I left her tied in the grove at Briceville. I'll have my walking for the day."

"I'm getting on the train," Betsy said, "I have a job." She took Jake's hand and started to the passenger car.

By the time the convicts were loaded into the boxcar and it was tied onto the train, Betsy had found her normal seat. She began her study of the books that Mr. Powell had given her and of the typewriter operation manual.

The eight guards, Mr. Goodwin, and Mr. Jenkins walked into her car and began to take seats. Betsy was the only woman in the car.

"I don't believe it's safe for a young lady to ride on the train today. We've got a boxcar full of convicts. You might want to get off," Mr. Goodwin said to Betsy.

Betsy recognized Mr. Jenkins who sat next to Mr. Goodwin. "I feel just as safe with them as I would with some mine owners or those who lease convicts," Betsy said and turned back to reading her books.

In Nashville, Governor John Buchanan sat at his desk and read the letter again. He had just received the bad news. Mrs. Jefferson Davis had declined his request to bury the deceased President of the Confederate States of America in Tennessee. His body would be exhumed from Louisiana and reinterred in Richmond, Virginia. The letter was dated July 11, 1891, and post marked from Mrs. Davis's hotel in New York.

The governor thought he could receive no worse news the whole year. Then the telegram came. It was laid on his desk.

Knoxville, Tenn., July 15, 1891

Governor Buchanan, Nashville, Tenn.:

A mob of 300 armed men overpowered the guards at the new prison last night and forced the lessees to carry convicts on to Knoxville. Sheriff says he is unable to protect men. Two or more military companies needed at once. Situation is serious. You had better come and bring military companies from Middle Tennessee. Answer.

E. P. Wade, Superintendent

The governor stood, went to his door, and called for his chief assistant. He also sent for George Ford, his new Commissioner of Labor.

"I don't need this bother. What are they trying to do to me?" he asked no one in particular. After a half hour conference with his assistant, he decided to call in his adjutant general, H. H. Norman, and prepare for the worse.

Telegrams began to fly back and forth between Nashville and Knoxville.

Nashville, Tenn., July 15, 1891

E. P. Wade, Knoxville:

Let Sheriff of Anderson County ask for aid if he is unable to preserve order and enforce the law.

John P. Buchanan, Governor

Knoxville, Tenn., July 15, 1891

Governor Buchanan, Nashville, Tenn.:

The Sheriff, by his deputy, was in charge of the force at the stockade and could do nothing to prevent the mob from carrying out their threats. Prompt and decisive action must be taken or the State is humiliated. Nearly all citizens of Anderson County around the mines are in sympathy with the mob. Hope you will act promptly, because this move, if successful, endangers all our other branch prisons.

E. P. Wade

Then another missive from the superintendent.

Knoxville, Tenn., July 15,1891

Governor Buchanan, Nashville, Tenn.:

Order Ford to Briceville. Knoxville parties say he has large influence there.

E. P. Wade

"Damn. Who is the sheriff of Anderson County?" the governor asked his aide.

"Rufus Rutherford."

"Send him a telegram and ask him if he can enforce the law. Does he need the military? Maybe by my asking, he'll request it. We can't have anarchy. Get Colonel Sevier. He's from East Tennessee. We'll take him and some of the militia in and settle those miners down," the governor told his aide.

Labor Commissioner George Ford walked into the governor's office just in time to hear the militia mentioned.

"George, get ready. We're going to Knoxville and then on

to Briceville. The miners are giving us hell."

The aide scurried out of the office while Buchanan filled Ford in on all that he knew. In an hour, the aide rushed in with the reply telegram from Sheriff Rutherford.

Clinton, Tenn., July 15, 1891

Governor Buchanan:

In this case I am unable to enforce the law. Need help.

Rufus Rutherford,
Sheriff, Anderson County

"That's the request we need! Get us a train. We'll pick up a couple of companies of militia in Chattanooga. Telegraph the Knoxville Rifles to have their company ready by the morning. Let's go," the governor said and bounded from his office with Ford and Colonel Sevier.

Within the hour another telegram was received at the governor's office. It was from Coal Creek and the miners' committee. It arrived too late for the governor to receive it. He was already on the train, heading toward Murfreesboro and Chattanooga.

Coal Creek, Tenn., July 15

Governor Buchanan, Nashville, Tenn.:

We, the miners, farmers, merchants, and property-holders of Briceville and Coal Creek and vicinity assembled to the number of five hundred, who have come together to defend our families from starvation, our property from depreciation, and our people from contamination from the hands of convict labor being introduced in our works by Mr. Morrow through the Tennessee Coal Mining Company, do hereby beg you, as our Chief Executive and protector, to prevent their introduction, and thus avoid bloodshed, which is sure to follow if their taking our livelihood from us is persisted in. Answer.

Eugene Merrill, George Irish, J. A. Newman
For the Committee

On the train, Governor Buchanan talked on and on to his labor commissioner about his dreams and hopes for Tennessee. He wanted progress. He did not desire a confrontation with a group of miners. He pointed to the map he had of East Tennessee and drew a line from Jellico at the Kentucky border to South Pittsburg at the Alabama line.

"This could be the greatest industrial area in the south. Coal and iron ore. Steel and iron, George. By the turn of the century, Tennessee could be a manufacturing giant. We could be bigger and better than the northern industrial states.

"From Jellico straight to Alabama we have seams of coal just waiting to be mined. Coke ovens in Bledsoe and Sequatchie counties. Iron works in Rockwood, Chattanooga, and South Pittsburg. We have to have peace between labor and capital," the governor finished and looked at his labor commissioner.

"Governor, we can't carry the industrial revolution on the backs of slave labor. You and I know that using convicts to mine coal is slave labor. However, the miners themselves are not much better off.

"The mines are dangerous. Slate falls kill someone every week. The air is bad in some of the mines. Miners have to stand or sit in water to dig the coal. They're treated shabbily by the owners—paid in scrip and cheated when the coal is weighed. They're forced to buy from the company store at inflated prices. Something's got to change," Commissioner Ford concluded and turned toward the window where the scenery of Rutherford County was passing by.

"This is your home county, isn't it, Governor? Would you want convicts sent in to take over your farm?"

"Sounds like you're on the miners' side, George. That's what I need. Someone they will trust. Someone who can get them back to work. Someone who can keep them from interfering with the convicts. That's you, George. I'm depending on you," the governor said and smiled at his companion. "Get some sleep. We're picking up two companies of militia in Chattanooga, and Knoxville will have another one. You and I and Colonel Sevier are taking those convicts back up to Briceville tomorrow on this train. And, you'll convince the miners to leave them be."

Tennessee's militia consisted of twelve hundred men who were part-time soldiers. A few of the older officers had served in the Civil War, but for the most part, they were soldier-boys who had dreamed up fancy names for their companies—the Chattanooga Lookouts, the Knoxville Rifles, and the Moerlin Zouaves. Since peace had reigned during the years after the Civil War, these young men had never raised their rifles against an enemy. It had all been target practice.

The train stopped long enough in Chattanooga to pick up the two companies that were not at full strength. About a hundred youthful, undertrained, and underequipped militia boarded the train. It pulled out for Knoxville.

In Knoxville, the boxcar full of convicts had created a great curiosity the day before. The prisoners sat in the car while the authorities tried to determine just what to do with them. Finally, after being imprisoned in the oven-like car until three in the afternoon, they were taken to the third floor of the Knox County jail.

News spread of the rebellion. The company of Knoxville Rifles, with just half its roster reporting, began to drill near the depot on the evening of the convicts' arrival while awaiting the governor. It was quite a show. The local ladies came out to watch the young men march and turn. The soldiers slapped their rifles against their palms and clicked their polished shoes together with decent military precision. It was the best entertainment in town on the depot side of all of the saloons.

On Thursday morning the governor's train was met at the Knoxville depot with great excitement. Nearly five hundred men, women, and children crowded the area to get a glimpse of Buchanan and the militia from Chattanooga.

The governor met with Superintendent Wade, representatives of the mine, and Ford during breakfast at the depot. "We'll leave immediately," he told the men. "We'll take the convicts back in the same boxcar they came in. A hundred and twenty-five soldiers should be enough to show the miners we mean business.

I'll go myself. I served under Forrest, you know."

A little before ten, the train with a boxcar full of convicts, three companies of militia, the governor and his entourage chugged out of Knoxville toward Clinton. Although no trouble was expected, the captains of the military placed watches of militia in the locomotive with the engineer and in the caboose. Orders were to proceed cautiously at half speed with no stops except for Clinton where Sheriff Rutherford would deputize all of the military. The governor wanted everyone to know he was coming.

In Coal Creek, the miners awaited the train. They now knew the governor had to send the convicts back. But they would also have an opportunity to tell him their side. He could look and see. He had been the champion of farmers and labor in the past election. Surely, he would not turn his back on this laboring group.

Jake Drummond shook his head in disbelief. If the committee leaders knew that the convicts would be returned, why had they gone through the trouble? What were they gaining? Surely the governor already knew their situation. His labor commissioner, George Ford, had been to Coal Creek and Briceville before.

The crowd at Coal Creek to meet the train was larger than the one at Knoxville. Over seven hundred miners, wives, children, merchants, and farmers stood on both sides of the track and depot when it arrived around noon. They saw the uniforms of the militia and the shiny rifles sparkling inside the passenger cars. The governor, in his own car, gave orders to proceed immediately to Briceville.

The train was switched onto the spur and was followed on foot by practically all of the crowd. For five miles the miners, who had trod the same steps the morning before to release the convicts, retraced their path from Coal Creek to the Wye past the Knoxville Iron Company mine and on to Briceville and the stockade.

Between lines of militia, the convicts walked back into the stockade at the Tennessee Mine. Two companies of the militia remained at the Tennessee stockade while the Knoxville Rifles boarded the train again to be taken to the Knoxville Iron Company stockade on the return trip to Coal Creek.

There, at the Knoxville Iron Company mine, Governor Buchanan took leave of the train to have dinner with the Chumbleys in the great white house that was the jewel of the area. It was covered with two coats of brilliant white paint every year. The massive Victorian, with its sweeping veranda, loomed over the road between Briceville and Coal Creek within pistol shot of the stockade of the mine.

John Chumbley was highly respected by the miners in the same manner that Jesse James had been respected by bank tellers. The Knoxville Iron Company mine that he oversaw was worked by a hundred and twenty-five convicts and a few free men. A hundred and twenty of the convicts were black. Many of them never saw the end of their sentences. Over a hundred were already buried in unmarked graves between the stockade and the mine.

While Governor Buchanan was enjoying the delicacies of the table of John Chumbley, Eugene Merrill started the rumor that the governor would speak to the miners mid-afternoon at Lafter's Grove near Thistle Switch between Briceville and Coal Creek. The story spread as it was supposed to, and a great crowd began to gather at the junction. Newspaper reporters from Knoxville converged on the site, ready with pen in hand to see what words of solace the governor would pronounce over the crowd of miners.

The governor, learning of the anticipated speech, thought it better for him to make an appearance than to depart for Knoxville and let the people believe that he was afraid to face them. Chumbley provided a horse and buggy for the governor's return to Lafter's Grove.

Merrill smiled when he saw the buggy bouncing down the road. He would be magnanimous and introduce the governor. A wagon was pulled into the center of the grove and used for the speaker's platform after the mule was detached. Merrill stood on a nearby stump and presented the governor to the crowd which greeted the chief executive with stony silence.

"Fellow citizens of Campbell and Anderson counties, I did not come to make a speech." There was applause, and a few guffaws of laughter rippled over the sea of miners. Merrill held his hand up to quiet them.

Jake Drummond stood next to Betsy and her father, listening to see if he could discern his future.

The governor continued.

"Every man before me in this vast audience knows the sad mission which I came to perform as the executive officer of the state. I had hoped during my term of office that law and peace would reign supreme. Law, peace, and order must not be violated and overthrown.

"I do not make the laws. They are made by men whom you and others throughout the state send to the legislature every two years. Send good men to the legislature where laws are made. They will redress your wrongs."

Betsy nudged Jake and tiptoed up to whisper in his ear. "Jake, he's right in that. You should seek the legislative seat and help change all this, legally."

Jake looked down at Betsy and smiled. "Me? In the legislature? I don't even have a high school education."

"It's not required. Most of them act like they have no education at all. You ought to run."

Jake shook his head and turned back toward the governor.

"The leasing of the convicts has been maintained for many years for several reasons. Owing to its financial condition, the state is unable to accommodate them. The lessees made arrangements to come here to one of the mines with some of them.

"Night before last three hundred men appeared at the mines, overpowered the guards, and sent the convicts back to Knoxville. I ask you, Is that preserving the law? I am not here to discuss the justice or equity of the laws. My duty is to restore peace.

"I have appointed one of your own class, Mr. Ford, to see that you had what the law demands in the way of ventilation, lights, and other benefits. I have worked for your interests, and I earnestly advise you to let the law take its course," the governor said and continued for another ten minutes.

When he finished and stepped down from the wagon, the shrill call of a bluejay from a distant thicket sang across the silent sea. Not once had the governor addressed the three issues that had brought convicts to Briceville in the first place—scrip, a check weighman, and the required signing of a contract that would make the miners give up rights given to them by state law.

Eugene Merrill would not let the opportunity pass to remind the governor of the real problems. He mounted the stump near him and began to speak in words more eloquent and forceful than the governor himself.

"Scrip is issued to the miners. This is unlawful. The miners should be paid in lawful money and be allowed to spend it where they please, or else they are not free men.

"When the cars are loaded by the miners in the darkness of the mines and are weighed a good mile away at the tipple, the proper amounts should be put on the sheets for the miners. The law says the miners shall have a check-weighman. But the company says, If you have a check-weighman, the mine will be shut down.

"We want to be men and not slaves. For a state to sustain such a system as we are subjected to here is a disgrace to a civilized country.

"Is there any redress? Will the governor and other officials do anything for us while they send the militia for Mr. Chumbley and Mr. Morrow? Will they be so prompt to send the militia on behalf of our wrongs?"

When Merrill finished, thunderous cheering rolled over Lafter's Grove as hundreds of miners and their families roared their approval. The call of the bluejay was drowned in the tumult.

Governor Buchanan turned to John Chumbley. "Who is that man?"

"Just a trouble maker, Governor. Merrill. A Frenchman from New Orleans, Illinois, and now, here. He'll never see another working day as a miner."

The governor shook his head. "I'm glad he didn't run against me for governor."

"There'll be another meeting of miners here tonight," Merrill shouted to the dispersing miners.

Eugene Merrill and Miners

Again

Nothing had been accomplished. It was now worse than ever. Not only did the residents of the mining valley of Anderson County have convicts in their presence doing the work of the miners. Now they had over a hundred members of the state's militia bedded down at the stockade to make sure that the miners did not remove the convicts a second time.

Governor Buchanan had departed on Friday morning, having promised the miners absolutely nothing. Old Buck was on his way back to Nashville, away from the little hell hole squatting in East Tennessee. On Thursday night some miners on their way home from a meeting at Thistle Switch had fired their guns into the air as they passed the Knoxville Mine stockade. The governor, who spent the night with the Chumbleys at their house nearby, rushed to the stockade and shouldered a rifle, believing they were under attack. "I fought with Forrest," he had told one of the militiamen.

"I didn't think it would do any good," Betsy Boyd said at the table on Sunday morning. "The state intends to stand behind the mine owners. They have more money—and power. You'll have to beat them in the legislature."

Daniel Boyd looked at his eldest daughter across the table. "I've always encouraged you to speak your mind, Betsy, but there's sometimes when you remind me you're still a child—ought to be seen and not heard."

His eyes told her that he was hurt. "All I meant, Papa, was that men that support your cause should run for the legislature. I think Jake should run. Everybody likes him. He could be elected." She smiled across at Jake who was now at his usual spot at the Boyds' table.

"Betsy, I told you I couldn't do that. I'd be out of place in Nashville. The farthest I've ever been is to Knoxville on the south and Jellico on the north. I've crossed the Clinch a few times, and I've walked the spines of the mountains, just hunting and looking." He peered down at his miner's boots. "Those dandy dressed dudes would laugh me out of the Capitol Building."

"You underestimate yourself, Jake. You could do anything you want. What do you do best?"

Jake thought for a minute. He pulled a pocket knife out of his pants pocket and a piece of wood. "I whittle pretty good. I can carve and make little animals for fun. I like to do that."

"Did you know how to do that when you first started?" Betsy looked at Jake who sat silent. "No. Of course not. You had to learn. And you can learn to be a spokesman for the miners. You could be as good as Merrill or Ingraham or Irish. Any of them. You're not a hot head. Yet you could speak forcefully for them."

Jake just shook his head back and forth. He looked more at the plate in front of him than at Betsy.

Matriarch Grandma Dolan surveyed all their faces from her perch at the head of the table. She had assumed the primary position when Betsy's family had moved in with Uncle Will and Aunt Ollie. No one had objected.

"Violence ain't going to solve nothing. Reason is, the gov'ment can be a lot more violent than you can. They got the men. They got the guns. They got the prisons. We ain't nothing to them.

"They think we're like a bunch of chickens—ain't got no brains. You ever eaten chicken brains? No, course not. You'd have to have a hundred to get a mouthful.

"Now pigs are different. They're one of the smartest animals. We all need to be pigs, and Jake there has a good start on it."

Jake looked up from his plate and put down the fork full of sausage, biscuit and gravy he was about to take to his mouth.

"Better listen to Betsy. She's wise beyond her years."

At Briceville, Colonel Granville Sevier watched his soldiers march around the stockade. He looked up to the mountains that towered above him on three sides.

It was precisely the worst place in the world to have a military fort. Forts were supposed to command the highest and most secure position. This place was an open invitation to attack. There wouldn't even have to be an attack. The miners could just take to the hills around them and pick them off with their long rifles like shooting rats in a rain barrel.

He took his pocket watch out and looked at the time. It was near noon. His orders were to be as friendly as possible with the surrounding population in order to defuse any dangerous situations. On this first Sunday of his encampment, he had determined to invite any curious townspeople into the stockade for a look around.

Some would say this would be inviting spies in who would then plan an attack. But when he viewed the high mountains, he knew they would not have to spy out his fortifications to know exactly what he had. They could just go to the nearest ridge and look over.

Sevier was a direct descendent of Tennessee's first governor, John Sevier. His family went back in East Tennessee history to the time before Tennessee was a state. John Sevier had also been the governor of the State of Franklin, which was never recognized and melted into Tennessee in 1796.

When he compared the troops under his command to the miners that he had already seen, Sevier shook his head. The miners were a hardened bunch. The older ones had fought in the Civil War while the younger ones had suffered the rigors of coal mining. They had hunted these mountains and were expert marksmen—just like John Sevier and the East Tennessee mountain men of a hundred years before.

His young troops were fuzzy-faced boys—some of them only seventeen years old—who were from the friendly confines of Knoxville and Chattanooga. They may have camped for a week as part of their training, but they were more used to momma's biscuits and soft quilts at night than the company of convicts and sleeping on wooden-planked beds. However, they had weathered the first three days in good spirits—only a third had asked when they would be relieved and allowed to go back to their homes.

A whole wagon load of Boyds left the Methodist Church in Coal Creek, with Jake Drummond in command of Nellie, and headed toward Briceville. Word had spread of Sevier's invitation. Betsy insisted on going, but Jake was hesitant.

"We don't want to get too friendly with the military," Jake said.

"Yes we do," Betsy replied. "We are part of the state. They're our military. Besides, it would be harder to shoot somebody you're friendly with than just a nameless face. They need to know that the miners have wives and children—that all they want to do is work.

"They'd probably rather be around us than those convicts and mine owners they've been with. Besides, I might just find me a nice soldier-boy in one of those uniforms," Betsy said.

"That's what I was afraid of," Jake said and snapped the line lightly over Nellie's back. The wagon jostled down the road with Jake, Betsy, Aunt Ollie, Sally, and Betsy's twin sisters, Belle and Estelle.

"Pleased to have you ladies join us," Colonel Sevier said to the Boyd women when they entered the stockade area. Jake tied Nellie to a sapling and walked around outside.

"Are you from a mining family?" Sevier asked Sally.

"Yes, my husband's a miner. We don't like having convicts here doing their work. These are my children and my sister-in-law," she said, careful not to give any names to the military.

"I understand your feelings, ma'am. These young soldiers would rather be some place else themselves. We're just doing our jobs. Go ahead and look around as much as you like." Sevier looked down at the four-year-old twin girls. "Lovely children. And excellent weather to go barefoot."

Sally looked down at her unshod girls. "It's not by choice, sir. They won't have shoes this winter unless their father gets back to the mines." Sally looked at Colonel Sevier's shoes. "Looks like you have yours right nicely shined."

While the women strolled about inside the stockade area, Jake made a circuit of the outside. It was nearing completion. He estimated that the stockade could be enclosed in another day.

Some of the militiamen were sitting on piles of stacked wood and large boulders near the perimeter. They were dressed in their nice blue uniforms, some wearing dress hats with feathers. They looked at him with squinted eyes. Was this one of the hideous miners they had been told about?

Jake noticed that most of the soldiers were no older than he was. Some were writing letters. Others were eating apples. A few were nodding toward some of the women visitors and making remarks to their comrades. There was laughter about.

It didn't seem real. It was more like a fairground than a battleground. They were boys just like Jake. He could have been placed in one of their uniforms and looked just like them. Except he wouldn't, he told himself. He would never occupy another man's territory and stand between him and his job.

One of the young soldiers approached Jake and held out his hand. Jake was slow to grasp it. "Are you a miner?" the soldier asked.

"I was," Jake said, "until I hurt my ankle. Then they locked the mine down. I'm still a miner; with no mine."

The soldier nodded his head. "I'm from Chattanooga. Live within a mile of the Read Hotel. You ever heard of that?"

Jake shook his head. "No. I've never been past Knoxville."

"I'm a brickmason apprentice," the soldier said. "I'm just in the National Guard for fun. Weekends and summer camp." He turned and looked around toward the stockade. "Some fun, huh? Say, what's it like to be a miner?"

Jake thought for a minute. He squatted down and motioned for the soldier to squat down also like he was going to whisper a great secret to him.

"This is the position we have to work in. Most of the seams of coal are from three and a half to four and a half feet thick. So we can't stand up in most of the mines. The tunnel is just as high as the seam of coal. We have to leave the slate ceiling. You don't want to start messing with it. It'll fall on you. That's how I hurt my ankle.

"We drill holes into the coal with long augers. We put powder in that and tamp it. You have to be real careful with that powder. Then we go around a corner or two and let it blast. Then we have to shovel it out into wheelbarrows, carts, or even buckets sometimes until we can get it to one of the little cars that the mules pull.

"The drivers take it on out of the mine to the tipple where it's weighed. That's the simple explanation, but you won't understand until you've been in a mine and worked. Nobody would."

The young soldier shook his head. "Sounds like hard work."

Jake nodded. "It's hard. We have to squat or stoop over for ten hours a day. The air has coal dust in it. It's dark except for the little light our miner's lamps put off. We often have to stand in ankle-deep water. The ceiling might fall in any time. We could get blown up with our own powder. Or bad gas from the coal could cause an explosion. At the end of the day you're covered with a layer of coal dust that eats into your skin."

"Why do you do it then?"

"Because my father did it until he was killed. His father mined. It's the only thing I know. If you work hard you can make three or four dollars a day. It's almost enough to pay off my account at the company store. We have to buy our own picks and shovels. Even the blasting powder. You oughta join us and become a miner."

The soldier grinned and rubbed his hand across his forehead. "Thanks, but I think I'll stay a brickmason. I like to be outside."

Jake started to walk away. The soldier grabbed his shoulder. "I'm sorry," the soldier said. "I didn't get your name."

Jake hesitated. "How old are you?" he asked.

"Eighteen," the soldier replied and pushed a lock of long blond hair back under his hat.

"I'm Jake. And I hope we can always meet on as friendly terms." He held out his hand and shook the young brickmason's.

Red clouds reflected the last remnants of sunlight over Vowell Mountain as the Lord's Day drew toward a peaceful ending in the valley. Shadows of the high ridges swept the stockade and the Tennessee Mining Company buildings in Briceville. The visitors had left, and the militia and convicts they were guarding retreated to behind the walls of the nearly completed stockade.

As soon as darkness cloaked the ridges and ravines, solitary figures began to walk the road between Coal Creek and Briceville toward another meeting of miners. They came alone or in clusters of two and three. Then a half dozen, a dozen, and a score.

From throughout the mining district of Anderson County they came on foot or horseback. Word had spread to neighboring Campbell County to the north, and the road filled with miners in sympathy from Jellico, Newcomb, and as far away as Harlan County, Kentucky. Long rifles, Winchesters, shotguns, and Colt revolvers found the hands of most of those who moved in silence down the road to the place they were told to meet.

A nod was exchanged when one passed another. There was little talk and no introductions. No names were bandied about. For this kind of work it was better to linger in anonymity.

They numbered over a thousand this time. Among them were Daniel Boyd who carried a Winchester, Dick Drummond with the Colt revolver, and Jake Drummond who came unarmed.

By four in the morning, all who were coming had arrived. Eugene Merrill, Captain Matthew Ingraham, and James Turner assumed command. Merrill gathered all who had rifles into one group—over five hundred. He selected three hundred of them to flank the stockade and take to the mountain on both sides. All those who would climb the ridges around the stockade would also carry an unlit torch with them. Daniel Boyd was one of the ones to start the climb.

Then Merrill arranged the remaining men into a marching corps that began to stretch out for a half mile along the road. The ones with rifles who didn't go to the ridges formed the front ranks, those with shotguns were next, then those with pistols, and finally those who were unarmed. Jake was five rows from the back. When the march toward the stockade began, Jake imagined himself as part of a huge black centipede. He was no longer an individual but just part of a beast that was slithering down the road.

For three hours Colonel Sevier's sentries had made reports to him on the movement of the miners. He could hardly believe the numbers. Five hundred, a thousand, fifteen hundred. Surely the miners could not enlist so great a number.

The colonel had his troops to take defensive positions. All fires and lanterns were doused. Clouds drifted overhead. There was little moonlight. He took his field glasses and peered down the road. He could see nothing. A sentry came with a report that the miners were taking to the ridges on both sides of the stockade.

Then he heard a sound. A steady but muffled beat. The slight rumble of nearly two thousand shoes and boots meeting the soft dirt of the road made little noise. Then he beheld the sight. A frightening host was coming toward him. They marched like corpses that had been lifted from graveyards. They rounded the bend in the road a half mile away. There was no end to their lines. He could barely make out the shouldered rifles.

The footfalls stopped. A lone torch was lit. Merrill, Ingraham, and Turner, carrying a white flag, proceeded on toward the stockade.

"Hold your fire," Sevier told his lieutenants and had them spread the word. He and two of his senior officers, Captain John

Patton of the Knoxville Rifles and Captain Henry Simmons of the Moerlein Zouaves, walked toward the three miners.

"We have come for the convicts, Colonel Sevier," Merrill said.

"How do you propose to take them?"

"I believe I have a sufficient number with me to take them if need be. But we want no bloodshed."

"We are sworn to protect them and keep them here, Mr. Merrill," Sevier answered.

With that, Merrill took the torch and waved it in a great arc. He nodded to the hills on both sides of the stockade and behind it. Sevier turned and looked.

The hillsides came alive as three hundred torches began to burn in a semi circle around and above the stockade. It looked like fireflies on the first warm night of summer as more and more torches awakened with orange light. Each tongue of fire moved in a slow arc as they glowed around and behind trees and rocks.

"With each torch is a Winchester, Colonel. It will be light in another hour and you will have no place to hide. We can do this peacefully. You're a good soldier. I'm sure you don't want to sacrifice one life or a hundred in an impossible situation," Merrill said.

Sevier nodded. "Let me confer with all my officers. You shall have your answer within a half hour."

The decision lingered. Some of Sevier's officers wanted to fight to the last man. More of them saw the reasonableness of accommodation. Before light, the deal was struck.

After another hour of discussion between the miners' committee and Sevier and his men, they agreed that Sevier's quartermaster would secure all of the militia's arms and ammunition. The soldiers would pack all their personal belongings and begin the short walk to Briceville where they would board a train of empty coal cars.

At eight the march began. Thirty-eight convicts, all of whom had been on this trip before, and a hundred and seven militia, most of whom were glad they were leaving, walked to the spur of the railroad at Briceville. They marched along the main street where women met them with buckets of hot biscuits and cool water. While the food and water were meant primarily for the visiting miners, the soldiers feasted on it too.

The train pulled out with striped uniformed convicts, blue uniformed militia, and ununiformed miners—all riding in the dusty coal cars. The miners were used to the dust stirred up by the little wind, but the militiamen got their first taste of real coal.

Adjutant General H. H. Norman and Labor Commissioner George Ford arrived at Coal Creek from Knoxville at the same time the train was leaving Briceville going toward Coal Creek.

General Norman and Commissioner Ford then began the five mile walk to Briceville, only to be met by the train and its strange cargo just a mile from Coal Creek. The General, who was the commander of the state's entire National Guard, flagged down the train and found out that three companies had surrendered and were being shipped out in coal cars along with the convicts. It was humiliating, but he climbed on board.

At Coal Creek the miners sent the cargo of convicts and militia on toward Knoxville after a delay to be sure the tracks were clear for traffic. General Norman remained at the depot and wired Governor Buchanan of the trouble.

As soon as the militia and convicts from Briceville were on their way, the miners turned their attention to the Knoxville Iron Company stockade just a mile from Coal Creek. They marched there to an unprotected garrison where just four nights before Old Buck had taken a rifle in what he believed to be the defense of the stockade. No soldiers remained.

The few guards meekly surrendered the convicts to the miners and asked only that the company property be spared. A hundred and twenty convicts marched out of the stockade and toward Coal Creek. This was their first trip to Knoxville. The fifteen hundred miners formed a walled escort for the convicts.

General Norman, embarrassed again by the release of the convicts, agreed to escort this group, with a few guards, to Knoxville. The governor was once again telegraphed about the trouble.

Five hours apart, two trains left Coal Creek carrying all the convicts and militia that had been in the valley. Not a shot had been fired. The miners from Jellico, Newcomb, and Kentucky departed on the northbound train. The Briceville and Coal Creek miners dispersed to their homes after stationing guards at the stockades to insure no harm came to the property.

Eugene Merrill summoned the committee to meet once again to decide the next course of action.

In Knoxville the first train was met by a crowd who had heard of the uprising. They looked on in wonder and amazement. The first witnesses saw the empty coal cars with pathetic figures inside but could not discern who or what they were until members of the militia identified themselves. They were fully coated with layers of coal dust.

One young soldier took off his military cap, letting locks of long blond hair fall down over a blackened forehead. He looked at his arms and hands. “Now I know a little more about what it feels like to be a miner,” the brickmason said.

More Troops

Governor Buchanan stormed out of his office and into his assistant's as soon as he received the first telegram that the convicts had once again been removed from Briceville. This time the miners had also offended the state by demanding and receiving the surrender of over a hundred of the state's militia.

"Dammit! Get General Carnes on his way to Knoxville with every company of our National Guard that he can roust out. I'll meet them there. Every damn militiaman!

"If a hundred soldiers aren't enough to keep the peace and the convicts at the mines, a thousand will. I want them all in Knoxville tomorrow. And tell him to bring those Gatling guns."

He looked at the telegram again and spoke aloud. "Sevier surrenders. General Norman joins the train that is carrying the troops and convicts. What an indignity! Jackson was right about those Seviers—they're more likely to run than to fight.

"Carnes will fight though. He's battle-tested. We're not going to allow some Yankee miners to mar the dignity of the state."

The assistant just nodded. He was afraid to give him the next telegram. "Sir, this is another dispatch from General Norman," he said, and cautiously handed the paper over the desk to the governor.

The governor's face turned red as he looked at the telegram.

His walrus mustache moved on his upper lip as though it had a life of its own.

"Now they've taken the convicts out of the Knoxville Iron Company mine. Hell, they've been there for fifteen years. I'm going to show those miners who's in charge."

By Monday night the call had gone out to all the units of the National Guard across Tennessee. They were to muster in to their company headquarters and then on to Knoxville. Special trains were called upon to carry the soldiers. Buchanan asked the Governor of Georgia about the possibility of bringing a couple of companies from that state and another Gatling gun or two.

General S. T. Carnes was in Memphis and the farthest from Knoxville. He left immediately with the units from the bluff city.

Nine companies of militia arrived in Knoxville on the morning of Tuesday, July 21. They included twenty from the Perkins Rifles of Franklin; twenty-four from Springfield; twenty-five of the Washington Artillery from Nashville; twenty-seven of the Nashville light infantry; twenty-three of the Buchanan Rifles from Nashville; thirty-five from the Murfreesboro Rifles; thirty-seven of the Shelbyville Rifles; twenty-eight from Tullahoma; and thirty-five from Winchester. Sevier's hundred soldiers were still in Knoxville.

They marched from the depot in Knoxville to the Knox County Courthouse at the corner of Main and Gay. There they took over the grounds, awaiting General Carnes and the word to invade Coal Creek and Briceville. Many of Knoxville's citizens met them and looked on with curious eyes when they made the march down Gay Street. The populace had not seen so many troops since the Civil War.

To the dismay of the Knox County Sheriff and others occupying offices in the courthouse, the soldiers came and went through the building as though it belonged to them. Cots and tents were set up on the grass and surrounding grounds. Large kettles began to boil in preparation for feeding the first three hundred of the troops. More were on the way from Memphis.

Biscuits and hams satisfied the appetites of the predominantly youthful group of militiamen. Stewards sliced the ham and made sandwiches with the biscuits. The mid-July sun beat down on the troops, and they found little relief from the sultry heat.

The bivouacked troops entertained themselves by watching the young ladies who would pass by on Gay Street or walk past them on Main. Others took the hardened and uneaten biscuits and played a type of baseball game with them throwing them about or batting them with the stocks of their rifles—until called down by their officers.

General Carnes arrived in mid-afternoon with four more companies from Memphis, consisting of about a hundred fifty men in all. He brought the two Gatling guns with him along with a mountain howitzer. The Gatlings could fire twelve hundred and fifty rounds per minute. The howitzer would lob explosive charges over a mile. From the depot to the courthouse, the line of citizens viewed the heavy fire-power of the National Guard.

Carnes meant business. In response to a reporter's question about what they were going to do with the military, Carnes replied, "I expect to be ordered to Coal Creek and Briceville tomorrow."

Rumors spread about the great battle that would take place in the serene setting of Anderson County. Soon, bodies would litter the valley. Coal Creek would run crimson with the blood of miners. Reports were that as many as five thousand miners and supporters from Tennessee and Kentucky were gathering to battle the militia if it marched into their home territory with the convicts in tow. The miners' backs were against the wall. Their freedom was taken from them. That's what they would fight for. Freedom.

By the time Carnes's companies joined the others at the courthouse, the number of militia had swelled to over six hundred. A speedy survey of the situation convinced him that they could not stay at the county courthouse, and so he ordered a march of a little over a mile to the campus of the state university. It was state property and had empty dormitory rooms and a place to store the arms and ammunition of the troops.

Dick DeArmond, custodian of the courthouse and grounds, was glad to see them go. "They ruined the lawns, broke a fence, and rode a gate to the ground. It'll take a lot of work to get it spruced up. I'm glad to be shut of them," he told anyone who would listen.

Old soldiers from Knoxville stood and watched in awe as the militia headed for the university grounds. "They look awful young," one said. "But in the War it was boys eighteen to twenty-two who could stand hard marching, loss of sleep, and loss of grub. We needed the old heads for commanders, but the War was won with the young ones."

General Carnes and the National Guard took up residence at the university. Near the corner of Clifton Street and Cumberland Avenue, the soldiers stored the big weapons and ammunition. It being summer, the grounds of the university were practically deserted except for a few professors and maintenance personnel. The militia took all the dormitories. General Carnes set up office on the first floor of the east dormitory and began plans for the invasion.

The blast of bugle and rattle of drums echoed from the hill at the university to the courthouse on Main. Sentries were posted to keep the curious at bay while the companies competed in shows of march and precision handling of weaponry.

Professor Robert Brimer walked down from his office at the science building and, in the manner of a citizen, inspected the troops as they marched. He found General Carnes's office and walked in.

"General Carnes, I'm Robert Brimer, a professor of history at the university. I want to welcome you here."

Carnes looked up from his desk where he had been studying maps and troop rosters. "Thank you, Professor. What can I do for you?"

"Sir, it's history in the making that you are here. What do you think the outcome will be? Do you think there will be serious trouble?" Brimer asked.

"I hope not. I know but little of the situation there, personally. Colonel Sevier seems to think there will be a serious time if we take the convicts into Coal Creek. I'm acting under the orders of the governor to enforce the law, and that's what we will endeavor to do.

"It seems to me, however, if the miners are as shrewd and

intelligent as I am told they are, they will precipitate no bloodshed. It certainly will do them more harm than good.

"I understand there's an armed force added to that region from Jellico and that most of them are miners from the Kentucky mines. If that's true, I should call that pretty nearly armed invasion and one that would justify taking extreme measures in dealing with," the general concluded.

While Governor Buchanan was on his way to Knoxville to take command of the troops from that vantage point, Eugene Merrill called a meeting of the leadership committee and all the miners for Lafter's Grove in an effort to head off bloodshed.

"They have over six hundred troops in Knoxville now. A thousand may be there before this time tomorrow. They have two Gatling guns and a mountain howitzer. We need to resolve this peacefully, before this valley is filled with widows and orphans," Merrill spoke to the hushed crowd.

"We can take them, Frenchy. We can take to the mountains and pick them off one by one. We can have ten thousand join us. We can't be defeated!" someone shouted from the back of the crowd of six hundred miners. Howls of agreement burst forth like the thunder after a flash of lightning.

Merrill held up his hands for quiet, as did the other leaders. "For every one we pick off, they'll send a dozen more. The governor will be in Knoxville tomorrow. Let's send him our demands, and see if this can be resolved."

Cooler heads prevailed. The miners adopted six objectives that they would submit to the governor.

They would allow the convicts returned to both mines from which they had been removed while any offenses the miners had committed would be pardoned. The contract at the Tennessee Mine with the convict lessees would be terminated and the convicts removed. The governor would call a special session of the legislature and recommend a repeal of the convict lease system. The miners would protect all property of the state and operators without the military being present. Once the lease system was repealed by the legislature, the convicts would be removed from Coal Creek and Oliver Springs. The miners would look out for the safety of the guards of the convicts.

The miners, as a group, approved the propositions, and named a committee of five to take the peace proposal to the governor in Knoxville.

Betsy would not be deterred from her job by all the ruckus of the miners sending the convicts to Knoxville. They would be back again just like they were before. She didn't like it any more than her father or Jake. But why did they think the governor would back down now?

Before the convicts were returned the next day. This time she expected to meet them on an incoming train as she traveled to Knoxville on Wednesday morning.

In the passenger car with her were the five men who had been appointed by the miners to go to Knoxville: W. T. Smith, S. R. Pickering, John Hardin, Joshua T. Thomas, and Samuel D. Moore.

They looked more like they were going to a funeral than to talk with the governor. Betsy and Joshua Thomas's daughter were friends. She could not remember ever seeing Mr. Thomas in a suit. Now here he was, with the other four, all spiffed up with suits, ties, and better hats than they normally wore. But their eyes were red, their mustaches downturned more than ever, and they cast their eyes at the floor as they rode along in silence. Was it their funeral or someone else's they thought they would be attending?

The more Betsy thought about it over the period of the miles stretching between Coal Creek and Clinton, and then Knoxville, the more she determined that she would just have a chat with the governor herself. All he could say was "No" if he wouldn't listen to her.

She wanted to tell him three things, sweet and simple: Take the convicts out of Anderson County; let women enroll in the University of Tennessee; and push for the right of women to vote.

Professor Brimer had mentioned the suffrage of women, and she had laughed at the prospect. But the more she thought about it, the better she liked the idea. This was especially true after she had witnessed what a mess men had made of the county and state. In four years she would be twenty-one. She would like to vote.

Professor Brimer slapped his hand to his forehead and let out a howl of laughter when Betsy told him what she wanted to tell the governor.

"Miss Boyd, I am so surprised. In less than three weeks, I have so contaminated your mind with these wild ideas of women getting to vote and being allowed into the university on a full and equal basis that you want to talk to the governor."

He came around his desk, stepped to the window, and then walked to where she was sitting. "Well, I'll tell you what. The governor is staying in the Palace Hotel. You have my permission, as part of your work for me and your studies for Mr. Powell, to go down there and talk to the governor—if you can. If they arrest you, send for me. I'm a halfway decent lawyer. Friday, you report to me what he said. Take your books and go."

He escorted her to the edge of the walkway from the building and watched her make her way round the marching units of the militia. He shook his head. What had he created in this Betsy Boyd from Coal Creek?

In a parlor near the dining room of the Palace Hotel, fourteen men sat around a large conference table. The slowly turning ceiling fans barely moved a layer of bluish smoke that hovered above their heads like fog above a warm river on a cool morning.

Governor Buchanan, Labor Commissioner Ford, State Attorney General Pickle, and an assistant were meeting with the miners' committee and another group of local business and civic leaders from Knoxville.

Buchanan played his forefinger and thumb through his mustache and squinted at the papers the miners' committee had handed him. When he finished each page, he handed it on to

Attorney General Pickle and then to Commissioner Ford.

The papers outlined the conditions under which the miners would agree to allow the convicts back into their county and their mines.

When the governor reached the last page, his eyes latched onto the language that the miners had used. He read and re-read it:

"It is unnecessary for us to refer to the gravity of the situation. Sufficient is it that it is so. We are neither of the school of the commune nor nihilist. We struggle for the right to earn bread by honest labor, and in principle are opposed to that system of labor which may be invoked to our degradation. For us and our families we invite the sympathy of a common humanity."

"Neither of the school of the commune nor the nihilist." Anarchists, nihilists, and communists were all getting their share of publicity around the country and throughout the world. Buchanan smelled the work of Eugene Merrill in the wording, or else the miners were more educated and better read than the majority of his cabinet.

"We need to pass these requests on to Mr. Goodwin who represents the lessees and to Mr. Jenkins of the mining company. We can't agree to take the convicts out for good unless they concur. I'll send for them. We'll meet again in two hours, men. Let's get this worked out," the governor concluded and rose. All the others scraped their chairs back and stood. The governor walked out the door.

In Coal Creek some of the floors of homes were still dirt, but when Betsy Boyd walked into the lobby of the Palace Hotel her shoes patted down on marble. The polished rock had been quarried just a few miles out of Knoxville. The pink and gray veined stone spoke to her of opulence in this new home away from home. The name befit it. Palace.

She walked toward the dining room where dark-skinned men in white coats and black trousers carried food and drink to the tables on silver trays held above their heads balanced on three fingers and a thumb. The tinkling of glasses and ice blended with the murmuring soft conversation as though no one was aware that her home valley was about to be invaded by state soldiers. It was more in keeping with an inaugural dinner than a wake awaiting bloodshed.

She turned past the clerk's counter and walked toward an area where several people were gathered in front of a cage-like contraption that was capturing men and women and lifting them to an unknown destination. She put her hand against the wall where the cool marble again ran to shoulder height. "Elevator" was stenciled in bold letters above the opening where the brass-colored metal cage had disappeared into a hole in the ceiling.

It then reappeared on its downward run with six other people standing within and a black man near the door with his hand on a large lever. He pushed it down and the door to the cage opened and the people alighted as though they had not been prisoners at all.

"Do you want to go up, ma'am?" the black man in the cage asked Betsy.

She stepped toward him and stared upward to see if she could see the landing for the cage and where it had disappeared through the ceiling. She could only see a dark shaft with what appeared to be ropes or cables attached to the top of the cage. "Will this take me to the governor's floor?"

The man leaned toward her but remained in the cage. He spoke in a conspiratorial whisper. "Are you here to see the governor?"

"Yes," she said and clutched her books nearer her.

"Business or pleasure?" he asked.

"Business. I need to inquire about a matter. Do you know his room?"

He waved her into the cage and closed the door. "Don't tell anybody I told you, but his suite is on the fifth floor and all the way to the right."

He closed the filigreed door with a clang of metal against metal and pushed the lever all the way down. With a lurch, the contraption began its upward ascent. Betsy's stomach did a half roll the same way it did on the occasions when she jumped from the hay loft to the ground.

At the fifth floor she departed the elevator, thanked the operator, and walked slowly to her right. She saw two uniformed men and several chairs toward the end of the hallway. Three men were seated near the door that she believed must be the entrance to the governor's suite.

The nearer she approached the slower she walked. She let her hand slide along the marble wall. It was solid—something she wasn't.

She looked up at the ceiling and admired the electric lights surrounded by lucent globes with a blue pattern. She walked by doorways to toilets. She was beginning to covet the niceties of city life. Running water through spigots that could be turned off and on. Electric lights. Toilets inside the building. Polished marble and burnished brass. She knew she could be a city girl if given a chance.

She took a seat, opened her American history book, and began studying. She would wait however long it took to see the governor.

Before she had read the first page, though, the guards snapped to attention, and Governor Buchanan walked down the hallway from the elevator with an aide. She knew it was him from the pictures she had seen in the newspaper. He was a large man, full faced, with the droopy mustache. He puffed on a cigar and frowned as he walked hurriedly along.

"Who are all these people?" he asked gruffly of his aide.

All three men waiting to see him stood, and Betsy joined them. Buchanan cast a sideways glance at her on his way past. Two of the men were together and introduced themselves. The third one shook the governor's hand, leaned toward him, and whispered. The guards opened the door, and the governor took the first two men in. Before the door was closed, he turned back and told the third that he would see him next.

He glanced again at Betsy. "Are you wanting to see me, young lady?"

"Yes, Governor Buchanan, sir," she answered with quivering voice.

"It'll be a while. These men had appointments."

She nodded and sat back down. She was used to waiting. Her mind was a whirlwind of activity. She plotted the best terms with which to approach the governor with her requests. She wanted to be forceful but deferential—logical but not argumentative—spirited but reasoned.

She read and practiced the words in her head. She turned in her history book to the Declaration of Independence. She studied the words—*"life, liberty, and the pursuit of happiness."* That was what she wanted to get across to the governor.

Each of the three principles she proposed had to do with Jefferson's words. Get the convicts out of Anderson County. This embodied all three words. Let women enroll at the university. Again it was the same. Let women vote. Liberty.

To Betsy it was a powerful message. She could hear the drum rolls as she mouthed the words. Bugles hailed the speech of a goddess. Fireworks should burst forth. The governor, being a half-way intelligent soul, should see the reason and justice in these ideas for which she was pleading.

An hour passed. The two men were let out and the lone gentleman allowed to enter. Betsy waited. She thought back to April and their march from Briceville to Coal Creek. Her father had said it: "There's three things in life you can't speed up: A man making whiskey, a woman birthing a child, or a sow feeding her young." She added to that "or a governor in conference."

In another hour, she had read her history, worked the math problems, and begun her English literature assignment. She read a partial scene from Shakespeare's *Richard II.*

Peace shall go sleep with Turks and infidels,
And in this seat of peace tumultuous wars
Shall kin with kin and kind with kind confound;
Disorder, horror, fear and mutiny
Shall here inhabit, and this land be called
The field of Golgotha and dead men's skulls.

She closed the book and shivered. She hunched up her shoulders as she felt a sudden coldness. It rode the length of her spine like an icicle thrown down the back of her dress in winter. She could see Lafter's Grove full of "dead men's skulls." She looked closer to see if her father or Jake lay there. The soldiers were on the university campus for the purpose of putting down the coal miners' rebellion, and the outcome could mean that her father or Jake, or both, might die.

A messenger bolted down the hallway to the governor's door. "Goodwin and Jenkins are here," he told the aide when the door opened. He turned and rushed past Betsy back down the hallway.

Within a minute, the governor emerged from the doorway with his aide and the last gentleman who had been allowed in. The governor looked at Betsy on his way by, "I'm sorry. There's a conference I need to attend. If you'd care to wait, I'll be back."

She sat back down. She had three more hours until her train would leave for Coal Creek. She would wait.

"We cannot accept the miners' proposals," Goodwin told the governor when he returned to the table. "We have sub-leased these convicts to Mr. Jenkins's mine. We are bound by that contract, and the state is bound to our contract."

The governor frowned. He turned to Commissioner Ford and whispered. Then he spoke to the miners' committee. "Before coming to Knoxville, I had determined to call a special session of the legislature to deal with the lease issue and other matters of urgency. There is nothing I can do under the circumstances except to enforce the law.

"Please return to Coal Creek and persuade your fellow miners to abide by the law and give us time to work this out through the legislature. I can do nothing more."

The five men on the miners' committee sat numbed by the news. They had accomplished nothing. The convicts were to be returned to both mines. The leases were still in place. Some time in the future the legislature might repeal the lease system.

Joshua Thomas turned toward the governor. "This is not

good. We gained nothing. Those waiting for our return will be incensed by the turn of events. It's not within our power to deter their actions. I have neither the eloquence nor reasoning ability to persuade them that we have achieved a thing. Someone else must tell them—persuade them—calm them."

The five men from the Knoxville business community included Chancellor Henry Gibson, William Rule, Dennis Leahy, D. A. Carpenter, and General J. C. J. Williams. They finally turned to General Williams and asked him to go with the miners' committee to Coal Creek. He shook his head. "It's a difficult task, but I shall attempt it. Will the governor go with me?"

Buchanan blew out a fountain of smoke. "Not this time, General. It's not wise that I should go without an agreement already being reached. It might incite the crowd. But I'll send Commissioner Ford with you. He has some sway there."

The two guards by the governor's door on the fifth floor of the Palace Hotel had grown tired of standing and joined Betsy in the chairs.

"Where you from?" one asked.

"Coal Creek."

The guards nodded. "You're too pretty to be a miner," one of them said and laughed.

"They don't let women in the mines. They're superstitious. It's bad luck."

"Do you have a beau who's a miner?"

Betsy blushed and lowered her head. "Kind of."

The clang of the elevator door announced the arrival of Governor Buchanan. The guards jumped to their feet and took their places at the door.

"Come on in, young lady," Buchanan said as he and his aide prepared to enter his suite.

The guards smiled at Betsy and showed her through.

"Have a seat," the governor said and motioned to a chair near the window. "What's your name, and what can I do for you?" he asked and sat down near her. The aide drew up another chair and flipped open a note book.

"Governor, my name is Betsy Boyd. I'm from Coal Creek."

The governor's head flinched. "You don't have a gun, do you?" He smiled.

"No. I have a summer job with Professor Brimer at the university. I came to ask you three things, Governor, because I respect you and your office. You are the most powerful person in the state."

The governor shook his head. "Sometimes I wonder."

"As governor, you have much to say about the policies of the university. I would like to attend, but they don't allow women to enroll." Betsy watched the governor nod. He didn't say anything.

"I also believe that women should be allowed to vote." This time a bit of color drained from his face, but he continued to nod and look at her.

"Lastly, I want to implore you to do everything within your power to keep the convicts out of our valley and to keep the groves from becoming fields of dead men's skulls."

The governor stood and went to the fireplace on the far wall and leaned against the mantel. He put the thumb of his right hand under his suspenders near the shoulder. He laid his cigar onto the mantel.

"Miss Boyd, you are correct. Our women need to be allowed into the university. I'm already working on that.

"Now, voting is a different business. Politics is dirty and is not the proper domain for ladies. Women won't be allowed to vote—at least not in my lifetime.

"The business with the miners is difficult. I must enforce the law. I want peace. But, until the law is changed, the convicts will work some of the mines. I will try to restrict it, but it's up to the legislature to repeal it.

"Please, Miss Boyd, when you go back to Coal Creek, talk to your miner friends. Ask them to give us time. There need be no bloodshed.

"I'm with you on two out of three, Miss Boyd, but I can't imagine women ever voting. That's not their place."

"I don't want to sound disrespectful, Governor, but, perhaps if women were allowed to vote, it would bring a measure of civility to politics that doesn't presently exist."

A boisterous crowd of over a thousand gathered the next day at Lafter's Grove to hear the report of the miners' committee. Rumor had preceded the committee that their requests had been rejected. Fear rolled in the stomachs of the committee members. General Williams, and Commissioner Ford also were ill at ease when they peered out into the drawn faces of the dejected miners.

"Let's fight it out."

"To hell with the governor and his toy soldiers."

"Not one concession."

These and other cries met the ears of General Williams as he stood to speak.

"I hardly know which way to turn. I see such a sea of faces before me, on either side of me and behind me. I want to say that I occupy a position toward you like that of the Queen of Sheba toward King Solomon. When she saw all the splendor and greatness of his kingdom before her, she threw up her hands and said she had heard a great deal about it, but the half had not been told.

"I see before me honest assembled labor that ought to wear a crown. You only have to be conservative and a great victory is within your grasp."

Williams spoke in low tones. He didn't shout. Of necessity, the miners had to draw still to hear his words. As he spoke, they came nearer and nearer. He was speaking of victory—not defeat. He seemed to be on their side. He asked them to try again.

The mood of the crowd changed just as surely as the tide changes with the power of the moon. Williams shone with the reflected light of the miners' travail and led them on to victory. He was soft and caring. He was powerful and moving.

Tempers that were as hot as a blacksmith's fire cooled to the steel of a horse's shoe in a mountain stream.

"By the eternal, this system must go out of existence. The legislature should stamp out this hydra-headed monster. We will get rid of this infamous statute and get rid of the zebras."

The miners agreed. They appointed another committee to draft alternate resolutions. They would compromise if the governor would.

They reduced their requests to four. The status quo would be restored. The militia would be ordered home from Knoxville. The governor would call the legislature into session and recommend the repeal of the lease system. An armistice would be declared for sixty days to give the legislature time to do its work.

Williams, Ford, and the miners rejoiced at the prospect of peace. They returned to Knoxville that evening on a late train with the good news for the governor.

At eight o'clock in the evening they met again with Buchanan.

"Absolutely not," the governor fumed when he read the last part of the resolution. "An armistice? I can't agree to that. It's like saying we are two equal powers at war. It's beneath the dignity of the state. There is no armistice. The convicts go back in. The miners obey the law. That's it. I will call a special session of the legislature."

It was a lost cause. The members of the committee shook their heads in collective disbelief. What they thought had been a good settlement had been rejected out of hand by the governor because of one word. "Armistice." Perhaps there had to be some real shooting in order to have an armistice. So far, both removals had been accomplished without firing a shot. If the governor wanted shooting, he would get it.

Commissioner Ford persuaded his mining friends to try one more time. He would go back to Coal Creek and help reword the resolution into something acceptable.

On Friday it was done. The miners had given in some more with the mere hope and prayer that the legislature would solve the problem.

Their resolution was reduced to two basic propositions: The convicts would be returned to the mines. The governor would call a special session of the legislature to deal with the matter.

George Ford wrote in his notes of the day: "The conference was concluded, and the miners departed, conscious that they had done right, while God cast the mantle of charity and love over the entire affair, with peace and good will to all engaged therein, and the sun went down beyond the western hills, shedding a radiant glow on the peaceful termination of what, at several times, threatened to bring sorrow, suffering, and death to our noble Volunteer State."

General Sam Carnes and Tennessee's National Guard marched to the depot in Knoxville on Saturday. They had yet to go into Coal Creek under battle orders.

Governor Buchanan waved at the women and children who stared from porches and windows as the train with the convicts threaded its way up the valley from Coal Creek to Briceville. The women and children waved back until they saw the dreaded cargo of convicts in the last cars.

Their smiles then turned to scowls.

The Mine

Huddled in a small conference room in Nashville, the penitentiary board ordered an inspection of the Tennessee Mine at Briceville to see if it was a fit place to work prisoners.

Ten days after the convicts had been returned there, Labor Commissioner George Ford appeared with his assistant for a tour of the mine that would take two days.

The miners had grown fond of the shoe cobbler from Pennsylvania who had become Tennessee's first labor commissioner. He was a friend of labor. He would not divulge their secrets, although he consistently urged restraint and resolution through peaceful means.

For the same reasons, the mine owners despised Ford. They said he was not qualified, not a practical miner, not trained in inspection. He was too thorough. He always carried pen and paper. He wrote down what people said, what he observed, his orders from superiors, and his requests of others. His task was to document, document, document. So when he appeared on Tuesday, August 4, 1891, the mine superintendent, with much trepidation, followed him to the mine opening.

"You want to go with me?" Ford asked the superintendent.

"I don't guess I have any choice."

Ford, his assistant, the superintendent, and William Carmack, a miner with over sixteen years' experience, entered the mine right at one o'clock.

The mountain soared over six hundred feet above the opening that had been punched into its side to follow the seam of coal. The wooden door swung open disclosing two young boys who worked as "trappers" to open and shut the door for miners, mules, and wagons.

"What're your names?" Ford asked.

"I'm Ben Morrison."

"I'm Johnny Manis."

"How old are you, Ben?" Ford asked.

"Eleven."

"And you, Johnny?"

"Nine."

Ford was writing all of it down. "Boys, why are you working here?"

Both boys shook their heads as though the question of why children of their ages worked in a mine was new to them. Was there any thing else they were supposed to do?

"My father's hurt. He can't work. I have six brothers and sisters younger than me. We need the money," Ben finally said.

"And you, Johnny?" Ford continued.

"I don't have a father. He died last year. I have a mother and two sisters. It's fun to work."

"Fun?" Ford said and looked down at the boys' feet. They were standing in ankle-deep water that was black and oily. Their faces and arms were covered with coal dust. Their eyes searched the faces of Ford and his companions for reassurance. "What are you paid?"

"Fifty cents a day," Ben said, and Johnny nodded rapidly in agreement. "It's cool in here and we only work ten hours a day," Ben added.

"We didn't know you were coming for an inspection today," the superintendent interjected.

"Obviously not," Ford responded and wrote some more. "Superintendent Davis, don't you believe it's bad to expose our youth to the company of such hardened convicts as pass through here at all hours? Let alone, the filth they have to work in?"

Davis didn't answer.

They squatted down and walked farther into the mine. Ben was right. It was cool. Ford had been in a lot of mines and they were all chilling to the outsider who was not working, but the miners who sweated with pick and shovel didn't notice.

The air in the Tennessee Mine not only was cool, but it felt thick against the skin. It was like Ford was putting on a layer of snake skin when he walked farther into the mine. It was clammy. He shined his light on his hand. Already an etching of coal dust was gathering on the pores.

Rooms led off right and left. In the darkness of those confining quarters, Ford heard the shoveling of coal.

At the seventh room, he stopped and took his anemometer for a reading of air current. He shined his lantern to the instrument. The paddle-fans were not moving. There was no air current. He sniffed. His nose told him the same thing his instrument did. The air was stagnant.

He took a measurement of the height of the room. Two feet and four inches. Yet he heard workers within. He turned his lantern toward the noise.

There were at least six convicts. They were lying on their sides or backs in two inches of water shoveling the coal toward the opening. Only the few streaks of white that remained on their striped garb allowed Ford to see them. Otherwise, their black bodies melded with the equally dark coal to become one.

Ford bumped his head on the ceiling and bent lower. He duck-walked down a hallway toward another entry room. This one was about the same height but much wider. He measured. It was a twenty-seven-foot wide opening with only one support throughout the whole expanse. He was afraid to tap the ceiling for fear of provoking a cave-in.

"You're supposed to leave more columns of coal for support and have more timbers for braces," Ford said to the superintendent who just nodded.

He looked at his notes of previous complaints about the mine's conditions. He stopped at room twelve. In January, Church Wright had his right leg crushed when about five tons of rock and fireclay fell on him from the roof while he was bringing in a car to load with coal. Wright had not worked since.

They walked down to another room on the left where Ford found John Bertree, a convict, and D. B. Cash, a free man who had not been locked out with the other miners, working together. Ford looked at the ceiling. “This could fall before we get out.”

Superintendent Davis put his hand up and examined the rock. “Yes, I’m afraid you’re right. We don’t need to linger here.”

By now they were over a half mile into the innards of the mountain. They walked into a passage where mud lay under stagnant water. The water came almost to the top of their boots. The seats of their pants were wettened as they squatted to go through.

“What is that smell, that stench?” Ford asked and turned his lantern toward the brackish water. There staring up at him were four eyes of two dead and bloated rats as big around as his thigh.

The men splashed out of there and toward the main entrance as fast as their tired legs would propel them. A miner sat near another room, staring toward the mine’s opening.

“What are you doing?” Ford asked him.

“Waiting for them to send me some supports for the ceiling in this room.”

“How long you been waiting?”

“Since Saturday.”

“But this is Tuesday,” Ford reminded him.

“I know,” the man said.

They found the ties and tracks which supported the coal cars that ran in and out of the mine. They were pulled by small mules, bred for that purpose. They could only maneuver through the main passageway which was four and a half feet high. In the lower ceilinged-rooms, coal was hauled out manually in baskets or wheelbarrows to be loaded into the small cars. Water and mud covered part of the tracks.

A bit farther along, a gang of seven convicts gathered at a passageway. Their lamps were burning with open flames. One of them was pouring blasting powder from a can into another container. Ford hurried on by and imagined the whole mine exploding through the carelessness of these untrained convicts.

He looked for the water-course that was supposed to be present in all mines to allow for the escape of water and to be an alternate escape route for miners who might be trapped by an explosion of gas or a fall-in. He crawled over rock and sludge scraping his back. Finally, he reached a point where the water flowed to the top of the opening. Neither he nor anyone else could escape through there.

Ford smiled when he saw the sunshine of day. He sat on a rock and made more notes. The Tennessee Mine now worked forty-four convicts and fifty-six free miners who were known as "blacklegs" to the miners who had been thrown out of a job.

A commotion erupted at the mine's entrance. Four black convicts came lumbering out. They carried another who was bleeding and unconscious. They hauled him to the stockade. Ford followed.

An hour later Ford came back out and sat on the same rock. He wrote into his notes: "Henry Cotton, a colored convict, was injured this day by a shot blowing out on him, burning his face and hands. He was an inexperienced hand, and did not know just how to carry on this kind of work."

Ford concluded his inspection the next day and made his report to the board the following. He found several faults with the mine.

There was no map. There was only one outlet. It was dangerous to work there because of the conditions. The mine was not examined prior to every shift in accordance to law. Ventilation was defective. Boys under twelve were being worked in violation of law. Accidents were not timely reported. Drainage was deficient.

Ford recommended the removal of convict labor from the mines because of health and safety reasons.

The penitentiary board made their own inspection the following week. They took statements from different parties.

John Goodwin, who represented the lessees, admitted a few deficiencies, but said, "We have a plumber here now, and will have the mine in apple-pie order in regard to water. The ventilation is in first-class order. Our stockade is large and airy, our buildings well ventilated and comfortable."

The steward for the stockade, T. J. Linn, told the board, "We are feeding convicts beef and bacon; beef three times a week, bacon the balance. Sometimes the bacon is boiled, other times fried. We have no molasses. We have only moderately good clothing. The majority of convicts brought two changes of clothing with them. There is no straw or mats for the beds."

S. M. Hoskins was the main mine boss. He was more forthcoming than the owners cared for. "The mine is not very well drained now, but better than it was. Men can get through the waterway when the water is not up, but it is generally up. Boys are trappers, but they are over twelve years of age. There are no set tasks, but we work the men ten hours a day. There's about fifty digging coal, and we get out about seventy-five to one hundred tons a day."

S. W. Jack, the warden of the convicts at the Tennessee Mine was quite frank. "The men come out of the mine wet. We have no night shirts for the convicts. They have to sleep in the same clothing they work in, although Mr. Goodwin has promised us some more clothing. We have no straw for the beds, but I have requested it. They sleep on wood-slatted bunks. The weather is warm so they don't need blankets.

"I'm not sure about the air in the mine. I've been sick and the physician told me not to go in. The mine, I understand, has water in it. I think they commenced working before being ready."

The board members also spoke with some of the convicts. Most of them asked that they not be quoted for fear of retaliation by the guards and owners after the board departed. However, the board did make note of four particular convicts and their comments.

Wood Diggs had been convicted of robbery and was in for five years. He had only served four months. "I work in water over my shoe-tops. The air is bad. It hurts me in my chest. I've had headaches and cramps. I haven't had anything fit to eat since I've been here. The meat is old and moldy. The potatoes have no grease on them. I'm wearing all the clothing I have. No socks.

I've never dug coal before."

Babe Hurt was in for a year on a petty larceny charge and had served seven months. "The mine is worse than the one at Tracy City. I have no coat, but the food is passable. I get out four or five cars of coal a day."

Obie Lewis had only been in for a month of an eighteen month sentence. "We have hard beds. No straw. There's some water in the mine where I work. They haven't abused us yet. There's been no whipping, but they say they will if we don't meet our task amounts when they set them."

The injured Henry Cotton could speak but little. "I worked in the mine for two weeks. I worked in water. Now I can't stand up. I got hurt blasting."

The board member interviewing Cotton made the note that he was "blowed up considerably. Doctor attending him now."

The board retired to Nashville and requested an opinion from Attorney General G. W. Pickle as to whether the board had authority to order the convicts not to be worked under such conditions.

Pickle wrote that "the convicts are not outlaws. They are entitled to protection of life and health during their imprisonment. The state cannot confer upon another absolute dominion over its convicts and their lives and health."

On Thursday, August 13, 1891, the board unanimously held that the convicts should not be worked under such conditions and ordered them removed from the mine.

Commissioner Ford followed that with a cease and desist order of his own to the mine owners, citing fourteen violations of law and safety regulations.

With a phalanx of lawyers, the mine owners and lessees of the convicts responded with a lawsuit to set aside the orders of the board and Commissioner Ford.

Commissioner Ford "is not a practical miner, as the law requires, and is entirely without experience. He is in sympathy with the movement to drive out the convicts and is incompetent to make an impartial investigation," they said in their court papers.

"The mine is not entirely free from water, but is as free as any mine in that section of the country. The stockade is not completed, but the walls are up, and the rooms inside are built. The bedding was imperfect, but since the inspection has been made good. The washing, bathing, and hospital facilities are being constructed and are, at present, sufficient for use," the papers continued.

The case was heard in Nashville. On August 26, the judge ruled that the convicts could stay at the Tennessee Mine stockade but could not work in the mine until it was in better condition.

The miners of the district would have to await the special session of the legislature to find any permanent relief from the canker that was growing in the Tennessee Mine.

The Mule

By the last Saturday of August, Betsy Boyd had completed two months of schooling under the tutelage of Jim Powell. Her test scores were excellent. In another month she would complete the tenth grade under his accelerated course structure.

Professor Brimer had told her that her hands danced along the keyboard of the typewriter to the same cadence of the wheels of a train over the sections of rail. He smiled when he said it, so she thought it must have been a compliment. The stack of papers that she had typed over the two months did make quite a heap on the corner of the table, but with the mountains left to type, she knew she had job security with him for the next summer.

Early this morning she had left the Boyd household outside of Coal Creek and walked the seven miles to Briceville. Her father needed Nellie for farm work so she had no choice. She didn't mind walking. But would Nellie be there for her when she began teaching? She needed a source of transportation. "God will provide," Grandma Dolan had told her before she left for Briceville.

The day before she had stopped at Clinton to see John Harding, the school superintendent. He gave her a bell. It was her very own brass bell with a wood handle. With it she would signal her students it was time to begin classes or to end recess.

She couldn't help it. She tested the bell on the train ride

home. When she saw a child in a yard or near the track, she thrust her arm out the window, flailed with her new bell, and yelled, "School starts in a month. Get ready. Miss Betsy Boyd is going to teach you to read and write."

When she thought on it this morning, she knew she had acted childishly, but she was so excited. She brought the bell to Briceville to show her friend. She had not visited with Sarah Thomas since the exodus of miners in April.

Sarah was the one with whom she had shared all her childhood secrets. Being apart for five months was too long. There was so much to tell her—Jake Drummond. She was going to be a teacher. She was going to be a high school graduate. And, if Professor Brimer had his way, she would one day be a voter.

This dreadful matter with the mine owners would come to a quick end when the legislature took action the next month, and she and Sarah would be able to renew their association on a more normal basis.

They talked on for hours that sped away like minutes. Sarah, too, had news. She would marry in the fall. Would Betsy stand with her at the church?

They laughed until they cried. They hugged, looked each other in the eye, and cried some more. They both wanted to hang on to the memories of their youth, but with new responsibilities, new relationships, and a separation of several miles, things would never be the same.

When she started home down the dirt road in late afternoon, Betsy was accompanied by a touch of melancholy. The miles slipped away under her feet while her thoughts stayed with Sarah and the years that had gone before. It was difficult to walk away, but she looked forward to what lay ahead for her—teacher, university student, and voter.

She clutched the silver dollars that she carried in a small leather pouch in a pocket of her dress. She was a woman of means. She had amassed a small fortune, seven silver dollars of her own. The remainder of her earnings she had given to her mother and father. She kept only four out of every twenty-four for herself—and that she did not spend foolishly.

She had bought her own dictionary for a dollar. It contained every word known to man and she would learn every one of them. Professor Brimer used so many words that she had never heard in Briceville or Coal Creek. She was becoming educated just by learning their meaning as she typed his papers.

On the left just ahead was the Knoxville Iron Company mine and its horrible stockade. She glanced over toward it and saw the striped garb of convicts behind the wall of cedar posts. Saturday was still a work day at the mine. She could hear the clatter of the cart wheels being pulled from the mine with their loads of coal.

A hundred yards ahead of her, the road was blocked. She peered closer. The figures first appeared motionless as though they were a creation of some unseen hand that had just placed them in the road as a monument. Then she noticed that one part moved but the other didn't.

There was a mule crossways in the road. She was kneeling, front legs tucked under and head down on the road as though praying.

Betsy walked faster.

Behind the mule there was a man from the mine. He yelled at the animal. He picked up a large tree branch and began to beat the uncompliant beast.

The mule did not budge.

The man threw down the tree limb and picked up a piece of discarded lumber from the side of the road. He swung it overhead and crashed it down into the mule's flanks. He took a pistol from his belt and fired off a shot into the air.

Betsy's heart began to pound. She clinched her teeth. Her feet broke into a run.

The man kicked the still-praying mule. He cursed the reluctant animal. "Move you worn out beast!" He was not aware of the fast approaching Betsy Boyd.

She felt in the little basket she was carrying and took out the only weapon she had—her school bell.

She ran toward the oaf, ringing the bell as though time had come to an end.

"What the he . . .?" the man said when he saw the flailing dervish approaching.

Betsy stopped before striking the man with the brass bell. "What are you doing to that poor animal?" she asked, not expecting to receive an answer that would explain the bestial behavior of the man.

"That mule is on its way to the graveyard," he finally said. "Who are you to interfere?"

Betsy walked to where the poor brown animal with the floppy ears had bowed to pray. Betsy looked back to the man. Her eyes flashed and her arms flailed up and down. "Balaam, what have I done to thee, that thou hast smitten me three times?"

The man took his hat off and scratched his head. "Woman, my name ain't Balaam. I'm one of the mule drivers for the mine. This animal is worn out and I'm taking her over to that ravine to shoot her. Then we'll throw some dirt on her. She's too old to pull a coal cart."

"Sir, each of God's creations is entitled to a little respect. Dumb animals do not need to be beaten. You come down to the Methodist church and you'll learn who Balaam was." She kneeled down and took the mule's head in her arms.

"Who are you?" the mule driver asked.

"I'm Betsy Boyd. I'm a teacher. And I'm a human being. Is this the way you treat the convicts and other miners?"

He drew his pistol back out and walked to where he could touch the barrel against the ear of the mule. "I can kill her right here and pull her off the road. You'd better move."

"I'll take her," Betsy said. "Give her to me, and I'll take her off your hands. You won't have to worry about burying her."

"You interfering, sassy child, I wouldn't give her to you if I had to dig a hole for her myself."

Betsy reached into her pocket, took out the leather pouch, and retrieved a silver dollar. "I'll buy her." She thrust the money toward him.

He looked back toward the stockade, put his revolver back into his belt, and jerked the money from Betsy's hand. "You just bought yourself a broken down mule." He stomped off back across the road.

Still, the mule didn't budge.

Betsy walked down the bank to the creek and searched along its bank until she found a large can. She filled it with water and walked back to her mule. *Her mule.* She owned something else.

She dipped her hands into the cool water and then put them to the mouth of the mule. She wiped the animal's face and stroked her ears. She eased the can toward the mule's mouth, encouraging her to drink. She still refused.

For an hour, Betsy's mule continued in her bowed position. Two men walked by and shook their heads at the sight. Finally, the old animal raised up, trembled a bit, and turned her head toward Betsy. She began to walk, and Betsy led her to the creek. There the mule assuaged her thirst with long drafts of the refreshing water.

The mule's ribs showed, and Betsy could have hung her bonnet on the animal's hip bones. With the pace of a death march, Betsy led her back up onto the road and toward Coal Creek.

At a feed and hardware store on the main street, Betsy bought a bag of dried corn and oats that was flavored with a hint of molasses. She took a double-handful and held it up to her mule. The animal snorted and then began to eat from Betsy's hand.

Betsy didn't want to feed the ravenous animal too much at one time. She wasn't sure her body could stand the shock of food.

Betsy hefted the bag of feed onto her own shoulders and started anew toward her house with her new possession.

"See your mule's got you trained to carry her feed," a young boy yelled at her. She paid no attention and walked on. The mule followed at the end of a small rope.

Grandma Dolan sat rocking on the porch when Betsy finally reached home.

"Where did you find that?" she asked her granddaughter.

"They were going to kill her. They were beating her with a board. I couldn't stand it. I had to take her."

"I saved you some supper. All the others have eaten. We thought something might have happened to you," Grandma Dolan said as though it was an every day occurrence to bring home a mule. "Did you have any trouble?"

"No. Nothing I couldn't handle." Betsy looked to see if anybody else was near by. "I'll take my mule to the barn, then I'll eat. Thanks for saving me something."

"Apple cobbler."

Into a vacant stall next to Nellie, Betsy led the mule. She scooped some more of the feed into her trough, then went to the hay loft and threw down a pitchfork full of fresh hay. She gathered it into her arms and carried it to the stall.

From a nail near the door, she retrieved a curry comb and began to brush the poor animal's coat. Handsful of hair came out. She continued to brush. She needed a name for her mule. Jake had Charmer who was black as coal.

Hmm. The mule came from the Knoxville Iron Company mine. She would be transformed by Betsy from a worn out animal to a thing of beauty—at least as beautiful as mules could be. Steel. As iron is transformed into steel, so should the mule be changed. She would henceforth be Miss Steele.

Betsy rushed back into the house ready to eat. Jake had just arrived, and only he sat at the table with her.

It was the best of seasons for home grown food. The table was still heaped with bowls of boiled corn-on-the-cob, green beans seasoned with bacon drippings, sliced red tomatoes, boiled potatoes, and a pan of fried chicken. In the center stood a still steaming bowl of Grandma Dolan's apple cobbler.

Betsy would as soon look at it and smell the aromas as to consume it. But eat it she did. The day had been long and arduous.

She told Jake about the man and the mule. She laughed when she told him she attacked the scoundrel with a school bell.

"I bet that really scared him," Jake said and took a bite of chicken.

"I wish I'd been there," Grandma Dolan said when she heard Betsy's story. "That man has less sense than the mules he drives."

All of the Boyds, Grandma Dolan, and Jake Drummond sat on the porch and in the yard after supper. The music of the crickets and frogs, occasionally interrupted by the howl of a hound, serenaded them as they entertained their own private thoughts or engaged in quiet conversation and jesting banter.

Jake looked at Betsy from where they sat together at the end of the porch.

"Betsy, the miners have selected me to go to Nashville. I'll be gone for two weeks. Me and two others will go and observe the legislature to see what they do about our mining problems. Will you miss me?"

"I told you they liked you, Jake. They see something good in you. Sure, I'll miss you, but you need to go. You might be in the legislature yourself next year."

Away from the eyes of the other Boyds, Jake and Betsy embraced.

The Legislature

Governor John P. Buchanan was true to his word in the call for the state legislature to meet. He assigned the body several tasks.

Among those was the request "to enact, amend, or repeal such laws with reference to the penitentiary of the state as shall be deemed promotive of the public good, as the leasing, working, and safekeeping of the convicts."

He also called for other considerations. He wanted specific authority to call out the military when he thought necessary. The prospect that he did not have power to call out the National Guard had haunted him from the first days of the problems at Briceville and Coal Creek.

The militia had to be compensated for their call-outs to the trouble spots, so he asked for an appropriation.

Since he had the legislature in session, Buchanan threw in a few other items for consideration. Included among those was a call for Tennessee to participate in the Chicago World's Fair to be held in 1892, which was officially known as the World's Columbian Exposition in honor of the four hundredth anniversary of Christopher Columbus's visit to the New World.

Buchanan's own Farmers' Alliance Party met in Nashville and endorsed the idea of doing away with the convict lease system.

The road seemed paved to abolish the system and relieve the miners.

Jake Drummond traveled to Nashville with Eugene Merrill and George Irish to monitor the actions of the legislature for the first two weeks. They would then be relieved by three others.

From Coal Creek, Jake and the other two men journeyed through Knoxville and Chattanooga on their train ride to the capital city. Jake kept his face turned toward the window to take in the new vistas he had only heard about. In Chattanooga, he walked to the Read House Hotel. Where did the blond-haired soldier live that he had met at the stockade in Briceville?

On Monday, August 31, the legislature came together at noon for the opening of what was limited to a twenty day session.

While Merrill and Irish went together to watch the senate in action, Jake walked up the narrow steps to the balcony of the state house chamber. Visitors were allowed to sit there and look down to the floor at their legislators in action.

The polished limestone of the railing was cool to his touch when he leaned over to get a better view. There was a flurry of activity on the floor. The legislators walked between desks and talked loudly to their neighbors. They were all men, white and bearded. Some gestured toward the gallery where many visitors sat.

Jake and his friends were not the only ones interested in the actions of the legislature. Here in the same balcony sat John Goodwin who represented the lease-holders of the convicts, and the mine owners had at least a dozen men in attendance.

In less than an hour after commencing, the house adjourned for the day. They had appointed committees to look into the matters, but there had been no real discussion. The only thing that passed was their appropriation for five dollars worth of stamps for each member's use during the session.

Jake looked at the clock. One hour. He was less than impressed with the amount of work they did on the first day. He assumed they would work longer and harder as they got into the discussion of the matter. A miner worked ten hours a day. The legislators worked one. Perhaps there was something to what Betsy said. Maybe he should run for the legislature.

He walked back down the steep stairs, sure that the senate was probably into the meat of the problem. Merrill and Irish were already waiting for him in the area between the two chambers on the second floor of the Capitol Building.

There was jovial banter among the legislators still in the hallway. Mine owners had collared at least a dozen of them and were busy in conspiratorial whisperings.

"That's it for today," Merrill said to Jake. "They are breaking down into committees to discuss the options and will meet again tomorrow. I don't think this is going to be easy." Irish nodded his head in agreement.

"Why?" Jake asked. "All the papers are condemning the system. There's been meetings across the state saying it has to go. Can't they see that?"

Merrill rubbed his thumb and index finger together. "It's money, Jake. Greed. Some are already saying it would cost too much to build a prison to keep the fifteen hundred convicts in. The way the system is, the state gets paid for their convicts instead of paying to put them up."

"It all comes down to who has the most money," Irish agreed. "And we're short in that regard."

"How does this work? What do they have to do to repeal the system?" Jake asked his companions while they were walking down the main steps to the first floor and outside.

"We need fifty votes in the house and seventeen in the senate. There are ninety-nine house members and thirty-three senators. Some are absent. But that doesn't make any difference. We still need a majority of all the members—not just the ones present.

"So, we have to get fifty representatives to vote to do away with the lease system or to buy out the lessees. It's easier to kill a proposition than to pass one. We can have a vote of forty-nine for us and fifteen against us, and we still lose."

The mysteries of the legislative process were just beginning to make their impact on Jake.

The next day in the senate, the first bad omen appeared. State Senator Russell Polk offered a resolution for the Senate's consideration:

Whereas, a state of rebellion does now exist in the county of Anderson, and the civil authorities are unable to enforce the law; and

Whereas the public safety requires that the military force of the state be used to suppress the same;

Therefore, Be it resolved by the general assembly of the state of Tennessee, That the governor be and hereby is empowered and instructed to call out such part of the military force of the state as he may deem necessary to suppress said rebellion and insure due execution of the laws and maintain the peace of the state.

"Rebellion? What rebellion?" Merrill asked Irish and Jake. "We're down here to redress our wrongs in a lawful manner. There's nothing going on in Briceville and Coal Creek. Our own miners are protecting those guards and convicts until the legislature does something." He took his hat and hit it against the railing. "This doesn't sound good."

The next day proved worse. A house member questioned from the floor the citizenship of the Coal Creek and Briceville miners. He said at least half of them were "foreigners who have recently come into the country and made trouble."

Jake reported it to Merrill who immediately wrote out a response and had the three to sign it in front of a notary public. He gave it to the house and senate clerks and to newspaper representatives.

"We do not know of one man in Briceville who is not a citizen, and only two who are not voters of the state of Tennessee, except for ex-convicts who have been released from the mines by reason of expiration of their terms. We don't allow liquor to be sold nearer than ten miles from us, and our county has but one man in the state prison. There is no dangerous or extremely ignorant class among us of any nationality, and 75 per cent are natives of Tennessee, and descendants of Sevier, Shelby and Crockett, men who defended the honor of their country and their liberties against England, France and Mexico, died in the Alamo in defense of liberty, home and just laws, and their teaching is exemplified in their descendants of today."

"I hope they get that last little hint about the Alamo and the teachings we have learned," Merrill told Jake and Irish.

Later in the week, the legislature began to go in all directions. Some were concerned about the World's Fair. Some wanted to tax the railroad property. There was a scandal that the doorman for the Capitol Building had illegally charged for tours of the building.

The legislators looked at criminal reform. One theory was to reduce the number of convicts and eliminate the pool of slave labor for the lessees.

Bills were introduced to have lesser offenders to serve their time in county workhouses. For other transgressions of the law, it was suggested that the whipping post be reinstated. Representative B. R. Thomas proposed that wife beaters receive no more than a hundred lashes while daytime burglars receive no more than forty.

Both the house and senate adjourned for the celebration of Labor Day on Monday, September 7.

Merrill, Jake, and Irish returned to Coal Creek for a quick report to the miners.

"Betsy, these legislators don't have the brains of those geese out in the back yard. Why did you think I would make a good one?" Jake asked on Sunday after church. He would head back on Monday morning to complete his two weeks of spying on the lawmakers of the state.

"Because you're brighter than most of them down there, Jake. You have a feel for what's right and wrong that they've lost. That's why."

"Maybe so. It looks to me like they just meet, squawk a little, and then adjourn to go out and drink. That's not my type of life. They haven't worked a full six hours the whole week we've been down there."

"Well, you just have one more week on your assignment. Then we'll go up to Briceville. Miss Steele may be strong enough to ride by then. She's looking better every day. I can't wait to ride by the Knoxville Iron mine and show that disgusting mule driver what a fine animal she turned out to be with just a little care."

Miners' hopes did not improve the next week.

A house member accused Labor Commissioner George Ford of being an "agitator, encouraging lawlessness, and responsible for the trouble at Briceville." A committee was appointed to investigate.

Taxes. If the lease system was done away with, the state would have to raise a million dollars in taxes to pay for a new prison and to compensate for the one hundred thousand dollars per year that was received from the lessees. A tide started to build among the rural representatives of farmers to leave the system as it was. No farmer could tolerate any additional tax. The miners were a small minority of the population of the state. They would have to turn to other occupations, if necessary.

Apparently fueled by mine owners and the lessees, Representative T. S. Alexander accused Merrill, Irish, and John Hatmaker of being criminals.

"This mob went armed with guns, pistols, and other weapons and released the convicts at Briceville and Coal Creek. Eugene Merrill, George Irish, and John Hatmaker did incite this rebellion against lawful authority. Their threats of violence and lawlessness are still freely made. They openly threaten to repeat the conduct of July. These criminals should be hunted down and prosecuted."

His resolution provided for a five hundred dollar reward for each of the culprits.

Merrill was in the gallery with Jake.

He stood. "Here I am, sir. You don't have to waste the state's money on any reward," he shouted down to Alexander who blanched at the retort.

Jake pulled Merrill back down into his seat. "Gene, be quiet. They'll arrest all of us."

"No they won't. That Alexander is a cowardly scoundrel," Merrill said and started to walk out. He looked back at Jake. "You could make a quick thousand dollars by turning me and

George in." He smiled and walked out of the gallery.

On the floor, other representatives came to the defense of Merrill, Irish, Hatmaker, and the other miners. Heated words were exchanged. There were cries of "liar" and "infamous liar," as though one was worse than the other. The resolution was tabled.

But the next day, matters continued on a downward spiral. Representative John Curtis introduced a bill empowering the governor to call upon the sheriffs of all counties to join him with a sufficient number of citizen draftees to put down any rebellion, mob, or riot. There was little doubt what was intended.

The only glint of sunshine on the otherwise stormy horizon came in the form of a non-binding request of this legislature to future legislatures. Representative J. L. Cochran introduced, and the house passed by a slim majority, a resolution expressing the sense of the body that there should be no further leases of convicts after the current one expired. The current one didn't expire until 1896. However, the senate killed the resolution anyway.

The following day, an opinion from Attorney General Pickle was read on the floor of the house. The attorney general pointed to a technicality in the lease law to help the miners. "In the lease law there is no direct nor indirect allusion to the giving of the lessees the power to sublease the convicts," he wrote.

Therefore, it followed that the convicts at the Tennessee Mine were there illegally. The mine would have to be owned by the original lessee of the convicts to be legal.

Jake was confused by all the dancing around the real issue. Would the legislature do anything to put an end to the lease system? Could the miners work without competition from convict labor? Would there still be a war?

The senate sputtered along. It rejected the whipping post as an idea whose time had come and gone. A proposal to punish anyone convicted of their second felony with life imprisonment was likewise voted down.

In a separate move by another arm of state government, the penitentiary board met in Nashville with representatives of the lessee, Tennessee Coal, Iron and Railroad Company.

Would the lessees modify the lease to allow convicts to work only in mines where they had worked before the Briceville trouble? What if the state needed some prisoners to work to help build a new prison? Would they be available?

Nat Baxter spoke for the company. He would call the bluff of the state. "We would be happy to surrender the lease," he said and looked around the room for reaction. "You can have all the convicts back."

The members of the board looked at each other. The state had over fifteen hundred convicts. They had no place for them. The convict lease system had been in place for so long that the state was not in any way prepared to take them back.

"You can have them all back." Baxter smiled. "But we can't change the lease one bit. I don't have places for them all either if we can't work them at Coal Creek and Briceville."

The board could not take the convicts back. They adjourned and the board hoped that the move by the lessees would not be made known to the miners at Briceville and Coal Creek. The problem fell squarely on the back of the state which was unprepared for an avalanche of convicts.

Jake Drummond's observation of the legislature for two weeks came to a welcome end. He now knew more than most people in Anderson County about how the state made laws. Or in this case, failed to make laws. He was educated if not impressed.

He had learned some new words. The phrase he coined in describing the legislature was as good as the eloquent Merrill could have done. "The legislative hall is a pavilion of perfidy," he told Betsy. She immediately went to her new dictionary.

The legislature continued to muddle on through for two more weeks of wrangling. One day a paper ball fight broke out among house members that took the speaker and the sergeants-at-arms ten minutes to quell.

The short time the military had been in Briceville, along with the travel to Knoxville, had cost the state over fourteen thousand dollars. Some legislators objected to appropriating the money for it because they said the governor had illegally called out the militia.

The senate wanted to start work toward building new penitentiaries immediately. West Tennessee representatives said they didn't want any convicts in their end of the state. The house voted to study the matter by appointing a committee to travel the state and make a recommendation to the next legislature.

What would the miners at Briceville and Coal Creek do with the inaction of the legislature? Many were asking that question.

An East Tennessee legislator said the convicts at Briceville and Coal Creek would be released within thirty days.

Commissioner Ford felt optimistic. "I believe they will control themselves and wait for the action of the next legislature."

Superintendent of Prisons E. P. Wade was not so sure. "I anticipate trouble. The sixty days armistice will expire on the twenty-fourth of September. At that time you may look for another uprising. I am firmly of the opinion that the authorities of the state will have to again proceed to Anderson County and, by decisive action, suppress forever the miners' outbreak against law and order."

Chris Cawood

The Convicts

Coal digging done for the day, Sam Farley scooted the wooden crate he used for a chair nearer the wooden crate that served as a table.

He and four other black convicts hunched over the big can of boiled potatoes seasoned with a hint of lard. They ladled the food into wooden bowls. At least it was still warm. The cornbread that sat beside it was cold and hard.

"Where do they get their cooks from?" one of the newer tenants of the small room asked Farley.

"They rotate them. If you're too hurt to go to the mines, you can still cook or do something else. If you break a foot in a rock fall, you'll be our next cook."

A sixth young black man lay on his wood-slat bunk bed that had a thin layer of straw. His arms curled over his head. He wasn't talking or eating. He'd only been at the stockade of the Knoxville Iron Company mine for a week. Farley was an old-timer, having dug coal for five years. He had five more to go.

Sam Farley was always having new tenants in his little room. The guards put newcomers who had bad reputations with Sam. He provided a calming influence.

The younger ones sometimes thought they could escape. They might not work as hard as Sam, or they questioned authority. But they soon learned better. The withdrawn one was going to get a lesson in obedience and meeting his assigned task this evening.

"Jim, you'd best get over here and have some food. You'll need it to carry you through the night. You'll have to work tomorrow and make your task. Else they'll have you out there again tomorrow night," Sam spoke to the sullen one.

The youth lay motionless. He had not met his assigned "task", or amount of coal he was supposed to dig since he had been there. Today he had cursed a guard who had a low limit of toleration. Jim would soon be whipped with a leather strap.

The guards warned all incoming convicts of the possible penalty and told them how to avoid it. "Work hard and behave."

All of the convicts had been walked past the arena of correction where four metal rings protruded from the ground. A malcreant would be stripped of his clothing and manacled to the iron rings face down in the dirt. Thus, bare, spreadeagled, and vulnerable, he would await the dreaded punishment.

A guard would stand above him. With a leather strap three fingers wide, a half inch thick, and attached to a wooden handle, he would lash the upper legs and buttocks of the helpless convict until bruised and bloody. The number of strokes depended on the offense. This youth had been sentenced to between ten and twenty, depending on the disposition of the guard.

Sam Farley, at fifty-one, was a father figure to some of the younger black men. He had been born in slavery in Madison County, Tennessee. This was his first term in prison.

As a slave he had picked cotton for his master. As a free black, he had picked cotton for his former master. Conditions were about the same. His large family would tend a portion of the owner's property. They would attack the cotton at harvest time with a ferocity that stripped many acres per day of the white fluffy balls.

Most of the convicts at the Knoxville Iron mine were younger. They were not former slaves. They were born in freedom to former slaves. But the same society that had enslaved them for three hundred years now enslaved them again under a different system.

Of the fifteen hundred convicts in the Tennessee prison

system in 1891, eighty per cent of them were black. At the Knoxville Iron mine, a hundred thirty of a hundred thirty-five convicts were black. The five white men roomed together.

Tennessee didn't always have a prison system. For its first third of a century, the state had managed to get by with county jails, fines, and the whipping post.

In 1829, Governor Sam Houston signed the bill that allowed the building of the first penitentiary.

The first prisoner sent to the penitentiary was from Sam Farley's home county of Madison in west Tennessee. W. G. Cook was a tailor convicted of malicious stabbing and assault and battery.

Cook said a man didn't pay him for a suit and disparaged his quality of work. So Cook attacked the man with his shears and hit him with his tailor's goose, an iron with a long wooden handle. His first work at the penitentiary was to make his own suit.

It wasn't until 1866 that the state allowed the convicts to be leased out for private endeavors. Under the administration of Governor William G. "Parson" Brownlow, the prisoners were leased for forty-three cents per day. After the ruinous Civil War, the revenue helped to balance the budget.

Close to three hundred prisoners were leased to do the jobs of coopers, carpenters, painters, shoemakers, harnessmakers, blacksmiths, wagonmakers, and shop tenders. Others cut stone, worked in lumber yards, cooked, aided at hospitals, or became yard hands. For the most part, the work was done at the prison in Nashville or nearby.

Governor Brownlow predicted that the prison population would jump. In a message to the legislature, he noted that the increase would result "from the demoralization of the war, and the remission of the colored race to the penalties of our criminal code instead of the summary treatment applied to them when slaves."

A study by the prison directors in 1868 showed that half of the convicts were in prison for petty larceny of less than five dollars each. Together they had stolen less than a thousand dollars. Yet, the state was forced to house and guard them in dollar terms far above what the convicts had stolen.

Of the three hundred convicts, the division was almost equal between black and white.

By the next year, the prison population had grown to five hundred fifty-one. It was costing the state eleven dollars per month to care for the prisoners. This amount included expenditures for food, clothing, shoes, tobacco, hospital care, and guards.

Until 1870, the convicts were confined to the penitentiary in Nashville and worked there. But with the changing of the lease to Cherry, Morrow and Company of Nashville, some convicts were employed on railroads, and for the first time, a hundred fifty went to the coal mines in southeast Tennessee.

In 1874, the Superintendent of Prisons recommended the building of "branch" prisons in the areas where the convicts worked. They erected stockades near coal mines or where they were building railroads.

The prison population pushed the thousand mark in 1876. Blacks outnumbered whites, two to one. With the large number of convicts being worked outside the prison walls, the frequency of attempted escapes rose accordingly. Two hundred fifty-seven succeeded.

It was in 1877 that convicts first came to the Knoxville Iron Company mine at Coal Creek. Their coming was not welcomed by the local miners. But the few incidents of shooting and vandalism soon died out. When the miners saw that the convicts were not going to be worked at other mines in the area, they tolerated the condition.

Nine years later Sam Farley was sent there from Madison County. He had been convicted of larceny.

One of the young black men looked at Farley. "Just why are you here?"

"I was convicted of stealing a pig."

"Did you do it?"

"That's what the law says. I confessed. Actually, my boy did it."

"Why did you confess to it then?"

"Cause I had always been a 'good nigger'. I didn't think they would do nothing to me. My boy had two little babies. He stole the pig for food for the family. It'd been a bad winter. There was no food. We shared what we had.

"He found this pig wandering down the road one day. He took it. Instead of just letting it go wandering by, he took it.

"They came looking for the pig. I told them I took it. I thought I might get a few days in jail or a fine. I got ten years.

"My former owner came and testified for me. Didn't do no good. They said to make an example out of me. They didn't need niggers starting to thieve around there.

"I can serve the time. I've shown them that."

Serving time is what the convicts did well. Very few were paroled early. The state's prison warden said in 1880, "As a reformatory I do not consider the penitentiary a success. Some few, perhaps, go out wiser if not better men; none go out with an improved moral character."

The penalty of prison came early to many. A report by the superintendent in the same year showed that the prison held many youths. There were two ten-year-olds, one eleven, fourteen twelve-year-olds, seventeen who were fifteen-years-old, twenty-two who were sixteen, and forty who were just seventeen.

The mines often worked them to death. They were buried in unmarked graves near the stockades. In 1884 and 1885, thirty-six died at the Knoxville Iron mine; and in 1888 another fifteen succumbed to the rigors of the labor.

The weakened convicts were subject to diseases that took their lives; some died in mine accidents. Very few died from the whippings—they only wished they had.

"You've got to show the white man the respect he wants. Else they can make it hard on you. Say 'Yassir' and 'Nosir' and you'll get along better. Do what they ask and you may make it out of here alive," Farley volunteered to the young men who shared his table.

"I'm going to get out and go back to Madison County. I ain't digging coal the rest of my life."

He leaned closer to the ones around the table. "You boys see those graves up the way toward the mine?"

They nodded.

"In the five years I've been here, there's been fifty bodies laid to rest there. They cover them up with a little dirt. There's no stone. Their families don't even know what happened to them."

Farley touched an index finger to the side of his head. "I've got it all up here. I knew each one of those fifty. When I get out, I'm going to look up as many of their families as I can and tell them where their fathers, brothers, and husbands are.

"If you're not careful, you'll end up there too. I'll be looking up your families," he nodded to each one. He had their attention. "Be smart. Do what the master says. You'll live. You'll get out."

The door banged open, knocking into one of the wooden bunks. Two guards burst in. Behind them stood another two.

One of them stepped to where Sam Farley was eating. The guard rubbed the top of the black man's head. "How's the food, Sam?"

"Excellent, sir. Best I've had."

The guard looked at the young black men. "Have you had any influence on these young bucks to make them good miners, Sam? Or are they going to be just lazy niggers?"

"I think we can make miners out of them, sir. It'll just take a little time."

The guard nodded and looked over to the youth on the bunk. "Well, that one's going to learn the hard way in just a few minutes."

The second guard stepped closer to Farley. "What did you think about your trip to Knoxville, Sam? Did you think you were going to get to go home?"

Sam shook his head. "No, sir. We just did what you told us to do. We went with those miners. Got a little train ride out of it. Saw some scenery between here and Knoxville. But I was glad to get back. I missed the mining—and the food." Sam and the guards laughed.

"Somebody asked me up at Knoxville what I thought about the situation," Sam continued. "I told them it didn't make no mind to me.

"I asked them right back. I said, 'Did you ever see two

dogs fighting for a bone?' They said, 'Yes.' I said, 'Did you ever see da' bone fighting or taking sides?' They said, 'No.' I said, 'We da' bone.'" Sam and the guards laughed again.

"It's time to go, boy," the first guard said to the young black man on the bed. All four of the guards stepped forward in the event they were needed.

The youth sat up on the bed and turned toward the guards. "Please, please, I'll get my task tomorrow. I'm sorry for cursing you."

"It's too late, boy. You'll get your task tomorrow, all right. Cause if you don't, we'll be after you again."

"You'd best go on with them peaceably, Jim," Sam told the youth. "Go ahead and take your lickin' like a man. You'll get over it."

The youth stood and began to walk toward the guards.

"You won't be needing your clothes. Take them off here," a guard said.

The youth turned, took off his prison garb, and laid his clothes on the bed.

"Here, we need to put these cuffs on you while you're in here. Hold out your hands."

The youth complied. Two sets of handcuffs were applied, one to each wrist, leaving the vacant part of the steel rings to be attached to the iron rings in the dirt. Similar ones were placed on each ankle. With a guard on each side, he was led from the room.

"You two come too," one of the other guards said and pointed to two of the others who were in the room. "You need to witness this so that you won't ever be tempted to not meet your task, try to escape, or curse a guard." The newcomers followed.

The door slammed shut, and Sam bowed his head. "Lord, give him the strength to endure. Let him come back alive. May his wounds heal quickly. Amen." He looked up to the two who were still left in the room with him. "You don't ever want to do anything to get a whipping from those guards. They'll take the hide off you."

Sam walked to the corner of the room where a bucket of water sat. He reached down and dipped a piece of towel into the water, wrung it out, and brought it back to the table. "We'll have to help Jim when he gets back. He'll barely be conscious, if at all." They all sat with their heads cradled in their hands, downcast, waiting for the sounds.

The guards threw the youth into the dirt at the ring of retribution. "On your face! Stretch toward the rings!" one guard shouted. Two others bent to their task of connecting the youth's handcuffs and anklecuffs to the four iron rings protruding from the ground.

Two hundred yards away, John Chumbley, the mine superintendent, and his family were being served supper by two convicts he used for house servants. A pink glow reflected off the white of the house from the clouds of sunset.

A fine table was set. Chicken, roast beef, corn, beans, sliced tomatoes, cucumbers, and three kinds of pie.

Chumbley offered the blessing. "Dear God, we thank Thee for Thy bountiful blessings. For this food and our family we give Thee thanks. We thank Thee for keeping us uncontaminated from these that we must deal with. We thank Thee that we are your called children. Amen."

The sound was like a crack of lightning hitting nearby. The report of a rifle would have been no louder. There was the explosion of cowhide against human skin. Then came the scream.

Mrs. Chumbley turned to her husband. She put down the piece of chicken she had taken from the bowl. "John, are they whipping someone again?"

"Yes, dear. One of the new niggers. Didn't get his task and cursed a guard," Chumbley answered and took another bite of roast beef.

The shrieks of pain continued to come through the Chumbleys' windows about every five seconds.

"I know those niggers have to be whipped, John. But do they have to do it right at our supper time? It doesn't make for delightful music."

John Chumbley motioned to one of the servants. "Joe, get your fiddle and play us a tune."

Just fifteen minutes after they had taken him, the guards

brought the penitent youth back. He slumped between them. The guards kicked the door open and tossed him in. He landed on the floor near Sam Farley.

The beaten youth's left arm flailed the floor. His head convulsively beat against the wood planks. The muscles in his thighs twitched involuntarily.

From the top of his buttocks to the backs of his knees, the leather strap had made its imprint over and over. Open welt overlapped open welt. Blood dripped to the wood planks and ran between them.

Ribbons of flesh hung from his buttocks like tiny black snakes whose heads had been flattened by the heel of a boot on the hearth and oozed out their lives' fluid. Beneath, flesh lay exposed. Everyone is red beneath the skin.

The two from the room who had witnessed the beating were tossed inside. They sat motionless on the floor in shock at what they had seen.

Sam Farley and the other two who had remained in the room carried the wounded one to his bed. They laid him on the straw. Sam checked the mouth of the youth.

"Just what I thought. He almost bit his tongue off." He took the wet towel and wiped the youth's mouth and cleaned the blood from his tongue.

"You two hold him. I'm going to have to clean his wounds. Else they might get diseased. I need to lap some of this skin back on. It might grow back."

The guards had left. There were but a few screams more from the youth when cloth met bare tissue. He lay unconscious.

The ones in the cabin were then serenaded by the chorus of katydids and crickets. And from the distance, the soft sound of a fiddle drifted through the night air to where Sam Farley played doctor.

The Shoes

Early on Saturday morning, the Third of October, Betsy Boyd left the breakfast table, walked out the back door, shooed the chickens away, and sneaked to the barn.

Once in the hay loft, she walked to the far wall and reached back to where some loose hay hid her prized possessions. She felt the wood handle and slid the guitar free of its covering. It was her birthday gift to herself.

The day before was her last one working for Professor Brimer at the university. The summer had sped by. And she had matured more during the last six months than for any period of her life.

She had learned more, worked more, rode the train more, accumulated more, and . . . loved more than ever before. She was becoming a different person. The previous Saturday she had turned eighteen.

No one had noticed or said a thing. Not her mother, not her father, and not even Jake. But how could he know? She hadn't told him. He would have done something special for her if he had known.

It was only Professor Brimer who had mentioned it. He had looked at her test scores with Jim Powell and noticed that her birthday was September 26. He had said the certificate that she had completed the tenth grade was a good birthday present. But, then he added it wasn't a present at all. She had earned it.

So when she received her final wages for her work, she had gone straight to West and Company on Gay Street in Knoxville. She was amused by the advertisement the store had printed in the Knoxville *Journal*. "Convicts Must Go!" it read. "So must the present stock of pianos and organs."

If the store backed the miners in their attempt to rid the valley of convicts, she would support the store with her purchase—small as it might be. The guitar cost her five dollars. It was a lavish, and probably sinful, expenditure for herself. But she had wanted it, perhaps even lusted after it, so much.

She sat in the hay and let her fingers play with the strings. Very softly she plucked the wires and leaned down to hear the sound of the vibrations. She knew she could play it. She just needed more practice.

All during the summer, she had listened to Professor Brimer strum his guitar. It seemed so relaxing. Then when he noticed her interest in the instrument, he had let her handle it and test her skill. When she rested from the typewriter, she soothed herself with the guitar.

Professor Brimer told her she was a "natural" with the guitar. Of course, he had said that about the typewriter too. Should she believe him? What was for certain was that she was in a world of her own when she played the soft chords of the instrument.

She was afraid to tell her mother or father about her guitar. Money was so scarce. There were so many needs that there was no room for things that were just for pleasure. Grandma Dolan would understand. She had often said that life was too short not to have some enjoyment, whatever the state of affairs.

Today was the twins' birthday. Belle and Estelle were five. Betsy determined that her little sisters' big day would not go by unnoticed as hers had.

She put the guitar away for the time being and reached to her secret hiding place in the hay again. She brought out the leather pouch that she had carried with her from Briceville. It still contained the scrip tokens of the Tennessee Mine.

She blew hay dust off the container and opened it. Into her hand she poured the brass pieces. She counted them. Eleven dollars. More than enough.

She reached in once again to the haystack and withdrew Jake's kerchief that still cradled the tokens the miners had thrown down at the big meeting. She untied the knot and spread the corners out. She had never calculated their worth before. She counted. Two hundred dollars.

Ignorant miners! They had thrown two hundred dollars in scrip into the dust. Even more probably. She had been unable to find all of it.

She folded the kerchief back around the tokens and tied the knot. This would be her bank. She didn't need that much today. Eleven dollars would be plenty. She would save the other for more dire circumstances.

She was a woman of means. A dictionary, a mule, and now a guitar. On Monday, she would begin her teaching career. There was so much to do and so little time.

With the guitar and Jake's kerchief safely back in their hiding place, Betsy clutched the leather pouch of scrip to her and descended the loft ladder.

When Betsy reached the house, she noticed Grandma Dolan and the twins were in front of the fireplace. Estelle and Belle sat at the knees of their grandmother on a small bench. Grandma Dolan's fingers were dancing across the small hands of the girls. She was chanting one of their favorite non-sensical rhymes and pointing to their fingers.

"William-a-William-a-Trembletoes,
He's a good fisherman, catches hens,
Puts them in a pen,
Some lay eggs, some none,
Wire, briar, limberlock,
Ten geese in a flock,
Clock falls down,
Mouse runs out,
'O' 'U' 'T',
Spells out goes he."

She finished and her bony forefinger of each hand found the soft skin of the twins' belly buttons. They giggled and begged her to say it again.

Betsy laughed and sat beside her sisters on the bench.

"Estelle and Belle, Grandma Dolan has played that tune with all of her grandchildren. You need to learn it and pass it on to yours."

The twins looked at each other. "Ours?" Belle asked. "We don't have grandchildren!"

"Someday you might," Betsy said.

"Where you been, Betsy?" Grandma Dolan asked. "You walked out after breakfast. I didn't know where you went."

Betsy looked around to see if anyone else was nearby. She leaned over and whispered to her grandmother. "I was in the hay loft."

"Not with Jake were you?" her grandmother asked and grinned.

"No. Listen, Grandma. What would you think if I told you . . ." she looked around again and then whispered lower "that I bought me a guitar?"

Grandma Dolan's jaw dropped and then she began to smile. A twinkle came to her eyes. "I'd say you'd better learn how to play 'Silent Night' on it before Christmas for me. I'm glad you got something you can enjoy. Praise the Lord."

"Don't tell anybody about it, Grandma. Not yet, anyway."

Betsy showed Grandma Dolan the pouch of scrip. "I'm going to take the twins to Coal Creek to get them some shoes and a piece of candy for their birthday."

Older children were given priority when it came to shoes. They had to work and shoes were necessary. It was natural for the younger ones to go barefooted in the summer. The prickly grass and warm dirt of walkways and roads felt soft and cool to young feet.

But as fall mornings brought cold dew and then frost, they all needed shoes. Belle and Estelle had outgrown and worn out the ones that had been bought the year before. The older ones stuffed paperboard or strips of leather inside when soles wore through.

One pair of shoes a year. That was in good times when Daniel Boyd worked full time as a miner. The past year he had barely worked a month. There would be no new shoes this year.

They would make do with last year's or do without.

The morning sun was warm on their faces, and a fall breeze barely lifted strands of their hair. The leaves on the trees along the road and on the distant ridges were beginning to turn the colors of fall—crimson and orange. It was Betsy's favorite season.

She walked in the center with the twins on either side, each holding one of her hands. The young girls were excited about going to town with their older sister. They skipped along and kicked at the dirt road while they made their way to Coal Creek and the company store.

Near town they turned down the lane where the Drummonds lived. Betsy now knew Jake's mother almost as well as her own. His brother, Dick, was a different story. A grunt was the most that she could get from him when she said, "Hello."

Dick Drummond had taken the mine closing more seriously than his brother Jake. Jake had Betsy, but Dick wasn't married. He had taken to drinking more with the small amount of money he made from odd jobs. He had taken his father's revolver down from the mantel and, more than once, threatened to use it on the mine owners.

"Is Jake home, Mrs. Drummond?" Betsy asked when she stepped onto the porch.

Jake's mother stopped her sweeping of the porch and leaned the broom against the wall. "No, Betsy. He's down on the river running his traps. You know, he's doing quite well as a trapper. Selling a few skins and making a little money. Lord knows we can use it. Winter will be coming on shortly."

"I was taking the girls to the store, and I thought he might want to walk along."

"Oh, I'm sure he would if he was here. He'll probably be over to your place before sundown if the last few months is any sign. Seems like you two are getting mighty serious," she said without smiling.

Betsy blushed. "Jake's a fine young man, Mrs. Drummond. You've done a good job raising him. He's real nice to me."

"He's a worker. He tries to put bread on the table for us. He always has since his father died. He had to become a man too soon. I'm glad he found you, Betsy. You're a good influence on him."

"Thank you, Mrs. Drummond. You're too kind. I'm going to take the twins on to the store. Tell Jake I was by." She took the twins' hands again and turned toward town.

Stores and businesses occupied the better part of two blocks in Coal Creek. Coal had made it a booming little village over the past fifteen years. It was not really a town. The citizens had turned down incorporation as recently as July.

There were the company stores of all the mines and other merchants who were not connected to the mines. Eight miles from the county seat of Clinton, the town was the last settlement of civilization in the northern part of the county. A few miles to the north in Campbell County sat the smaller village of Careyville. Another thirty miles to the north through steep mountains lay Jellico and then the Kentucky border.

Both passenger and freight trains stopped at Coal Creek. It had a main line and two side tracks. The spurs led off at the Wye to Briceville on the left and Black Diamond Valley on the right. Each day carloads of coal came from both spurs into Coal Creek awaiting their shipment to Knoxville and beyond.

The rich coal seams that laced the mountains to the west of Coal Creek appeared to go on forever. There would be work for the miners for a hundred years or more.

The stores clustered around the junction of the railroad and spur. A block of wood-framed two-story buildings running north and south intersected with another block that ran east and west.

Saturday was the busiest day. The working miners were into and out of the company stores buying everything from sugar and salt to clothing and shoes. It was one stop shopping for everything they needed. The stores stocked flour, coffee, tea, meal, side-meat, and oil along with the wearing apparel.

The miners purchased not only their everyday living essentials there but also their work tools they used in the mine. Picks, shovels, oil, and even their own blasting powder and fuse wire had to be bought at the company store. If the miners didn't have any scrip, they could put it on their tab and have it deducted from their pay at the next payout. Some became indebted beyond any reasonable expectation of escape. They owed their lives to the company store.

Each company store would take its own scrip or real currency. Most miners used their scrip. The "chips", as the brass tokens were known, were devalued at regular stores. If they were going to spend real money they would go to some other store where the prices were better. The farmers used the other stores because of the value they received.

The Tennessee Mine had two company stores. One in Briceville where the mine was and another in Coal Creek where many of their miners lived.

Horses, buggies, and wagons lined the short streets in front of the stores. Dogs barked. Neighbor greeted neighbor with loud yells across the bare dirt thoroughfares. Wooden sidewalks, elevated a bit from street level, bordered the front of the stores and only ended at the intersection of where the row of stores stopped.

Betsy and the twins mounted the sidewalk and started toward the far end of the block where the Tennessee Mine store stood. The twins, their dresses reaching to the rough planks, had no embarrassment at their unshod feet. It was all they knew. They scrunched their toes against the crevices of the boardwalk and held tightly to Betsy's hands.

Only an occasional building had a coat of paint. In boom times they would paint or whitewash and then go years before the boards saw another coat. The wind and dust did a good job in sandblasting. Most structures had lost what paint they had years before. Graying wood planking was the most common siding.

Betsy tiptoed up and looked into the first window of the Tennessee store. Her hands braced against the wood sill of the window that was dust covered. It was dark inside but she could see the store was still stocked. Boxes of shoes were on the first aisle from the window.

They walked on to the door. A shade was pulled down over the glass of the entrance. A handlettered sign was wedged between the glass and the shade. "CLOSED". In frustration she banged on the door glass. There was no response.

She walked to the far side and peered in another window. She saw a figure moving in the store. A woman. She knocked on the window until it rattled in its frame, but the woman went about her work as though she didn't hear.

An old man sat on a bench near the window whittling on a cedar stick. His cane leaned against the store wall. Betsy grabbed it and beat on the window. The woman finally came to see what was making the racket.

"We want to buy some shoes," Betsy said loudly through the closed window. She reached over and pulled up the dresses from the feet of Belle and Estelle.

"We're closed," the woman on the other side of the window mouthed and pointed to the sign in the door.

Betsy climbed onto the bench behind the whittler to where her nose pressed against the window pane and came face to face with the woman. She took her leather pouch, opened it, and showed the scrip to the woman.

"I have chips. You have shoes. My sisters need shoes. Please open up and let me buy them," Betsy said.

The woman frowned, looked around to the back of the darkened room, and then motioned Betsy to the door.

Betsy jumped down from the bench, took the twins' hands again, and stepped to the door. She heard the latch slide and saw the door open just enough for them to squeeze in.

Inside she faced the woman who towered above her. She had seen her before but had forgotten her name. The Boyds shopped at the company store in Briceville most of the time. This was only Betsy's second stop at the store in Coal Creek.

"We're closed. I'm here only to pack up. We're shipping everything back to Knoxville. There's not enough free miners at the Tennessee to keep one store open, let alone two," the woman said.

"My sisters need shoes. They have none. The mornings are cool and winter's coming on," Betsy said. She made her way to the boxes of shoes, quickly sat the twins down in the floor, and began to fit them with shoes.

The woman stood over Betsy and looked toward the back

of the store. "My husband runs the store. He told me not to sell to anyone. He's already counted the inventory. He would have to refigure if we sold anything."

Betsy found shoes that fit the twins' small feet. They fidgeted as she was lacing them up. "Stand up," she told them. "Walk around and tell me how they feel." Belle and Estelle walked up and down the aisle. "How do they feel?" Betsy asked. The twins held their arms out to their sides with their palms up and their lower lips rolled out.

"What are you doing, woman?" The voice was rough and loud.

Betsy looked up into the eyes of a bear of a man. He was taller than the woman. His teeth were clinched and his hands made into clubs of fists.

"This young woman needs shoes for her sisters," the woman tried to explain.

"We're closed!" the man said. "She's a miner's woman. If their men would work, the store would be open. They could have shoes. They don't want to work, they don't get shoes. Now box those shoes up."

"Sir, sir, I have my tokens," Betsy said and held out the pouch to the giant. "They're Tennessee Mine chips, sir. My baby sisters need shoes. They have none," Betsy explained again.

"I don't care. I just don't care. Get me those shoes off those urchins' feet, or I'll take them off myself."

Estelle bolted one way and Belle the other.

"Please, dear, let them have the shoes. I'll recount for you," the woman spoke softly to her husband.

"Don't you take up for them, woman." He swung his arm out and the back of his hand knocked the woman to the floor beside Betsy. Her mouth began to bleed. The man turned in the direction of Belle and started down the aisle. Belle ran to the end and around the corner.

Betsy took a cloth and wiped the woman's mouth. She then jumped to her feet and dashed after the storekeeper.

Around the corner, the next aisle over, Belle and Estelle came together and joined hands. The crazed man towered above them. They both kicked at him with their new shoes. His sweeping arm knocked their little legs out from under them and they came down hard on their backsides.

He kneeled down. With one huge hand the man pinned a leg each of Belle and Estelle together while he began unlacing the new shoes. The girls screamed and began to cry. But then they looked up and suddenly stopped their wailing.

Betsy stood on a nail keg behind the man. She raised an iron fireplace poker in both hands and brought it down with all the force in her body. The thunk off the back of the man's head sounded like a rock being thrown into a tin cup.

He tumbled over and onto his side. His eyes flickered but no harsh words came from his mouth. He didn't make change when Betsy dropped six dollars' worth of chips onto his chest.

"Four dollars for the shoes, a dollar for the poker, and a dollar for your trouble, sir," she said and took her sisters' hands. She carried the poker with her through the doorway and into the bright sunlight.

They sprinted as fast as the little legs of Belle and Estelle could go. Up the middle of the dusty street and on toward the safety of their own lane.

A half mile out of town, Betsy took the twins and sat beneath a reddening tree. They breathed heavily. Her sides hurt. She looked back toward town and then looked at the new shoes.

She started to laugh. Uncontrolable waves of laughter swept over her. The twins looked up and the merriment was contagious. They laughed until their breath left them, and they rolled in the warm grass. Betsy kissed the faces of her sisters.

She caught her breath. "They'll call me the 'Terror of Coal Creek.' First I attack a muler with a school bell, and now I flog a storekeeper with a poker." She laughed some more. "He shouldn't have called you *urchins.*" She looked at her sisters. "Sometimes girls you may just have to grab a poker and fight till you die!"

All Hallows Eve

Warm air currents swirled up the valley of Coal Creek, lifting hawks as they circled silently on widespread wings high above the crests of Vowell Mountain and Walden's Ridge. The heat was unusual for the third week of October.

Betsy Boyd sat astride Miss Steele on her daily ride home from school. The first three weeks of the session had been hectic. She first had to reclaim the children from the reverie of the summer to the routine of class. With forty pupils, ranging in age from six to twelve in the first four grades, it was a challenge.

Some of her charges still looked upon her as just another student. Indeed she had been in school with all but ten of them the preceding year. Now she was the teacher and the relationship had changed. Her bell and an occasional stern look from her had helped to quiet the ones who were loud.

Mr. Burroughs had the upper grades, from fifth through ninth, and he maintained control with a calming voice and the sight of a "discipline stick," as he called the hickory switch that leaned against the corner wall. He had about the same number of students who ranged in age from eleven to seventeen.

The two-room school house squatted on a knoll just a quarter mile from Coal Creek toward Briceville. Each room had a coal-burning stove. The older students brought the coal in and stoked the fire the first thing on cool mornings. The coal was donated by one of the nearby mines. The outhouses, one for the boys and one for the girls, sat fifty yards away at the edge of a pine thicket.

In the school house, the children sat on benches and shared books. They were the same ones that Betsy had studied during her nine years. Their edges were tattered and bindings frayed. But they were still precious possessions. The older students would cover more of the pages than the younger. There was no money for the schools to provide school books, and few of the families around Coal Creek felt that they could "waste" what precious money they had on things they couldn't eat, wear, or ride.

Most parents didn't expect their children to be educated beyond the basics. The girls would grow up to be wives and mothers. The boys would find work as miners or farmers. The options were few and the education limited.

Betsy didn't feel that way. She wanted to give every girl and boy the desire and ability to go on in attaining more education. A high school diploma at the school in Clinton, or perhaps, as she wanted, a college education in Knoxville.

While her mule bounced her along on the ride home, she imagined a day when all her students would go on to high school and college. They needed some basics first, however—books, paper, pencils. Shoes, also, were missing from the feet of ten or so of her students just as they had been from her little sisters until she "purchased" them at the Tennessee store in Coal Creek.

She remembered the kerchief full of scrip that she still had hid in the loft of the barn. Two hundred dollars would buy some books, paper, pencils, and shoes. She wouldn't dare spend the money on herself. She had gathered it from depressed miners, and it should go to relieving the burdens of their children.

She thought back to the poker she had to use to obtain the shoes for Belle and Estelle. She was above that now. Scrip was supposed to be redeemable in currency or at least in goods of the company. It was the law. She shouldn't have to depend upon brute force. This was the age of reason. She was a young woman of reason.

Professor Brimer knew the law. He was a lawyer in addition to being a history professor. She would take her little problem to him. Next time she would be prepared. The companies owed the miners for the scrip, and she would collect—legally.

The last week of September had seen the sixty days of the supposed *armistice* between the miners and mine owners come and go with no violence. There were rumors. There were always rumors. They flew up and down the valley faster than Jake

Drummond could gallop on Charmer.

The miners had met in small groups and large gatherings. What would be their next step? They had guaranteed the convicts' safety through the period that the legislature met, but the legislature adjourned without an ounce of relief for the miners. Apparently no one was taking them seriously. More and more, the violent element was taking control.

Convicts were now working at three mines in the valley. At the Cumberland mine in Oliver Springs on the far west end, a hundred and fifty were behind the stockade walls. The Tennessee Mine had another hundred in the middle of the valley. Coal Creek, with the original sore of the Knoxville Iron Company mine, worked a hundred thirty-five. Nearly four hundred miners' jobs were taken and given to convicts.

If it continued, the miners feared it would reach to all the mines any time there was a labor dispute. They would be locked out and the stripes brought in.

Eugene Merrill sat in the back room of his store in Briceville with others of the main committee of miners. George Irish, Matthew Ingraham, and James Turner turned their faces toward the floor while they discussed the outcome of the events upon which they had embarked in July.

"George Ford's done everything for us that he can," Merrill said. "The mine owners, the courts, the legislature, and the governor haven't done a thing. The men are frustrated. Their frustration breeds anger, and anger turns to violence. I don't think we can control their actions any longer. What about you?"

The other three nodded in quiet agreement. "There's going to be war. And the governor has himself to blame," Turner said.

"The rank and file of the miners want to release the convicts and burn the stockades to the ground. They would have done it sooner if we hadn't calmed them," Irish said.

Merrill looked at Ingraham. "Captain, a lot of the men look to you as the military genius. Do we have a chance in a war?"

"In the short run, yes. In the long run, no. We could produce fifteen hundred to two thousand men. That's more than the state militia has altogether. Their weapons are much superior.

They have Gatling guns, howitzers, and unlimited ammunition. We'd have to hit and run. Blend into the countryside. It wouldn't be so much a war as continued skirmishing."

"Would the people of East Tennessee support us if we turned to gunfire and the torch? So far they have. But so far we haven't fired a shot." Merrill looked at the drawn faces for answers. There was none.

"I don't think we will have to make that decision," Irish said and motioned with his hand to all of them. "The men out there in the hills and valleys have already made up their minds to do it. Where does that leave us? We're the leaders of the committee."

"That's right," Merrill said. "The legislature almost put a bounty on our heads—mine, yours, and Hatmaker's—last month. Once any violence occurs, you can bet they'll have a reward for the arrest of all the committee members for treason or such."

"Well, we better end the business of the committee and disband before the men take to doing their dark business," Irish said and looked around the room for agreement.

"Let's get a final report together and give it on Tuesday night when the meeting's set for. We'll end the committee and turn everyone loose to be guided by their own consciences," Ingraham said.

"Guided by their own consciences, or guided by their own torches and Winchesters," Merrill said.

When Betsy neared her house, she saw her father and Jake standing by the road talking with a lone horseman. She put Miss Steele in the barn and, by the time she reached the house, the horseman was gone. Jake and Daniel Boyd were seated at the supper table.

"Who was that man?" she asked.

"Just another unemployed miner," her father said.

"What did he want?"

Jake sat with his face downward looking at his plate. He didn't answer.

"Another meeting," her father said. "The miners are having another meeting on Tuesday. See where we go from here."

"We'd all probably be better off if we went into farming full time," Betsy said.

Eugene Merrill took to the stump one more time. The meeting was more somber than some of the others had been. This was the end of open organization and the beginning of underground violence.

There were no women and children at this gathering although there were newspaper reporters. The committee wanted it well established that it was coming to an end. From now on, the miners would have no leaders. It would be every man for himself.

Jake Drummond stood between Daniel Boyd and his brother Dick just a few rows back from Merrill and the rest of the committee. Dick Drummond had once again brought his revolver. Most of the five hundred miners present had done the same, except for Jake.

"We have worked hard since the first of July and for nearly four months have never had a chance to do a day's work for ourselves, having expended our energies on behalf of the miners," Merrill began.

"Of the extra session of the legislature, it is needless to say anything, except this. Working men must be sent to represent working men, regardless of political parties, or we need not expect more attention paid to our interests in the future than we have received in the past.

"I agree that we need to fight the lease system through the courts. We can't do it alone. We need to raise money throughout the state to do that. It will take time.

"The press of the state and beyond has been kind to us and reported accurately our condition. I want to especially mention the Memphis *Commercial*, the Louisville *Courier Journal*, the Knoxville *Sentinel* and *Journal*, and the Coal Creek *Press*.

"The committee has raised over a thousand dollars for the relief of destitute mining families and we thank those who gave to that cause."

Merrill paused, turned, and looked toward Coal Creek and then toward Oliver Springs.

"Now, in conclusion, we give you as our parting advice, as the state has so willed it, and is prepared to enforce its will with the bayonet and the Gatling gun, that you peaceably give up your work, your homes, and your sweet memories that around them cling, and, like Hagar, be driven out with your helpless ones apparently by the power that should shelter and protect you; driven out by the dictation of the penitentiary ring, which has now indeed been proven stronger than the state, and may you, as Hagar did, find a protection in a Divine Providence for surely you can find none elsewhere.

"With sorrow too deep to express, we ring down the curtain on the last act in the Briceville drama by tendering to you our resignations," Merrill said and motioned for the other committee members to come forward. They all signed the statement.

"Defeat never! Down with the stockades! The torch and rifle!" Shouts arose from throughout the mass of miners. Muzzles spit flames as shots were fired into the air. Dick Drummond raised the revolver and squeezed off four rounds near Jake's ear.

The committee members walked among the crowd urging the miners to disperse and go home—for tonight. Think on it before they did anything.

On Saturday, October 31, after sundown, horsemen, their faces wrapped in scarves and hats pulled down, rode throughout the valley into every ravine and onto every hill. They stopped briefly at homes of miners. The message was the same. "The time for talking is over. Get your hoss and gun and meet us at the Tennessee Mine."

On Vowell Mountain, there appeared a coven of witches and wizards. They began to stir a cauldron. They danced around in merriment, chanting the curses of ages past. The mixture boiled with the heat of sufferings and oppression until it emitted the evil mist of violence and lawlessness. The next day would be All Saints Day. The night was All Hallows Eve. It belonged to the mystery of darkness.

When the brew was thick, they exchanged their hoods for hats, their wands for Winchesters, and their sticks for steeds to carry them to Briceville.

No militia guarded the convicts at any of the "branch prisons" at the Tennessee, Knoxville Iron Company, or Cumberland mines. The boys of the National Guard were safely in their homes. The ones who leased the convicts kept only enough guards to prevent escapes from the inside or to mete out punishment to the incorrigibles. There were not enough to resist the will of hundreds of determined miners.

While the militia had been at the Tennessee Mine in July, block house fortifications had been built. Thick wood boards sandwiched a middle of slate rock to form walls a foot thick. Portholes were cut just large enough to fire rifles through. Two of these stood at either end of the stockade. The palisade walls were completed to a height of twenty feet and white-washed. All of this would not help the guards to fend off the miners.

There were no leaders. The miners migrated to the Tennessee Mine along the road from Coal Creek just as birds, led by an inbred sense, go south in the winter. It was time and everybody knew it. Some on horseback, some on foot, some with rifles, some with none—just like in July— the miners returned to the source of their trouble.

A torch here, one there, like the beginning tongues of flame licking at tender, so were the gathering miners. A half moon cast pale light on the silent procession while darting behind clouds.

Without ranks and rows and the leadership of Merrill, Irish, and Ingraham, the two hundred appeared more like a mob than an army. By nine o'clock they were at the doors of the stockade.

Despite the fortifications, the half dozen guards did nothing to prevent the entry of the miners. Warden Brit Cross was speedily given the ultimatum. "Give us the convicts and get out."

The hundred sixty-five convicts exited the walled prison expecting another train ride to Knoxville. Instead they were told they were on their own. They complained that they would be caught and sent back if they didn't have clothes that were less noticeable than their stripes.

They entered John Chumbley's company store. The miners showed the prisoners where the supplies were and told them they could have all they could wear. They took as many civilian clothes as he stocked and the supply of shoes was depleted as rapidly as the convicts could throw off their work boots and put on the new.

Jake Drummond and Daniel Boyd stood in the back of the mob of miners. The convicts came through and started their escape toward Coal Creek. Some stayed on the road, others walked the bank of the creek, while still others took to the railroad track. Striped clothing began to litter the sides of the road, stream, and track.

The warden and guards were told to leave. They did. The torches the miners used for lights were then used to ignite the buildings of the stockade and the mining company.

With the first flickering flame inside the buildings, yells went up from the miners, shouting with glee that the convicts were gone for good and the buildings that housed them were being cleansed through a baptism of fire.

Commissioner of Labor George Ford sat in his hotel room in Briceville writing another report to the governor on a routine mine inspection when he heard the sound of the celebrating miners. He went to the window and looked toward the source of the noise. Instantly, he knew it was from the Tennessee Mine.

An orange reflection of the flames bounced back from a few low clouds. The brightness grew. He went back to his desk, took his pen, and crossed out his last entry: "All is quiet in the valley."

"They're burning the Tennessee stockade," he told his assistant. "You go to Coal Creek and telegraph the governor. I'll stay here and see what I can do."

The torch was put to ten buildings—the quarters for the convicts, the company office, the kitchen, the guards' room, dining room, and store room. The thick walls and solid wood placed there to withstand an attack by miners could not withstand the inferno. The portholes for rifles disintegrated into nothingness. Tongues of fire leaped as high as nearby trees as though they were trying to mate with the clouds above.

The only shooting was in celebration when rifles were raised toward the heavens. Dick Drummond took his revolver from his belt and fired wildly overhead until it was empty.

With the buildings caving in on themselves, the miners turned their attention toward Coal Creek and the Knoxville Iron Company mine. It had started there with working convicts in 1877. It had been tolerated for fifteen long years. The sore had festered too long. This night, those convicts would be liberated too.

George Ford found no leaders. If Irish, Merrill, Ingraham, or Monroe were there, he didn't see them. He was pushed along with the crowd down the road for the five miles toward Coal Creek. There was no room for compromise. They were determined to scrape the wound open and see if it would heal.

"Let's burn Chumbley's white house," someone yelled when they neared the Knoxville Iron mine. There were shouts of agreement. "Yes, the stockade, the other buildings, and the house." First they would free the convicts.

Sam Farley heard the noise of the approaching mob. Inside his quarters with the five other convicts, he crawled to the wall and peered through the cracks. Flickers of torches were beyond the main wall. He heard the voices of many miners.

He shook the other younger convicts who were in deep sleep after a hard day's work. "Get your clothes and shoes on. The miners have come for us again. I guess we'll be taking another train ride to Knoxville."

They all crawled to where Farley had seen the flames and heard the voices. "They're not going to lynch us are they, Sam?" one asked him.

"No. The miners were much kinder to us last time than the guards. They know we don't have no stake in their troubles. They'll just send us to the Knoxville jail. The governor will send some troops in, and we'll be back digging coal in a few days. Might as well enjoy the holiday while we can."

Warden Charles Yokely came to the gate with his seven guards when he was alerted that the miners were there and making demands. He looked for a miner he knew but saw none. They all had their faces cloaked with masks or scarves of some type.

"Bring us the convicts. Get out with your guards. We're burning the place."

Yokely ordered the guards to round up all the convicts and bring them to the gate. "My wife," he said and tried to find someone he thought was in charge. "My wife has taken to bed with a very serious illness. Mrs. Chumbley is caring for her. Please don't burn our building. She couldn't stand to be moved."

The miners looked at each other. Their purpose was not to kill or harm anyone. Yokely was an honest man. He was only there because Captain Chumbley used convicts in his mine.

"You're lucky, Yokely," one of the miners told him. "We just burned all the buildings of the Tennessee Mine. I guess we got a little of that out of our system. We'll leave them standing until your wife is well. But if any convicts come back up here, we'll be back."

Sam Farley was among the hundred thirty black convicts who were liberated from the Knoxville Iron Company stockade. He didn't get his train ride this time. The miners told them which way was toward Kentucky and which way was toward Knoxville. Civilian clothes were given to as many of the convicts as were available.

Farley didn't take any. He told his younger friends to take them and head for Kentucky. "I'm an old man. I've always been a good nigger. I'm going to walk toward Knoxville and turn myself in. I can serve out my time and be a free man." He and a dozen others who were older joined in with Richard Hunt, a black man who had some education, and began their walk along the railroad tracks toward Clinton and Knoxville.

The miners, satisfied with their night's work, began to blend back into the hills and ravines. They had accomplished what they set out to do without leaders, without names, and without faces being recognized. None of them would even tell their family members who else participated in the All Hallows Eve celebration.

The next morning only chimneys and small plumes of

smoke from the smoldering ruins pointed toward the sky when the sun shone onto the otherwise gray scene. On the hills, wildflowers bloomed their last before a hard frost, and the leaves that hung wet with dew shone bright crimson and orange in the early morning light.

Curious citizens of Briceville walked around the stockade area. A few stooped to pick up a tin cup, a fork, or knife from where the kitchen had been. A lone lamp post with its oil light still ablaze stood like a sentinel near what had been the wall of the stockade. A section of the white-washed palisaded wall of about fifty feet in length leaned like an old man against his cane, waiting to fall, its support having burned.

On the road between Briceville and Coal Creek, the striped clothing of the convicts lay abandoned. A few women went along picking up the castoffs. The stripes would find their way into quilts that would be handed down to their children.

On the road and near a lane that led up a ravine, a passerby found an odd display. A dead hog had been attired in prison stripes, laid on its back, and a pipe stuck in its mouth. The miners left no question as to what they thought about the convict lease system.

Governor Buchanan caught the first train from Nashville as soon as he was wired about the troubles. He would meet Attorney General Pickle, Prison Superintendent Wade, and Labor Commissioner Ford in Knoxville.

"There's a five thousand dollar reward for the leaders of this insurrection, two hundred fifty for any participant, and twenty-five dollars each for every convict captured," the governor announced as soon as he arrived in Knoxville.

"What are you going to do, Governor?" reporters asked.

"I don't know yet. I'm here to confer with those who know more about the situation. It's a knotty problem."

"Governor, it's rumored that the convicts at Oliver Springs will be released next. Will you order troops to that point?"

"If I knew for certain they were coming and when, I

would—if requested," the governor said and excused himself to his room at the new Schubert Hotel. He was tired and drawn. Property had been destroyed and convicts released to roam the country. And he was up for reelection in a year.

The governor took counsel of all those he came to see, determined to return to Nashville the next day and decide his course of action. He went to bed a weary man.

While the governor slept in Knoxville, a hundred miners on horses and armed with rifles and pistols swept down the valley from Briceville to Oliver Springs.

There, near mid-night on Monday, the stockade of the Cumberland Mine met the same fate as the Tennessee. So quietly was the deed done that the citizens of the small town that prided itself on healing waters were unaware of the action until the sunshine of morning. The horsemen of the night set free another hundred fifty-five convicts and burned the buildings and stockade. The small contingent of guards offered no resistance.

Again clothes were given to the prisoners, and they were sent on their way to pursue their own type of freedom.

Governor Buchanan departed Knoxville on an early train unaware that the convicts at Oliver Springs had been liberated.

The headlines of the Knoxville *Journal* on the following day summed up the situation: **Liberated! A Clean Sweep Has Now Been Made. All Branch Prisons Gone. And Every Convict in East Tennessee Freed.**

Many telegrams awaited the governor when he arrived back at the capitol. Among them was one from Sam Farley's friend Richard Hunt.

To Governor Buchanan, Nashville

Me and ten of us who was working at Briceville and Coal Creek was turned loose last night by miners. They burned up everything at Briceville. We are loose at Clinton together. What shall I do?

Richard Hunt, colored, and ten others.

Christmas

Each child in turn scooted up against the door facing between Betsy's room and that of Mr. Burroughs. They would stand as tall as they could barefooted, and Betsy would dutifully mark on the wood each child's height. One would slide out and another move in. They laughed.

Betsy taught them about growth in trees and animals and was making a practical demonstration with each pupil. She put their initials next to their marks. The following year she would measure them again and show them how much they had grown.

Next, she had each one go to a tree and bring back a small branch. Betsy took a piece of brightly colored ribbon and tied around the stems. There she wrote the child's name. Then each child would hold a foot out while Betsy measured the foot against the twig. She broke the twig to match its length against that of each foot. Next year she would also show them how much their feet had grown. When finished, she tied all the twigs together into one bunch.

While she was measuring the feet, Betsy noticed once again how many of her students lacked the basic necessity of a decent pair of shoes. They all wore something now. It could have been a brother's or a sister's hand-me-down pair. On some children, the right shoe didn't match the left. A flat piece of leather was laid inside several shoes to cover holes in the soles.

She noticed some of the children looked away when she took their shoes off to measure their feet. Most of the time they covered up any embarrassment they felt.

A full month had passed in the valley of Coal Creek

without convicts in the mines. Governor Buchanan had indicated they would be back. But when, no one knew. It was a little over three weeks until Christmas, and more miners were employed in the coal mines than had been for the past year. There might be enough money for food to make it through the winter. But there was none for new shoes.

Betsy received a month's pay at the end of October and just the week before at the end of November. Of each twenty dollars, she gave ten to her mother and father. She would have given more but she found herself compelled to buy things for the school—some supplies, something to write on and with, a dictionary, a volume of short stories by Robert Louis Stevenson, a book of poems.

She wanted her students to begin to see that there were places and people beyond Coal Creek and Briceville. If they would just become interested in reading, she knew their journeys could be endless. She thought back to the hard task she had of learning Professor Brimer's typewriter. But now she was thankful for it. She had learned more words in the short three months than she had in all her previous years.

The dictionary she had purchased for herself had become a source of great joy. In addition to the words in Professor Brimer's papers, she had mastered at least one new word per day. She would be a lady of letters and words before she graduated from the great university in Knoxville.

On three separate occasions since the first of December, Betsy made the trip to Knoxville to sit outside the office of B. A. Jenkins, president of the Tennessee Mine. Each time she had brought with her Jake's kerchief with the two hundred dollars' worth of scrip. A hundred eighty was that of the Tennessee company. She was determined to redeem the scrip for legal currency. At no time had she been allowed to see Jenkins.

Betsy visited Professor Brimer on the same trips. It was a busy school year at the university and much different from the lazy pace of summer. Professor Brimer had taken her into one of his classes and allowed her to listen to part of a history lecture. She dreamed of the day when she could be a real student and study history under him.

She had controlled her temper at Mr. Jenkins's office. Not once had she bounded, uninvited, into his presence and attacked him with a bell or a poker. She had acted very civilized—most ladylike.

Today it would be different. It was Christmas Eve and she had waited long enough. He would see her before she left, or else he would know that she had been there.

Walking from the depot in Knoxville to Jenkins's office just a block off Gay Street, Betsy passed the gaily decorated stores and shops. Women in colorful dresses and men in their nicest suits walked briskly in and out, shopping for Christmas gifts for their loved ones. She put her nose to the large glass windows of each store she passed. They fogged up with her breath but not before she glanced at the treasures that lay inside. Gold and silver bells. Green and red crushed paper. They were all filled with the holiday spirit. People were happy and kind. Greeting met greeting.

Tiny bells strung to the frames of many of the buggies passing by tinkled out a merry tune of celebration and happiness. The men she met along the sidewalk doffed their hats to her and smiled. Young children, clinging to the hands of their mothers, giggled with an excited expectation of a bright tomorrow.

Betsy saw no one in Knoxville from Coal Creek or Briceville. Their prospects of a cheery Christmas were dim. It would be a day off from the mines that were working and a week off from school. But just the week before, there were stories in the Knoxville newspapers that the convicts would be returned to the mines soon. More men would again be out of work.

Mr. Jenkins and the Tennessee Mine had their Knoxville office at the corner of Gay and Asylum in a new three-story brick building. By now Betsy knew the gentleman out front by name—Mr. Pickering.

He looked up from his huge roll-top desk when she opened the door. He pulled the green visor up from his forehead and laid his pencil down. "Miss Boyd. I'd wager you're back to see Mr. Jenkins."

"Yes, Mr. Pickering. What are my chances?"

He came around the desk, took her coat, and hung it on a rack near the window. "Miss Boyd, it's the day before Christmas. I don't know whether Mr. Jenkins will be in today."

"Did the mine produce coal yesterday?"

"Yes."

"Are there figures he hasn't seen?"

"Yes."

"He'll be in, Mr. Pickering."

He nodded his head. "Yes, I suppose you're correct, Miss Boyd."

"I'll just sit and wait, Mr. Pickering. I brought me something to read." She sat down, placed Jake's kerchief full of scrip on her lap, and opened a book. "Have you ever read *A Christmas Carol* by Dickens?" She looked up at Mr. Pickering.

"No, I can't say as I have. Should I?"

"Yes, it's quite enlightening. Do you have a son or daughter, Mr. Pickering?"

"One of both."

"Your son's in good health, I hope."

"Yes, as far as I know."

"Good."

The bookkeeper stooped back to his work. Betsy read the story of Scrooge and the ghosts of Christmas and watched the passersby on the street.

In two hours, Mr. Jenkins walked in from the street and went directly to the desk of Mr. Pickering. He was accompanied by two other gentlemen.

"How do the figures look for yesterday, Pickering?"

"Good, Mr. Jenkins." He pushed the papers to where Jenkins could see them.

Jenkins nodded. "Hurrumph. We'll have to do better. But that's pretty good." He looked at Betsy who had closed her book and was preparing to stand. "Are you here to see me?"

"This is the young lady I was telling you about, Mr. Jenkins. She is Betsy Boyd from Coal Creek. She's been here three times before, but you were busy," Mr. Pickering said.

Jenkins pulled out his pocket watch. "Well, I have ten till noon. I have to meet some gentlemen for dinner down at the Palace at twelve-thirty. Come in Miss Boyd, but you'll have to make it quick. This is your lucky day."

Betsy left her book in the chair and followed the three men into Mr. Jenkins's office. Mr. Pickering nodded and smiled at her as she passed by.

"Miss Boyd, this is Mr. Gordon and Mr. Judd. They are stockholders in our little mining business. What can I do for you?" He sat behind his massive cherrywood desk and lit his pipe. Betsy took a seat in front and the two men sat along a papered wall.

Betsy laid the red and white kerchief on the front of the desk and untied the knot. She peeled back the cloth and displayed the pile of brass tokens and punch-outs.

"Mr. Jenkins. I've had a problem redeeming your scrip at your store because it was closed down. I'd like for you to redeem it for me in United States currency."

Jenkins blew out a huge puff of smoke that hung about his head and laughed loudly. The other two men also offered a little nervous laughter.

"Are you a miner, Miss Boyd?"

"No. But my father is. He worked at the Tennessee until . . ."

"Until what? Until they refused to work? Until they released the convicts I had working? Until they burned up my buildings? Until I suffered losses amounting to over four thousand dollars?" He stood up and walked to where the other men were seated. "These men lost money because of people like your father and others of his kind."

Betsy breathed deeply. She clasped her hands together. She had promised herself that she would not allow Mr. Jenkins to rile her.

"My father, and men like him, are just trying to make a living, Mr. Jenkins. They don't get to come into a fancy office and check their figures everyday to see how much they've made. Their offices are three feet high. They dig coal on their hands and knees in dirty water. They come home dirty, tired, and wet.

"I'm just asking for what is due me according to law."

Jenkins looked at the two men and then at Betsy. "Where did you get that much in punch-outs?"

"I took a collection," she said without hesitating. "There's a hundred eighty dollars in Tennessee Mine scrip here. We need the money. Some of the miners' children don't have shoes. There'll be no Christmas for them."

"You can go to the store in Briceville and exchange that for goods," Jenkins said.

"I live in Coal Creek. The last time I went to one of your stores, the manager was rude to me. I don't want to go back to your other store. The law says I'm entitled to United States currency."

Jenkins reached into his pocket and pulled out a wad of bills. He peeled one off the top. "Here's a twenty. I'll give you twenty for the whole pile and I won't even count them."

He smiled. She didn't.

One of the other men coughed and then spoke. "B. A., give her however much she has in scrip. Tomorrow's Christmas. It's obvious this young lady is knowledgeable, sincere, and dedicated. It would be a goodwill gesture to her and the miners."

"Hurrumph! They owe me more than that in damages! If we could ever prove who burned the stockade. She had her chance," he said and put the twenty back into his pocket. "I'm not paying her a damn thing."

"B. A., watch your language in front of a lady," the other man said.

Betsy pulled four long sheets of paper from the handbag she was carrying. "Here's a copy of what I will be filing before the end of business today if this scrip is not redeemed," she said and handed the papers to Jenkins.

Jenkins began to read the documents and moved back to his chair. He turned through each page. His face flushed. He laid his pipe down on his desk, snorted, and handed the papers to the other men.

"It's suit papers," he said, "signed by that crazy professor over at the university. Robert Brimer. Wait till my lawyers get finished with him. He won't even have a job." He got back up and paced the room while his companions continued to read.

"B. A., this could cost us in court and in the public's eye. You know what the law says. This Brimer's cited every law and case in the papers. He's going to file it in Gibson's court. You know how he feels about convict labor. He's just waiting for a chance to nail us.

"Give her the money and save ourselves a lot of time and wasted effort. I'd rather pay her than go through a court case." The man reached into his pocket, took out a few bills, and began to count them out.

"No reason for you to do that, Gordon." Jenkins brought his wad of currency back out. "Here, Miss Boyd, is two hundred dollars. Twenty extra. Just leave the scrip and get out. Please."

Betsy reached for the kerchief. "I need to take this. It has sentimental value." She put the money into her handbag. "Good to meet you Mr. Gordon and Mr. Judd. Good to do business with you, Mr. Jenkins. I hope your mine stays open . . . with free miners." She turned for the door.

"Miss Boyd," Mr. Jenkins said and smiled. "I want to apologize for my language. And by the way, if the miners had used you to negotiate their problems, there probably would've never been a dispute."

Betsy picked up her copy of Dickens's work, smiled at Mr. Pickering, and headed for the street with her bounty of currency. She said a little prayer for Mr. Scrooge and gave thanks for Robert Brimer.

She went to the first store on Gay Street that sold shoes. When she told the clerk what she wanted, he was delighted to serve her. From her oversized hand bag, she retrieved the bundle of sticks that had been the measuring rods for the feet of her students. She and the clerk matched each stick with a pair of shoes of the same size. She allowed another half inch for growth.

From a different part of the store, she bought a sheet and started dumping the shoes into the middle of the cloth. With a name and sticker on each pair, she wouldn't forget whose they were. Then with her own money, she bought shoes for her brothers, a scarf for her mother, a hat for her father, and for her Grandmother Dolan a pair of warm mittens and socks to match.

She trudged back onto Gay Street with the bundle of shoes slung over her shoulder. She walked to Market Square where vendors sold fruit and vegetables from open stands. She bought six dozen oranges and two scoops of hard candy. If by some chance Santa Claus missed the valley of Coal Creek, Miss Claus would be there riding among the miners' cabins upon Miss Steele.

The sun was moving ever lower in a hazy, gray sky, but she had one more stop to make before going to the depot. She had thought about what to get for Jake. She went to a hardware store and asked the clerk to show her his best pocket knives.

"This is a fine knife. The carbon steel blades will remain sharper longer than most," the clerk said, opened the blade from the handle, and handed the knife to Betsy.

"Would someone who whittles and carves like it?" she asked.

"Yes. Definitely."

The knife was twice as much as a pair of shoes. But Jake was worth it.

The conductor gave her an odd look when she boarded the train with the great white sheet full of shoes.

Darkness had captured the valley by the time the train arrived at Coal Creek. Betsy left her precious load of shoes with the clerk at the depot and made a mad dash for home. She needed Miss Steele to go with her through the valley to the homes of all her students.

Even at Miss Steele's top gait of a fast trot, Betsy was four hours in making her deliveries to the students' homes. She placed an orange in one shoe of each pair and a handful of candy in the other. She knocked on doors or placed the gifts on the porches with a note stuck in the shoes with the child's name. She knew there would be some brothers and sisters of her students who would be left out. She did only what she could do.

A smattering of parents balked at taking the gifts. They weren't "charity" cases they told Betsy. But she persuaded them she knew that. She was one of them. And this was a gift from heaven. They should take it and be thankful, not to her, but to the Lord.

Jake waited for her at the table. It was late when she returned from her rounds. She hadn't eaten. Grandma Dolan saw to it that she had food left from supper. Betsy stashed the remainder of her oranges and candy at the barn when she bedded down her mule. There would be enough for every member of the family.

Grandma Dolan, the young children, and the rest of the family sat around the fireplace and sang Christmas carols while Jake and Betsy finished their meal. By the time they joined them, the twins were beginning to nod off. Jake and Betsy sang along with the others until one by one the youngsters drifted to bed.

A half hour before midnight, only Jake, Betsy, and Grandma Dolan remained. Betsy whispered to her grandmother, who was dozing in her rocker in front of the fire, and wrapped the quilt snugly around her. She grabbed a large quilt from beside the hearth and motioned to Jake.

"Let's go to the hay loft. I have something to show you."

Jake took from beneath his chair a small package that was wrapped in brown paper and followed Betsy out the door.

He pulled his coat tighter around him when the cold air that whipped up from the river met him. They walked beneath a tree where two roosters were perched for the night. All the other farm animals were bedded down in the barn on layers of hay. There was no sound except for the lone baying of a hound in the direction of Coal Creek.

Betsy climbed the ladder to the hay loft with Jake following closely. She walked to the far wall and opened the hay door to the loft that looked out toward the river. In the summer they would fork hay directly from the wagon into the loft from that door.

Then she stepped to her secret place and motioned Jake to sit down. She reached into the space between the wall and the hay and pulled out the sheet which had been the bearer of shoes for her students. It still contained the ones for her brothers and the gifts for her other family members. She showed them to Jake.

"I bought all this in Knoxville. I love their stores. They have a much better selection than we do here. I had enough for oranges for everyone. And candy." She handed him an orange and a piece of candy.

"Look. I have a hundred dollars left. I spent a hundred on things for my students and have a hundred left." She wrapped the bills in Jake's old kerchief and then placed them in the pouch she had used to carry the scrip from Briceville. She placed it back in her hiding niche. "I may need that later on."

Jake shook his head. "Where did you get all that money?"

"The scrip the miners threw down at the meeting. Remember? I borrowed your kerchief to put it in. I persuaded Mr. Jenkins to redeem it for currency. He did and threw in twenty extra to boot."

"You persuaded?"

"Yes," she said and reached back into the crevice and took out her guitar. "The law and I persuaded him." She looked at Jake and smiled.

"Here. Sit back and wrap us in that quilt. Just give me room enough to have my hands on the guitar." After some maneuvering they arranged it. Jake sat against the stack of hay. Betsy leaned into him, her back on his chest. They both were able to gaze out into the clear night. Jake wrapped the quilt around them both and she felt the warmness of his chest against her back.

The moon was straight up. Their breath crystallized in the cold air. Betsy began to strum the strings of her guitar.

"Jake, did you know there is a legend that the animals in the barn talk at midnight on Christmas Eve? We should go down and see if it's true. See if Nellie and Miss Steele are talking to each other."

"I'm too comfortable. I don't want to get up. They probably wouldn't speak if they saw us anyway."

Betsy returned to her guitar.

"I believe I about have this one down. I learned it for Grandma." Her fingers played across the strings and in a low voice she began the words to "Silent Night."

She played on while Jake listened. He leaned closer to her neck and began to kiss her with lips as soft as butterfly wings.

Betsy enjoyed the feeling but didn't want it to go too far. She turned her head toward him. "I like that . . . too much. We better stop."

Jake pulled her closer. "I have you something for Christmas."

She smiled. "What is it?"

"Here's part of it," he said and handed her the small package.

She took it in both hands and began to peel the paper back. She took the hard cold object and laid it in her opened hand. She moved nearer to the opening where the moonlight poured in on her gift. The exquisitely carved wood mule was no larger than the palm of her hand.

"It's Miss Steele," Jake said.

"I know," Betsy said and hugged his neck. "It's beautiful. I'll keep it, always."

"I have something for you too." She reached once again into her hiding place and brought out the small package. She handed it to him. "I hope you like it and can use it."

Jake's eyes widened when he saw the shiny steel of the knife. "Oh, this is a good one. I didn't know that you knew your knives. This is great." He opened the blade and ran a finger up and down the sharpness of the edge. He closed it and put it into his pocket.

"I have something else for you, Betsy." He took her hand in his.

Betsy felt her face flush despite the coolness of the air. "What is it, Jake?"

He looked into her eyes. "Will you marry me?"

New Year's Day

Betsy lay in her bed. She was like a caterpillar in its cocoon. On top of her and around her were layers of blankets and quilts. Six in all. Their weight and thickness were such that little of the cold air could get in and her body heat remained captured.

She felt her ears. They were like cold, unfeeling flaps of cowhide. She didn't remember her head having been out from under the cover, but obviously it had. It was dark beneath the quilts, but it was warm. On either side, Belle and Estelle attached themselves to her like leeches. They shared the one bed in the loft of the Boyd farmhouse. On cold winter mornings when breath hung in the air like spiderwebs, the only real heat was near the fireplaces or in the kitchen in front of the stove.

She raised her hand and felt for the opening at the top. She would test the air. It was still cold. She raised the cover and peeked out. The sun shone in the near window. She smelled the pungent aroma of sausage cooking and heard the grease sizzling. She should be downstairs helping. And she would as soon as she could collect her thoughts.

On the shelf on the wall past the foot of the bed she looked for her wooden mule. It stood there facing her. It was the gift that she could accept from Jake. The other she could not—not now anyhow. She had said "No," and tried to explain. But he would have none of it. Was she being obstinate or mule-headed? Her eyes fastened on the carving.

She loved Jake Drummond. But marriage was not in her plans now. It had to wait. She had other things she wanted to do first. He didn't understand. The university and teaching would be difficult enough for a single woman. Marriage and babies would make her goals impossible. He didn't want to wait. She did.

He would help her do all those things, he had told her. They could wed and she could still pursue her dreams. She wasn't sure. She didn't know any married women who went to school. Even the high school did not allow married women. They were a bad influence. They might secretly tell the other young girls about the pleasures of the marriage bed and all of them would run off and become wives.

She would ask Professor Brimer. What was his opinion of the chances of a married woman being admitted to the university? What did he think about marriage, period? She didn't even know if he was married. If he had a wife, had she attended any college? It was all a mystery to her. She just didn't want to be shoved into a situation that she couldn't control.

Jake had galloped home on Charmer. He hadn't been back in the week since Christmas. Betsy had walked to his house. He wasn't there. His mother told her he left Christmas morning to go to the river to run his line of traps and had not returned. She hoped he was all right. Betsy worried about him, but there was nothing she could do.

A shout and the sound of hoofs like muffled drums shook Betsy from her thoughts. She crawled up to the top of her bed and looked out the window toward the road. A man on horseback was talking with her father and motioning toward Coal Creek. He galloped on and her father came back toward the house.

"They're here," Daniel Boyd yelled when he came back in. "The troops are coming in on the train. They say they have the Gatling gun too. I'm going to the depot."

Betsy grabbed her housecoat and climbed down from the loft. "What troops?" she asked of her father as he started toward the door.

"The ones we knew were coming sooner or later. There's going to be more trouble. You can bank on it. I'm going to see if they have the convicts with them." He slammed the front door and walked briskly toward Coal Creek.

Jake Drummond was already at the depot when Betsy's father arrived. He and another two hundred men and boys were surveying the New Year's Day gift the governor had bestowed on the valley.

A special train stood at the siding, its engine puffing and hissing. Three passenger cars carried eighty-four troops of the National Guard of Tennessee with the hierarchy of its command. Adjutant General H. H. Norman, General Sam T. Carnes, of Memphis, and Captain Keller Anderson, inspector of rifle practice on the governor's staff, were all strutting about.

Two baggage cars held tents, supplies, and provisions for a long encampment. On a flat car were mounted a Gatling gun and a mountain howitzer. The commanders displayed them for a show of force and to emphasize to the miners that the state meant business this time.

There were no convicts in sight.

"You soldier-boys going to dig the coal now?" someone shouted out of the crowd.

General Carnes did an about face and snarled in reply. "We have come to restore peace. We aren't here to dig coal or to protect the convicts. They have their own guards. We are here to guarantee that they will be able to go about their lawful work."

When Jake looked, he saw that General Carnes was speaking about a group of fifty men who were just getting off the train. They would guard the convicts. But where were the zebras?

The train was turned toward the Briceville spur and started slowly up between the gap in the ridge. It stopped just a half mile outside of Coal Creek near the stockade of the Knoxville Iron Company.

"That's the mistake we made," Dick Drummond said to Jake. "We should have burned that stockade the same night. Now they're going to use it as a fort."

The crowd followed at a discreet distance. The troops

unloaded and made their way onto the grounds of the Knoxville Iron Company and behind the walls of the high fence of the stockade.

Carnes, Norman, and Anderson huddled at the stockade entrance with their maps. Carnes gestured to Vowell Mountain behind the stockade.

"We can camp here tonight. But we need the high ground. This stockade is vulnerable to an attack from above. The miners could sit up there in those thickets and pick us off. They're good squirrel hunters. That's where we need to be." He pointed to the crest of the mountain directly behind the stockade.

"Tomorrow, we'll have the troops start clearing the ridge between here and the summit. We'll build embankments at the summit, move our tents up there, and start work on some basic buildings."

By noon, a cold rain began to fall. The soldiers were busy unloading the train cars and setting up their tents. The rain turned into a downpour and the road between the track and stockade oozed with mud. Wheels of carts became mired in the slime. The soldiers' pretty shined shoes were sucked off by the gripping black goop.

A fog rolled down off the hills. What had been a sunshine-filled morning became a cloak of bone chilling numbness. Gray and wet. Fingers turned stiff. Noses began to drip. Icy water ran down the soldiers' backs while they made their tents. Cots were set up on mud floors and sank inches into the water-soaked soil. Soldier turned to soldier and questioned the wisdom of camping in such a God-forsaken hole.

The officers went to John Chumbley's house and had dinner.

Next morning, the chunk-chunk of axe heads slamming against trees and the quieter buzzing of the back and forth action of cross-cut saws accompanied the soldiers and guards clearing the slope between the stockade and the crest of Vowell Mountain. The rain had stopped, but the temperature dropped to near freezing. The soldiers welcomed the activity. Their first night had been miserable.

General Carnes, General Norman, and Colonel Anderson climbed the mountain. With a field engineer, they roughly laid out the area where the fort would be located on the summit. They would dig earthworks and erect a wood palisade. Tents and rough-hewn cabins would dot the top of the mountain. They were preparing for a long stay.

Carnes and Norman planned to leave the next day. Colonel Anderson would be in charge of the fort and the valley of Coal Creek.

"The convicts will be returned in two days," Carnes reminded Anderson. "The troops can stay in the mine stockade until then, but this needs to be completed as soon as possible. It'll be rough for a while. But the men are good soldiers. They'll get used to it."

After surveying the top of the hill and seeing first hand the view they would have of the village of Coal Creek and the stockade of the Knoxville Iron Company mine, they agreed on the placement of one Gatling gun and the mountain howitzer.

To the east, the summit provided an unobstructed view of the gap in Walden's Ridge and the business district of Coal Creek. The howitzer could lob shells as far as the depot if necessary. Below and to the south was the Knoxville Iron Company's stockade. The Gatling would be placed at the southeast corner of the fort where it would have access toward the stockade, the railroad tracks, and the Wye.

Work progressed at a rapid pace that day and the next. Earth was moved at the summit to provide a relatively level area for the fort. Trees were felled, sawed into twenty-five foot lengths, and stood in trenches five feet deep to make the wall of the fort. Log buildings began to spring up at the corners with portholes for rifles. Berms were heaped up from the excavated earth on the outside of the walls. The soldiers could fight from there or retreat to the wooden walls of the fort if necessary.

On Monday, January fourth, a train moved between Knoxville and Coal Creek with a load of one hundred twenty convicts and thirty more guards. Among the convicts was Sam Farley. For two months he had been first in Knoxville and then at Nashville after turning himself in to the authorities.

In a way, he was happy to be back at the Knoxville Iron Company mine. The conditions he had endured at the Knoxville jail and at the main penitentiary in Nashville were as bad as anything he had suffered at the mines.

With the release of over four hundred fifty convicts on the last day of October and the subsequent rounding up of about two thirds of them, the state prison was packed to a dangerous and unhealthy over-capacity. The state was not equipped to house all of its prisoners. They would die if contained under such conditions at Nashville. The "branch prisons" were necessary until new facilities could be built.

Farley looked out the crack in the wall of the freight car when it came to the depot at Coal Creek. Outside, another group of curious miners and their families peered at the closed boxcars, trying to catch a glimpse of their cargo. They believed, correctly, that it would be the convicts. Sam Farley merely wished that he would get the same little room at the stockade that he had called home for over five years.

Over the next ten days, the convicts eased into what were familiar surroundings for some and totally new to others. Before they started to dig coal again, they were used for work on the fort.

With two hundred men scrubbing brush off the mountain-side, cutting the bigger trees with axes, and banging together logs into the shape of barracks, Fort Anderson neared completion.

General Carnes and General Norman departed for Memphis and Nashville, leaving Colonel Anderson in charge. He was a hardened veteran and liked a challenge.

He did miss a couple of things. He liked good liquor and bad women and sent out a few of his men to scout the area for both. By good fortune, the young soldiers stumbled across Dick Drummond who told them where satisfaction of the colonel's needs could be found in abundance.

There had been no disturbance since the soldiers arrived this time, so Anderson invited Drummond and a few local men behind the walls of Fort Anderson. Lieutenant Perry Fyffe warned the colonel that these men could be spies, but Anderson insisted on enlisting the good will of the citizenry and learning where his lusts could be quenched.

Dick Drummond took off his hat and shook Anderson's hand. "These miners aren't as bad as you've been told. I know my way around the valley, Colonel, and I wouldn't mind sharing my knowledge with you."

Drummond turned and pointed to the village of Coal Creek that lay six hundred feet below. "That house has good liquor. Of course, they wouldn't serve a soldier unless he was with me or somebody they knew."

Anderson took Drummond aside, away from the ears of Fyffe and others. "And what about women, Drummond. I heard there's a house or two in Briceville. Is it safe for me to go there?"

Drummond shook his head. "Only with a miner for an escort, sir. I'd be happy to oblige if the need arises."

"I'll think on it. Come back and visit with us in a few days and bring me a sample of that liquor. You'll be compensated for it."

The next day, Colonel Anderson was so pleased with the progress of the fort, its walls, buildings, and fortifications, that he sent for a photographer from Knoxville to record what soldiers could do when working together. A history of the fort that people, especially the military higher-ups, could see would be beneficial to the National Guard and to him personally.

W. E. Singleton was a photographer of note in Knoxville. He arrived on the morning train the next day and set about, with the aid of five soldiers, carrying all of his gear to the top of the mountain for the viewing of Fort Anderson. Although the tripods and cameras were bulky and heavy, by noon he was set up in the midst of the bustle of the fort.

"I like action in my plates and photographs," he told Colonel Anderson.

"Yes, yes. Action! Make it look like we're in a great war and withstanding the assault of two thousand," the Colonel said and imagined the photographs in his report to the governor.

They wheeled the Gatling gun and howitzer to the edge of the earthworks and stationed soldiers around them looking into the far distance as though they were staring into the jaws of death. For two hours he worked with the cameras and made at least a hundred exposures. The military would pay.

"What else might your soldier-boys do that would entail action?" Singleton asked.

Colonel Anderson thought. He pointed down the hill to the stockade where striped uniforms were evident on convicts walking to and from the mine opening. "We could be called upon to hunt down an escapee," he said.

Singleton closed his eyes for a minute. "Excellent. Bring a couple of convicts up here and we'll have your boys gather around them like they've brought them to bay after a hard night's chase."

The guards were leery of bringing convicts up the mountain without a large escort. They might escape, or there might be a miner attack. Colonel Anderson was in charge, so the stockade superintendent named two convicts he knew would be safe to take to the summit.

"They're going to make your photograph, Sam," John Chumbley told the old convict.

Sam Farley and another old black convict trudged up the steep slope of the mountain toward Fort Anderson. Sam had never been to the top. For almost six years now, he had worked in the bowels of the mountain tracing the black fingers of coal.

He caught his breath when he reached the summit. He looked around and liked the view. He peered toward the southwest, over the rolling ridges and bare trees, and imagined he could see all the way to Madison County. There his wife and children awaited his release.

The young soldiers pranced about in a jocular mood and posed here and there in groups of two or three with their rifles. Perhaps the photographer would choose one of them for the next shot. Some lounged about in the tents while others rolled the howitzer and Gatling gun from corner to corner.

"I need about seven soldiers," Singleton said. "We'll put

the convicts a little ways in front and have the soldiers draw down on them with their rifles."

The photographer arranged the group of military and then motioned for the guards to position Sam Farley and the other convict up front. He looked through his viewfinder on the camera. The convicts were too far down the hill. He moved them back. Still too far out of range.

Finally, he found two tree stumps. He stood Sam Farley on one and his fellow convict on the other. Now he could get the soldiers and the convicts in one frame.

"You convicts look scared and lean over like you're running. You soldiers look serious when you aim your rifles." He stepped behind the camera.

Sam Farley positioned his arms like a runner in a sprint and stared straight ahead over the mountain.

The seven blue-uniformed men stood like toy soldiers, in position with their rifles aimed at Sam and his companion.

At that moment another young soldier walking nearby tripped over a tree root and plunged into one of the seven posed soldiers. The soldier's Springfield rifle fired, sending a single forty-five caliber round into the back of the skull of Sam Farley. He toppled forward, dead before he hit the ground.

John Chumbley rushed to Sam while everyone else stood stunned. He looked at the unblinking eyes of the fallen convict and felt for a pulse.

He turned to Colonel Anderson. "You've killed my best nigger. You've killed my best miner."

Colonel Keller Anderson

Spring 1892

Dogwoods and redbuds dueled for supremacy along the creek banks and ridge slopes. The valley echoed with the velvety violet of the redbuds and the cushiony white of the dogwoods. Pure white battled the color of blood mixed with water. Which would be victorious? Valley residents wondered.

By April, Fort Anderson stood on the north knob of Vowell Mountain with white tents visible beyond the wooden walls.

Viewed from the depot in Coal Creek in the rays of the early morning sunlight, the flapping tent coverings gave the appearance of angels or giant moths ready to take flight. There was still a question as to whether the angels would be "killers" or "guardians."

Below, on the flank of the mountain between the mine opening and the stockade, the fresh mound of dirt covering the body of Sam Farley was the newest addition to a cemetery that contained the bones of over a hundred of the convict miners. Only Sam's was marked. John Chumbley had ordered a cross of rough-hewn wood placed at the grave. White paint spelled out his name and said merely "killed in accident, January 15, 1892."

The secret graveyard was kept that way for a purpose. No one was to know the number of convicts buried or the manner in which they died. A garden took up the surface area. A few of the prisoners knew that below lay the bodies of many other convicts mouldering away in stark anonymity. For fifteen years, those who operated the Knoxville Iron Company coal mine had added to the cemetery when convicts died natural deaths or were killed in mine accidents.

Since the coming of the soldiers with Colonel Anderson, the valley had settled down once more into a resignation that the militia would be with them for a while. Convicts had been returned to the Knoxville Iron coal mine at Coal Creek but not to the Tennessee Mine at Briceville. The stockade there was not rebuilt, and the mine was worked with free men. While the contract problem had not been resolved, conditions there were better than having the zebras take the miners' jobs.

In Oliver Springs, the leasing company bought the mine and rebuilt the stockade. Convicts worked there.

At night, throughout the time, a few miners here and there would walk along adjoining ridges and take wild shots at the fort. It had evolved into a war of nerves. The occasional shot of the miner was returned with a volley from the Gatling gun or a few rounds from sentries with their Springfield rifles.

Colonel Anderson walked down regularly from the fort and into Coal Creek. He had taken up with some of the more outgoing miners, including Dick Drummond. Anderson liked a good card game as much as the working men, and when he was with some of the miners, the Colonel was welcomed at the houses in Coal Creek that stocked liquor.

Dick Drummond had taken him to Briceville and introduced him at the house where the women lounged about in bright dresses and painted faces. The other soldiers also developed tastes for the pleasures of Coal Creek and Briceville, such as they were. Fort Anderson was a lonely and boring place. Soldiers came and went daily on the trains to and from Knoxville. Terms of service would expire with one group of militia replacing another.

Eugene Merrill had not deserted the valley. Now, he and his former committeemen met in secret to discuss what could be done to drive out the militia and convicts. He continued to caution against precipitous violent action, but younger miners and some who had drifted down from Kentucky counseled rebellion.

For Betsy Boyd, the end of March had meant the end of her first term of teaching. School ended with the coming of spring when children would be needed more by their farmer parents. At her first opportunity, Betsy took the train to Knoxville and visited Professor Brimer. She was ready to go to work again. She longed to be in the eleventh grade. The first of May she would renew her efforts at both.

"Professor Brimer, do you believe it would hinder my progress if I married?" Betsy asked from her chair in front of his desk.

He scratched his head and peered at Betsy. "Marriage? You?" He walked around his desk and looked out the window toward downtown Knoxville. "I suppose you could get married and still attend the university. I mean as far as there being a rule prohibiting it. But what about your time? Would your marriage obligations take all your time to where you couldn't study?"

Betsy nodded her head. "I've thought about that. I don't know. There'd have to be an understanding, I suppose. My husband would have to understand my desire to go to the university. He'd have to allow for it."

"I'm just curious, Miss Boyd. Is this purely hypothetical, or do you have someone in mind that you might marry."

"It's more like the someone has me in mind," Betsy said, smiled, and looked down at the floor.

Jim Powell knocked on Professor Brimer's door and entered when he saw Betsy and the professor.

Professor Brimer put his arm around Powell's shoulder. "Jim, Miss Boyd is considering marriage. Would that delay her progress through your high school?"

Powell sat down next to Betsy. "Well, in regular high school, we don't allow married students. But since I'm doing this in an unorthodox manner, I suppose no one would have to know. You're not married yet are you, Miss Boyd?"

Betsy shook her head. "No, no. I was just asking. I don't

want to do anything to knock me out of being able to go to the university."

"Well, if it happens, just don't tell everyone. Keep it a little secret," Powell added and looked for approval to Professor Brimer.

Brimer nodded. Powell gave Betsy three books and several pages of paper that outlined her assignments for the year.

"How's the mining situation at Coal Creek? Have you been to Fort Anderson?" Professor Brimer asked.

"Tedious," Betsy replied. "Everybody's just waiting for something big to happen. The soldiers are arrogant. The miners have young hot-heads who want to fight. I expect trouble. Everybody does."

"I hope it won't interfere with your work and schooling," Professor Brimer said.

After his feelings had a little time to heal, Jake Drummond renewed his courtship of Betsy, determined that she would not again say "No" to his marriage proposal.

His brother's association with Colonel Anderson and frequent visits to the fort rubbed on Jake. Why had Dick become such friends with the soldiers when before he was ready to shoot the mine owners and those who brought the convicts to the valley? He spent more and more time away from his brother. If Jake wasn't at Betsy's, he was riding the countryside on Charmer talking with mine families and scouting.

Could he run for the legislature? He was asking himself and those he rode to see. Convinced that the soldiers would not leave at the point of a gun, he began to believe that what Betsy said was the correct course of action. Through the legislature, the convicts could be driven from the mining region.

As he rode, Jake had hours of time to think. He remembered the halls of the Capitol where he had watched last September. He could do as well as the ones he saw. Most were older, but he remembered seeing a young legislator or two. He received encouragement at each house where he stopped.

There would be a county convention to choose the party nominees in August and then the general election in November. He had to decide what he was. A Democrat? Or a Republican? He didn't think of himself as either. He was a miner, but he would have to affiliate with one party or the other in order to have a chance to win. Independents didn't fare well.

"Sure, Jake, I'd vote fer ye." The voice of support was followed by a stream of tobacco juice as the old man spit out over his long beard. "My whole family. I'd ask them. Betcha they would."

"I'm just checking, Mr. Phillips. Trying to see what my chances would be," Jake said and shook the old man's hand.

Day after day he rode from Coal Creek to Briceville and then on into Clinton. He was known in the mining region, but in Clinton, the county seat, he knew very few people. There he met with more stares than voices of support. He went to all the office holders in the courthouse and told them of his interest. Some told him that someone from Coal Creek wouldn't have a chance. The job belonged to Clinton. Others encouraged him.

Within the miners' committee, he found almost unanimous support. Merrill, Irish, Ingraham, and other old-timers said he would be a good example for the younger miners. They needed to put away their guns for a year and give the legislature another chance.

By the first of June he had made up his mind. If Betsy Boyd, daughter of a coal miner, could go to the university, Jake Drummond, a coal miner's son and coal miner himself, could run for the legislature.

Fort Anderson From Stockade

August War

Governor John Buchanan faced up to reality and announced on the last day of July that he would not seek the Democratic nomination for a second term in office. He left open the possibility that he would run as an independent. The Democratic Party had turned its back on the Farmers' Alliance governor who two years before had formed a coalition that had given him the nomination.

The convict lease system had nagged at him for over a year. More recently he had jumped into hot water again when he reduced the sentence of a Memphis murderer who was saved from hanging by the stroke of Buchanan's pen and given life imprisonment instead.

News of Buchanan's withdrawal from the Democratic nomination fight would have been met with more excitement in Anderson County if it wasn't for the one who wanted to succeed him.

Peter Turney, who had practically wrapped up the nomination, had been the chief justice of the state supreme court when decisions were made that were not favorable to the miners. In November the decision for governor would be made among Buchanan, Turney, or the Republican George Winstead.

In Anderson County, a fresh young face grabbed the nomination for state representative when the Democrats met in convention during the first week of August. Jake Drummond beat out three other contestants. He would have three months to get his name known in all the county before the November election. He and Betsy celebrated with a cake that she had made with the help of Grandma Dolan.

At Fort Anderson, military discipline gave way to boredom. Many of the young soldiers were not used to being away from home, from their jobs, or from wives or girlfriends for so long a period. Liquor and bawdy women followed the movement of the militia. From Knoxville, a madam brought several young women of easy virtue to Coal Creek. They set up shop in two houses near where the town creek flowed beneath the railroad tracks. It was not long before the young soldiers found their way to these houses. Now they didn't have to walk all the way to Briceville to satisfy their appetites.

Local citizens deplored the deteriorating conditions which were condemned by preachers in the churches and editorials in the local newspaper.

The war of nerves worsened with the continual bombardment of the fort by miners who sniped away at night. The soldiers traveled together in larger numbers during daylight.

On the first Saturday in August, several miners were playing cards beneath a trestle of the railroad where it passed over the creek. A squad of soldiers marching along the track saw the miners and stopped. They aimed their Springfield rifles at the unarmed miners.

"We've been given orders to shoot you if you say just one word to us," a lieutenant told the suddenly still miners. He laughed, cursed the miners, and motioned his troops on.

A half hour later, the sound of the mountain howitzer echoed against the ridges. People on the streets of Coal Creek quickly took cover inside the store buildings. A mud-filled oyster can crashed down into the middle of the street and splattered its contents over the sidewalks. It was just another little game the soldiers on the ridge played with the townspeople, a reminder. If the howitzer could hurl the used cans into town, live shells could take the same course.

On the second Saturday of August, the scene of conflict shifted. Convicts now worked mines in four cities in Tennessee. Coal Creek and Oliver Springs were the two where the trouble during the past year had been confined. But in southeast Tennessee at Tracy City and Inman, convicts were now also displacing free miners.

On the torrid mid-summer morning, the miners at Tracy City followed the example of their northern Tennessee brethren and stormed the stockade. Three hundred ninety convicts were loaded onto a train and sent toward Nashville for Governor Buchanan to deal with. The torch was put to the branch prison.

On the way to Nashville, some of the convicts were able to detach a car from the remainder of the train and make their escape. The deed was done. Governor Buchanan was powerless. His soldiers were in Coal Creek.

The insurrection at Tracy City was brief. The convicts were gone and so was the stockade. The miners melted back into the hills and went about their jobs. There was no one for the soldiers to fight nor to protect even if there had been militia available.

When prisoners arrived in Nashville, they were sent to the main prison that was fifty years old and built to accommodate three hundred men. With the Tracy City convicts, the number swelled to over seven hundred.

"They'll be dying like sheep," one of the prison officials told a reporter. "It's too hot, there's no ventilation, and disease will spread like wild fire."

Once again Nat Baxter, vice-president of the Tennessee Coal, Iron, and Railroad Company that leased the convicts, agreed to surrender the lease if the state wanted the convicts back. The state didn't. There was no place for them.

Matters got worse on Monday. At Inman in Marion County, miners marched on the convict stockade there. The mine was owned by Nat Baxter's company and worked only convicts. Thirty guards were overpowered, and two hundred seventy convicts were loaded onto railroad cars and shipped to Nashville. The miners did not burn the stockade, as it was near a railroad trestle, but dismantled it board by board and pole by pole. Then they carried the boards and poles into the hollows and ridges for use by anyone who needed them.

In the course of one weekend, Governor Buchanan had six hundred sixty convicts returned to Nashville and two branch prisons either burned or dismantled. He took to his bed with illness.

There were now two places that remained in Tennessee where convicts worked in competition with local miners—Oliver Springs and Coal Creek. Both of those outposts had militia protecting the mines.

Governor Buchanan, never one for timely announcements, released a letter stating his intention to run for re-election as an independent. His platform had four planks which were more national in scope than state: Free coinage of gold and silver; an increase in currency circulation; abolition of the national banking system; and the enactment of a graduated income tax.

The governor had little time to wallow in self-pity. Two points of convict labor had been wiped out. Now, at the two spots where they were left, the worst was anticipated.

From his home, the governor ordered his adjutant general to send Colonel Cator Woolford from Chattanooga with the Third Regiment of the National Guard to Oliver Springs immediately. There they were to join about thirty members of the militia from Knoxville who were already behind the walls of the stockade.

At daylight on Tuesday, about a hundred miners moved down the road from Briceville to Oliver Springs and then the three miles farther to the stockade. They demanded the surrender of the convicts as they had done the previous November. This time they were met with defiance by the soldiers and an equal number of guards who believed they could repel the miners. A pitched battle ensued. Hundreds of shots were fired by the miners from the woods surrounding the stockade. The soldiers responded with fire from their Springfield rifles.

After an half hour, the loosely led band of miners hauled out a white flag, retrieved their wounded, and retired to the hillsides, disappearing as fast as they had arrived. Shouts that they would return were met by the victory whoops of the soldiers. For the first time, the miners had been repulsed.

In Chattanooga and Knoxville, the riot alarms were sounded from the courthouses. In Chattanooga Colonel Woolford prepared to board a train with his contingent for Harriman and then on to Oliver Springs. In Knoxville word spread quickly that the governor was calling out all the militia to go to the scene of trouble.

Fellow Kentucky miners heard of the rebuff at Oliver Springs and came in droves to Jellico. There they commandeered a freight train and ordered the engineer to take them to Clinton. By midnight hundreds of miners were on, in, or clinging to the freight cars pulled by engine No. 450 with engineer Caz Seivers at the controls. At Coal Creek the number of miners swelled to over a thousand. Two more train engines and empty cars were seized and the engineers given orders at the point of Winchesters and shotguns to head immediately to Clinton and on to Oliver Springs.

Just before dawn, the three trains arrived one behind the other at Oliver Springs and deposited their cargo of fifteen hundred miners. They began the walk to the stockade, not caring who knew they were coming.

Sergeant Lee Huddleston of the Chilhowee light infantry was on his way to the stockade himself to see what reinforcements they needed when he heard the sound of marching coming from the bend in the road ahead of him. Thinking it was advancing soldiers, he walked right into the mass of miners and was taken captive.

"Come here young man," Huddleston was ordered by one of the leaders of the miners. Huddleston looked him over. The leader was a white-bearded, grizzled short man who carried a sword in a sheath held around his waist by a string.

"Who's with you?" the leader asked and looked down the road.

"No one, sir. I just came from Knoxville."

Three of the miners rushed forward and seized Huddleston by the arms.

"Get away from him," the leader said. He drew his sword. "I'll cut off the head of the first person who lays a hand on the soldier." The miners backed off.

By daylight the stockade was in sight. A committee negotiated the surrender of the convicts. As soon as the warden of the branch prison saw the numbers they were up against, all thought of resistance took flight. He informed Major John Chandler and Colonel Leonard McBath who commanded the thirty soldiers. All agreed. The soldiers marched out between rows of miners and turned over all their weapons.

When all the convicts, guards, and soldiers had departed, the miners once again torched the stockade and its buildings. Sixteen miles away in Harriman, Colonel Cator Woolford had arrived with reinforcements at three o'clock in the morning. Instead of proceeding immediately to Oliver Springs, he decided his troops would breakfast at the Cumberland Hotel. By the time breakfast was over, the stockade at Oliver Springs was in ashes.

The miners headed back up the valley to Coal Creek which was now the last bastion of convict labor in the entire state. From there the miners sent a telegraph to the governor. It was short and to the point. Unless the soldiers at Fort Anderson were removed with the convicts, the fort would be attacked by the whole force of miners now concentrated at Coal Creek.

The sun's early morning rays reached the bright white tents of Fort Anderson before the news of the fall of the outpost at Oliver Springs. Now the miners' only remaining target sat majestically on the low mountain overlooking Coal Creek where miners were already gathering at the depot. They pointed to the sunlit summit where the soldiers were dug in behind earthen barriers and wooden walls.

Captain Keller Anderson and Lieutenant Perry Fyffe both gazed through their field glasses to the southwest. A strange smoke rose in the far distance where the stockade at Oliver Springs was still smoldering.

"Nobody leaves the fort today," Anderson said to Fyffe. "We're supposed to be receiving reinforcements from Knoxville and Nashville. General Carnes is on the way. Tracy City and Inman have fallen, and I don't know about Oliver Springs."

"Colonel, we need to give the immediate order to shoot to

kill anyone approaching the fort," Fyffe said and looked to Anderson for approval.

"Just tell everyone to be alert. No one leaves. No one enters. I'll give any lethal orders if we're attacked or fired upon," Anderson replied. "We still have friends among the miners. I've come to know quite a few of them during the last seven months." Anderson turned his glasses toward Coal Creek and looked at the house where he had played cards and drank liquor. "There's still time to reason."

"They're going to attack us, Colonel. I'll get the men ready," Fyffe said and turned away from his commander.

"You do that, Lieutenant. And, by the way, you're in charge *if* anything happens to me," Anderson shouted after Fyffe.

Betsy, Jake, and Daniel Boyd sat huddled at one end of the table while Grandma Dolan sat at her usual place at the opposite end. All the others had finished breakfast and were going about their chores.

"Today's the day, Jake. There's going to be nearly two thousand miners in the valley from as far away as Harlan County in Kentucky to Grundy County down at Tracy City. They're going to attack the fort," Daniel Boyd whispered.

"Papa, you can't let that happen. They'll never win. You're not going are you? Or you, Jake?" Betsy asked. A tear slid down from one eye.

"Betsy, I have to go. I'm a miner. We have to stick together," her father said.

Jake shook his head back and forth. "There's got to be a better way, Daniel. Why can't we give the legislature one more crack at it. That's why I'm running."

"They may trust you. But you'll just be one of over a hundred. If you get elected. The men have seen the victories in Tracy City and Inman, and if what I heard is right, Oliver Springs should be liberated by now. There's only Coal Creek left. This is where it started. This is where it'll end."

"Your life, Papa. Your life might end if they shoot you

with that Gatling gun or those big old rifles they carry. Please don't go."

"Shush, Betsy. You're going to rile up Grandma Dolan. She doesn't know what's going on," he said and looked toward the other end of the table.

Grandma Dolan glared up from her plate. "The hell I don't, Daniel Boyd. I'm just hard of hearing, not deaf. I've been through one war. Buried two sons from it. For nothing. For nothing. Crazy to rebel."

"What about you, Jake? What are you going to do?" Betsy asked.

Jake stood up and walked to the fireplace. He leaned against the stone mantel and stared away. He then looked back at Betsy. "I have to be there. I don't want them to fight. Maybe something can be worked out."

"Worked out? I think it's too late for that."

"Dick, my brother Dick, has been friendly with Colonel Anderson. I'll ask him. Maybe he can go to the fort and talk to Anderson. Maybe it can be worked out."

"The military is not going to give in," Betsy said. "They're holed up on the mountain. They're trained to fight. That's what they came here for. Now they'll have their chance. I don't want you getting killed." She got up and walked to him. She took his hand. "Please don't do anything stupid."

"I won't. I want to live as much as anybody. More than some."

"They've cut the telegraph lines to Knoxville already. My train won't be running. I can't go to work at Professor Brimer's."

"Just study your books at home. I'll be safe. I'm going to talk with Dick. I won't shoot, and hope I won't be shot at," Jake said. He gave Betsy a kiss on the cheek and headed out the door.

Jake found his brother at the depot. Dick Drummond nodded when Jake asked him to help negotiate a settlement with Captain Anderson. "Sounds like a good idea. They should give up without a fight. Look at all these miners. Some from a hundred miles away."

Jake turned and looked at the railroad tracks. To the north and to the south, miners lined the side of the tracks. Most stood while some squatted. Guns were everywhere. Some were being cleaned. Others were being trained on the fort that loomed above and behind them.

"We've sent a telegram to the governor. We'll give him today for an answer. If we don't get the answer we want, we're attacking in the morning."

"What about talking to Anderson?" Jake asked.

"Yeah. I'll do that tomorrow. I've hefted a few bottles with him. Maybe he and I can settle it all in a card game." Dick Drummond laughed.

In Knoxville, Colonel Cator Woolford awaited orders. He and his hundred twenty-five men had finally made it from Harriman. The Knoxville sheriff was rounding up a posse of civilians to aid the effort. Governor Buchanan requested all local sheriffs to do the same thing.

By noon on the seventeenth, General Sam T. Carnes had received his orders in Memphis. He and over three hundred militia were on the train and headed for Chattanooga within the hour.

Meanwhile the Knoxville posse was organizing under the field direction of three leaders. David Anderson, clerk of the supreme court and a former Confederate officer, took one squadron.

Major D. A. Carpenter, a former sheriff of Anderson County and now a Knoxville businessman, led another contingent. "When I get to Coal Creek and let out my war whoop, the miners will take to running," he told those who would follow him. Among those in Carpenter's group was John Walthall. He had moved to Knoxville from Abingdon, Virginia, five years before. He was twenty-three and a clerk in the freight office of the East Tennessee Railroad. Lawyers, constables, clerks, and livery men filled out the ranks.

Colonel W. L. Ledgerwood, an ex-Union officer, led the final third of the posse.

They waited all of Wednesday to see what progress General Carnes was making. The Knox County sheriff bought or confiscated all the guns and ammunition from every hardware store in Knoxville to give to the members of his posse.

When General Carnes reached Chattanooga early on Thursday, he added to his ranks another hundred twenty-five men from the first regiment and another sheriff's posse of over a hundred men.

Dick Drummond left the depot the next morning after giving the governor a full day to respond to the miners' requests. They had heard nothing back from Nashville but had heard of the posse forming in Knoxville and rumors that General Carnes was on the way from Memphis.

"Here, Jake. Take the revolver. Just hold it for me. I know you don't want to shoot anyone. But I want to show Colonel Anderson and the soldiers that we're unarmed." Jake reluctantly took the pistol and stuck it down between his belt and trousers.

Dick Drummond, Thomas Hatmaker, and two others with whom Colonel Anderson had played cards and partaken of liquor, began a slow walk from Coal Creek, past the Wye, and up the ridge toward Fort Anderson. They held a white flag, torn from a sheet, in front of them.

Lieutenant Perry Fyffe saw them first. "Four miners approaching the fort, sir," he told Keller Anderson while he kept his eyes on the group. "They have a white flag, but I don't trust them, sir. Shall I order our men to fire?"

"Give me those glasses," Colonel Anderson said, took the field glasses, and gazed down the mountain. He smiled. "I know those men. That's Drummond and Hatmaker and a couple of my card playing friends, Lieutenant. They're harmless. I'll go out and see what they want. You keep an eye on me."

"No, sir. I don't think you should go out," Fyffe said and shook his head.

"Now, now, Lieutenant, everything's going to be all right. If they kill me, you're in charge." He walked around the entrenchments and past the last sentry. He waved to the four miners.

"Colonel Anderson. There's a large contingent of miners

down at the depot. I believe if you come down and talk with them all this can be resolved without a shot being fired," Dick Drummond told his drinking buddy.

"Me? Talk to a thousand miners? I couldn't do that, Dick."

Dick Drummond leaned closer to the colonel and whispered. "Come on with us. We'll have a little to drink, play a few hands, and then you can tell your people you tried to reason with us and I can do the same. I'll guarantee you safe conduct. There won't be any fighting today."

Colonel Anderson looked back toward the fort. He turned to Drummond. "Lieutenant Fyffe's so worried. He wanted to shoot you on sight. Let me tell him where I'm going."

Anderson walked back to the fort and within minutes returned to the group of miners. "Let's go," he said and smiled. "A little liquor should make us all more agreeable."

In a back room of the Arbor Hotel in Coal Creek, the liquor flowed freely. Within an hour Colonel Anderson was drunk enough to lose his military hat on a bet in a card game. But Dick Drummond and Thomas Hatmaker kept plying him with alcohol. In another hour, the colonel passed out.

"Carry him out to the mountains and hide him," Drummond told Hatmaker and the others. "It's time to attack the fort."

The limp colonel was carried out and through lines of miners who wanted to string him up immediately. "No. He's our ace we're holding back," Drummond told them. "He's worth more to us alive than dead." The other miners backed off and allowed him to be carried through.

A thousand miners took to the two other ridges that faced Fort Anderson and began firing away with their rifles.

Inside the fort, Lieutenant Perry Fyffe finally was able to give the order to fire. The Gatling gun and mountain howitzer were turned toward Walden's Ridge.

Bullets from the miners' rifles thumped into the wood palisade and threw up dust where they hit the ground. As soon as the Gatling gun began to spew forth its rounds, the miners stood motionless behind trees and rocks. When it stopped, they stepped back out and fired some more.

A haze of gunpowder smoke drifted lazily off the mountain in the hot summer air. A soldier was struck by a bullet and fell to the ground. Blood oozed down his arm. Comrades rushed to him and dragged him to a corner of the fort where he could be treated.

Three other soldiers rushed to move the howitzer into position. One carried a charge to put into the gun, but it exploded prematurely sending its full force into his head. He died instantly. Now the soldiers crawled and squatted more than running upright. Bullets were raining down, but most fell harmlessly onto the ground or pounded into the wood.

On Walden's Ridge, miners gathered up three of their wounded, slung them over their shoulders, and started back down the ridge. They could get no nearer than a hundred yards of the fort. The Gatling gun did its work well.

A try was made by a hundred of the miners for the stockade of the Knoxville Iron mine. As they neared, the now familiar rat-a-tat-tat of the Gatling spitting out another blistering wave of bullets was heard. They first bit into the road ahead of them and then inched ever closer until the attackers scattered and jumped into the ditches along the road. They retreated on their bellies.

There was a quiet lull. Lieutenant Fyffe looked out through his field glasses. "Where is Colonel Anderson?" he asked no one in particular.

Dick Drummond met with D. B. Monroe at the depot. "We have to wait them out," Monroe said. "Going up that mountain against the Gatling gun would be suicide."

Drummond nodded. "Yeah, we just need to keep on flanking them. Fire a few shots here and a few there. They'll finally give up. We have their commander."

"He could order them to surrender," someone said.

"He's too drunk to do anything for a few hours," Drummond said. "He doesn't even know where he is."

Jake came up to his brother. "Why the attack? Why didn't we negotiate?"

"Jake, this is what we're negotiating with now," Dick said and held up his Winchester. He looked down at the revolver in

Jake's belt. "You keep that. Make our father proud. You'll probably need it before this is over."

Word reached Knoxville of the attack on Fort Anderson while General Carnes was still on his way from Chattanooga. Colonel Woolford, with his one hundred twenty-five militia and the sheriff's posse of over a hundred, boarded a special train at 3:30 p.m. and headed for Clinton. Traveling slowly with soldiers on the front of the engine as lookouts for traps and torn up rails, the soldiers and posse made it to the county seat of Anderson County in two hours.

"The tracks are dynamited ahead," someone warned them. "You'd better wait here for General Carnes. The miners have over a thousand waiting for you in groups of a hundred between here and Coal Creek."

"Hell, I know these mountains better than the miners," Colonel Carpenter said. "We can go as far as Knapps on the train. Then I'll take my part of the posse over the mountain and come up on the back side of Coal Creek."

A miner standing in the crowd at Clinton listened attentively to Carpenter's brag, went to his horse, and galloped off toward Coal Creek.

It was almost dark when General Carnes reached Knoxville with his nine-car train loaded with nearly five hundred militia and posse. From Knoxville on, all lights were doused, muzzles of rifles laid in the windows of the train cars, and the men of the military and civilian posse sat in the floor and between seats.

"Fire back immediately if you're fired upon," General Carnes said. The train moved slowly toward Clinton. Carnes hoped to catch up to Woolford and go into Coal Creek together.

At Coal Creek, Dick Drummond searched for his little brother Jake. The rider from Clinton had given him the news. Darkness was now complete. Clouds masked the moon and stars. Only the camp fires from Fort Anderson and the miners' small fires on adjoining ridges gave any color to the night.

"We need ten men to go up on Walden's Ridge and let us know if any of the Knoxville posse is getting close," Dick told Jake when he finally found him. "You don't have to shoot anybody. We just need some spies. I need you to go, Jake. You're a miner. It's about time you took a part in this. Don't disgrace our family name."

Jake looked at his older brother and spit into the dirt. "Me disgrace the family name?"

"Yeah, you. You act like you're afraid to fight for your rights. I had to almost force you to take our father's revolver. He used that in the Civil War. He fought for what he believed in. I don't know about you, Jake. What do you believe in?"

"I believe in the rule of law. All of this is hopeless." Jake took the revolver out and pointed to all the miners and toward the fort. "We can't win this way, Dick."

"Dammit, Jake. Just do your part. Scout for us. I'll be there to back you up."

"I don't need you to back me up, Dick. I know Walden's Ridge a lot better than you." He put the pistol back into his belt. "I'll go scout, but I'm not going to shoot anyone. I have to live with myself. I don't drink myself into a stupor every day."

They gathered up another eight miners to go with them and started toward the Wye from the depot. They would divide up and take to the ridge on their left to see if anyone was coming in the back door to Coal Creek.

Fatal Rock

Just outside of Clinton a mile or so, the Knoxville posse left the train to the remaining militia with Colonel Woolford and began the climb of the ridge that would lead them in the back way to Fort Anderson and Coal Creek.

It was ten o'clock and they wanted to be to Fort Anderson by daybreak.

The little cattle trail they began to follow ended in nothingness, and only the steep ridge, undergrowth, and brush lay before them. A flash of lightning signaled the coming storm. In their haste to leave Knoxville, the posse members brought no rain gear or clothing fit for fighting the mountain vines and leaves.

Rain, that first started as a drizzle, quickly began a steady beat on the bodies of the posse. Leaves on the ground became slick. Wet limbs slapped the faces and arms of the untrained soldiers. The ridge was steeper than what D. A. Carpenter remembered. His breath came in short gasps, and he wondered if he would be able to give his war whoop when he made it to Coal Creek.

The men began to use their rifles as walking sticks, pressing the stocks into the deepening mud while they tried to climb the hillside. One rifle discharged accidentally, barely missing the ear of one young man.

The farther they climbed, the more depressed they became. The mountain seemed to rise forever. Feet would find a secure place to push off only to land in another slimy hole. Clothes, first drenched with water, became layered with mud as each man fell every few feet. They began to crawl up the mountain more than walk.

Not used to the absolute darkness of the mountain on a rainy night, one member of the posse would become separated from another. There was little sound except for heavy breathing and an occasional shout for help. Some bowed their heads and prayed for dawn.

On the opposite side of Walden's Ridge, Jake Drummond and the other nine miners had spread out to take to the spine of the ridge. They had all hunted the ridge in daylight and dark. Their hounds had chased foxes and raccoons up and down the ravines. Still, it was a hard climb when the rain came.

Jake pulled his hat down to shield his eyes from the blowing rain and raised the collar of his coat up around his neck. He felt for the Colt revolver to be sure he hadn't lost the family heirloom. Surely the soldiers and posse in Clinton wouldn't try an assault over Walden's Ridge in weather like this.

He stopped about half way up and looked back toward Fort Anderson and the Knoxville Iron Company stockade. The rain blew in such sheets that he could barely make out the small campfires of both places. He could see a faint glow come from the windows of John Chumbley's house. He squatted down and rested.

Why had it come to this? Why was he climbing a mountain to scout for a posse? Why did an army and posse want to invade what had been a peaceful valley a little over a year before? Why did miners want to work in cramped holes that were dirty and wet? Why was he carrying a gun?

He shook his head and water flew from his hat. All of it was crazy. He would go to the top and wait. He wasn't walking the ridge to Clinton to look for a non-existent posse. City boys would have more sense than to go into a forbidding mountain on a night like this.

General Carnes received the same news as Colonel Woolford when he reached Clinton. There were rumors that a bridge a mile farther down was loaded with dynamite. Then he got worse news. A telegram from Knoxville:

"Rumor Anderson captured. Decoyed from his garrison by treachery. Run carefully, and look out for trouble between Offuts and Coal Creek."

It was a terrible night, but he had to make it to Coal Creek. His old buddy had been captured. He'd show the miners who was boss when he got there. If he had to hang twenty of them to get Anderson released, so be it.

Carnes's train had its nine cars filled with nearly six hundred militiamen and members of the Nashville and Chattanooga posses. He brought two more Gatling guns and other field pieces on a flatcar.

At Clinton some of his men carried on a stretcher a soldier who had accidentally shot himself. Another, wounded by the same bullet, was led to a local hotel to be treated by a doctor. So far, they were the only casualties.

The general ordered the train to move slowly out of Clinton and to Offuts where he would review the situation. At Offuts, he made the same decision that the militia had made earlier. They would detrain and go to Coal Creek through the mountains and ridges. They could be too easily ambushed along the track of the railroad.

General Carnes secured the guidance of a local farmer, unloaded the field pieces, and set out with his six hundred men up a dirt cattle path. With no horses or mules, the going was slow pulling the bulky fieldpieces up the steep road.

When it began to rain, the road turned to mire, the wheels of the pieces they were pulling sank into the mud, and exhaustion gripped them. Even with the troops alternating the pushing and pulling of the heavy equipment, it seemed hopeless.

After a constant struggle for a period of three hours, Carnes found himself and his troops going downhill. Shortly, they were back at the railroad tracks. Their guide was gone. They had pulled the field artillery for five miles up and down the ridge only to end up a mile in front of the train they had left hours earlier.

He sent back for the train.

Once Jake Drummond reached the summit of Walden's Ridge, he lost track of where his brother and the other eight miners were. All had agreed to divide up, but he wondered if they had gone farther on the ridgetop and were already to Clinton.

He knew the ridge by touch. Somewhere nearby he remembered there was a large rock. He would find it and wait out the rain until daylight. When he hunted the ridge, the boulder served as a place to rendezvous for him and his hounds.

He couldn't see, but somewhere just ahead in the inky blackness was the jutting stone that had been a place of rest so many times before. He squatted and stepped in short lengths hoping for a lightning flash to blaze the path for him.

For another quarter mile he hugged the ridge and trudged through the darkness. Then a series of three flashes of lightning lit up the huge boulder just in front of him. As tall as he was and three times as wide, the rock stood like a small fort. Jake walked to it, surveyed around it to see if anyone else had found the place of solace, and then took the side that gave him the most protection against the driving rain. He sat with his back braced against the hardness of the rock, folded his arms over his chest, and lowered his head until his hat almost touched his chest. Here he would wait for morning's light.

John Walthall's heart beat fast. He was lost. He had not seen nor heard another posse member in the past hour. He was afraid to shout. Somewhere on this ridge there could be miners. They had guns. He was used to stocking freight and writing tickets for shipping parcels. What had seemed like an exciting adventure when they were gathering the posse in Knoxville, now had become a wet, muddy, and exhausting nightmare.

He felt for his revolver. Mud dripped from its handle, from where he had fallen so many times. He stood still for a moment and then turned slowly all the way around. He looked and listened.

Nothing. At least he had accomplished one thing. He was on top of the ridge. But which way to go?

Suddenly lightning streaked across the sky in pulsing flashes. Not more than a hundred yards in front of him, a broad figure that was at least as tall as he was jutted from the ground. It was not a tree. He walked toward it until a wet limb slapped him in the face. Then he took to his hands and knees and crawled toward the giant object that he had seen. It was either a small cabin or a large rock. Whichever, he would rest there, wait until daylight, and let the remainder of the posse find him.

Another flash of lightning showed him that he was almost there. With his hands he found the nearest side, turned his back to the enormous rock, folded his arms, and went to sleep to the sting of raindrops against his face.

Near daylight the rain stopped. Jake's head jerked up. The rhythm of the rain had lulled him into a fitful sleep. Its end was like a whistle, awakening him to reality. He kept his arms folded, raised his head, and looked out into the first hint of light.

The mist rising from the warm leaves met the fog overhead, cloaking the top of Walden's Ridge in a white blanket that reminded him of loosely spun cotton. Still there was no sound. Even the insects were holed up from the rain. He waited a half hour for more light.

On the opposite side of the rock, John Walthall slumped over on his side. He opened his eyes and sat up, then shivered. He rubbed his hands up and down his arms and onto his face. He wanted to stand up, but his arms and legs ached from the night's march. He got to his knees and his revolver scraped against the rock.

Jake heard the sound. A raccoon or skunk was on the other side. He drew his father's revolver from his belt and tapped the barrel against the rock. The sound would send the animal scurrying.

John heard what he thought was the scraping of a tree limb against the far side of the rock. He looked up. There was no tree near the boulder. His hand trembled when he put it to his gun.

"Who's there?" His voice was low, hoarse, and gravelly.

More and more light filtered through the mist. Jake pressed himself to the rock when he heard the voice. "Who's there?" he asked, as though in a delayed echo.

The voice sent John Walthall slinking back down into the mud. "One of the posse. How about you?"

"No. One of the miners."

"I've got a gun. I'm not scared," Walthall answered and tried to wipe the mud off his revolver.

"I have one too."

"Is anybody with you?"

"There's a hundred of us on this side of the rock," Jake answered.

Walthall smiled. "Yeah? I have a hundred and fifty here. You stay on your side. We'll stay here."

"Good idea," Jake said. "What's your first name?"

"Johnny. And yours?"

"Jake. You lost?"

"No, I'm on top of the ridge. I just don't know where I am."

"What do you do when you're not out hunting miners on top of ridges and you don't know where you are?"

"I'm a clerk for the railroad shipping department. Have been for three years. I'm twenty-three. Came down from Abingdon, Virginia, to work in Knoxville."

"Johnny, who talked you into coming onto this ridge?"

"Ah, just some old men at the railroad. They won't talk me into anything like this again. How old are you, Jake?"

"Twenty-two."

"You're not aiming to kill me are you, Jake?"

"Not unless I have to in self defense. Where's the rest of the posse?"

"Somewhere, all along this blasted ridge. How do I get back to Clinton?"

"Turn around. Go along the ridge for about a mile. There'll be a trail heading off down to your left. Take it to the railroad and follow the tracks to town."

Johnny Walthall put his hands to his stomach. The pain there matched the ones in his arms and legs. "I'm hungry, Jake. Do you have anything to eat? I haven't eaten since breakfast yesterday."

"No," Jake said and then felt for his coat pockets. He had forgotten about the four biscuits he tucked away from his own breakfast the day before. "Wait. I may have some biscuits if the rain didn't soak them."

He pulled a packet from his coat and unwrapped the waxed paper. The biscuit on top had turned to mush. The second one was wet. The last two were dry. "I've got a couple of dry ones, Johnny. I'll toss them over the rock."

Jake lobbed the hard biscuits over the rock to the opposite side and Johnny caught them. Walthall began to eat, taking half of the first biscuit in one bite. "You have some left, Jake?"

Jake looked at the soaked mush he had already thrown to the ground. "Yeah. Don't worry about me."

Jake sat in silence while Johnny finished off most of the two biscuits in short order. "Thanks, Jake. That hit the spot."

"Those were Grandma Dolan's biscuits."

"Your grandmother sure is a good cook."

"She's not my grandmother. My girlfriend's."

"You going to get married?"

Jake thought back to his Christmas Eve proposal and the mule he had carved for Betsy. "I hope. Someday. You married, Johnny?"

"In two weeks."

For a half hour they sat on their respective sides of the huge boulder and talked. Family, jobs, Betsy Boyd and Johnny Walthall's soon-to-be bride. Jake learned more about Johnny in the few minutes they talked than he knew about some of the boys he had grown up with in Briceville and Coal Creek.

The first rays of sunlight hit the tops of the trees and diffused down through the dark leaves. Jake looked up and listened. On the slope of the ridge below them he heard the muffled tread of men.

"You hear that, Johnny? Is that some of your posse?"

They both strained to catch the distant sounds. "Could be. I don't know anybody else that's on this ridge."

"Actually, Johnny, there were ten of us scouts. I haven't seen any of them since we split up. But I better get out of here if that's your posse. Don't shoot me, okay?"

"Sure. I'll head down toward the posse. You get away. . . . Oh, Jake?"

"Yeah."

"Thanks for the biscuits. And Jake, if you can get out of Coal Creek, come to my wedding. Two weeks from Saturday. First Baptist Church in Knoxville. Just a block down from the courthouse. The name is Johnny Walthall."

Jake shook his head and smiled. "Johnny Walthall. Sure. I'll try. Johnny, I'm Jake Drummond."

The noise from the hillside was getting closer. Johnny Walthall stood and stepped toward the slope of the ridge to rejoin the posse.

A blast caused Jake to hit the ground as though he had been shot. He hadn't. It came from behind him. He looked back. Smoke was still coming from the barrel of Dick Drummond's Winchester.

"Dick, what were you shooting at?" Jake shouted.

Dick Drummond smiled. "I think I got me a member of the posse." He nodded beyond the rock and toward the slope.

The bullet had hit Johnny Walthall in the back of his neck and exited at his throat. Only his hand moved where he lay on his back on the wet ground fifty feet from the rock.

Jake jumped to his feet, looked around the rock, and saw his companion of the last hours. A red streak of blood flowed from his throat.

Jake turned back toward his brother. "Why did you shoot Johnny? He's my friend!" He took his revolver from his belt, aimed it at Dick, hesitated, and then flung the weapon as far as he could down the side of the ridge. He ran to the fallen posse member.

"Johnny, Johnny!" Jake cradled the young man's head in his lap. "It wasn't me. I didn't shoot you."

Johnny Walthall tried to speak, but blood was running down his airway. There was only the gurgling sound of a man drowning in his own blood. He took Jake's hand. The last piece of biscuit was still in his. He barely nodded his head, and he was gone.

Dick Drummond still stood behind Jake. The smile was gone.

Others from the posse stormed up the ridge. The rest of the scouts from the miners closed quickly. Gunfire rang out as though it was on top of Jake. He saw Dick fire his rifle toward the slope of the ridge and saw the other miners aim their guns.

Jake crawled back to the rock, to the far side. There were screams and cursing from the posse. The shooting was wild. A member of the miners yelled, "We have them surrounded boys. Kill every last one of them."

The posse began a speedy retreat down the slope of the ridge. Some fell headlong and rolled until they thumped into the trunks of trees. Another of the posse fell fatally wounded. A miner was shot and slumped to the ground.

Jake didn't want to leave the body of Johnny Walthall on the top of Walden's Ridge, but all the fighting was directed in that area. He crawled, then walked, then ran through the thick forest along the top of the ridge toward Coal Creek.

He sprinted until his sides ached. He stopped and leaned against a tree to catch his breath. Tears streaked his cheeks. His legs picked up the chase again as though they were propelling him along with no guidance from his head. Branches and limbs slashed at him. Blood oozed from the scratches on his face and hands. All feeling had left him. His mind was on Johnny. Johnny Walthall had somebody who wanted to marry him, and he was dead on Walden's Ridge.

General S.T. Carnes and Staff

Occupied

The retreating Knoxville posse stumbled down the fog cloaked ridge, finally reaching the railroad track. Exhausted and without the breath to give any orders, let alone yell out his famous war whoop, Colonel D. A. Carpenter begged a farmer to borrow a wagon. He climbed in, lay his head on a sack of corn, and was transported toward the position of General Carnes. His two sons sat on either side, holding his hands and consoling him.

"Everybody load back on," General Carnes told his troops when the train arrived. Wet, muddy, hungry, and fatigued, the troops went about the tasks of reloading the heavy cannons and field artillery pieces back onto the flatcars. The rain had stopped but the fog continued to soak them with added discomfort.

The bedraggled posse walked down the tracks toward the general's troops.

"The miners are upon us! Shoot to kill!" a soldier said when he saw the dark, shadowy figures of the posse.

"No, no, no, we're the Knoxville posse!" one of those in front yelled, preventing a disastrous shooting by their own friendly forces.

They gave Carnes the story. They had been attacked on Walden's Ridge by a greatly superior force—at least five hundred, probably as many as three thousand miners. With courage they had withstood a withering fire from the sharpshooters and managed to bring down several of their number while marching to the rear.

General Carnes peered up the tracks toward Coal Creek. "If they're on the ridge, then we may be safer to proceed on up the tracks. We can't make another try overland." He dismissed the posse members and let them return to Knoxville.

Carnes placed one detachment of soldiers in front to march ahead of the train. All the others rode with their rifles resting in the windows and the militiamen hunched down out of sight or lying in the aisleways. The train chugged on. No trouble was encountered, and in an hour and a half they had reached the coal chute just south of Coal Creek. The general ordered the train to stop.

He took his field glasses and looked to the ridge on his left. The fog was beginning to lift. He could make out the rays of sunshine hitting the tops of trees and the summit of the ridge. In the forest he would see a figure, then two, a half dozen, and then they would be gone. Was it the trees or the miners?

He ordered all the troops out of the train to take positions on the right of the cars. With all those who had joined him in Chattanooga and Knoxville, Carnes had a force of nearly six hundred regular soldiers plus the remaining posse members from Nashville and Chattanooga.

He sent Colonel Granville Sevier with a company of troops down the tracks and into town under a flag of truce.

"Tell whoever you find and perceive to be leaders that they shall surrender the town and Colonel Anderson to me. If they refuse, tell them to remove all the women and children for I shall begin to fire within fifteen minutes."

Colonel Sevier moved out and toward the depot. The field artillery was unloaded again and positioned with barrels aimed toward the businesses of Coal Creek.

In a half hour Sevier returned. "They surrendered the town to you, sir. They say they believe Colonel Anderson is in the mountains with some miners who are protecting him from a more radical group. They will deliver him by one o'clock."

General Carnes pulled out his watch. "One o'clock? That's four hours. All right. We'll give them four hours." He sent

Sevier back with his troops to the depot. He ordered another hundred to march to the relief of Fort Anderson. The remainder would stay along the railroad tracks and begin an encampment.

Jake hunkered beneath an apple tree near the base of Walden's Ridge. He pulled an apple from the tree and bit into it. The tart, juicy flesh of the fruit was the only food he had eaten in a day. He had lost his hat on the mad dash down the ridge. His hair became matted with water and bits of leaves and branches. He shaded his eyes and squinted toward Coal Creek.

The gap in the ridge where the railroad came from Coal Creek and branched off toward Briceville was a quarter mile ahead of him. He looked up toward Fort Anderson and saw pieces of the white tents, shredded by hundreds of bullets in yesterday's battle, flapping wildly in the morning breeze. There were few soldiers in sight. No sound of gunfire was heard.

Then, through the gap in the ridge, marched the first of the troops that General Carnes had sent to relieve Fort Anderson. Most wore mud-flaked uniforms, remnants of the previous night's march up and down Walden's Ridge. Jake lay down flat against the ground and kept his eyes trained on the soldiers.

They wound around the path that snaked up the hill toward the fort and disappeared from sight within a few minutes. He looked behind him and up toward the ridge that he had recently descended. He had not seen Dick or the other miners since the skirmish sent him on his retreat. Where were they? Was his brother dead? Did he find his end beside Johnny Walthall? Or had he escaped?

He looked back toward Coal Creek. Through the gap came three men. They walked along the railroad track and took the branch leading toward Briceville. Jake edged down to where he could intercept them. He was sure they were miners.

"What's happening in Coal Creek?" he called out to them. They motioned for him to join them. He looked behind him then scurried down to the tracks. They continued to walk toward Briceville while they talked.

"The soldiers have taken Coal Creek," one said and glanced back toward the gap. "Must be a thousand of them. Say they're going to start shelling the town if Colonel Anderson ain't returned. I'm heading to Briceville and to the hills."

"Are they shooting anybody?" Jake asked.

"Not yet. But they're likely to shoot or hang anybody who gets in their way. If you're smart, you'll head toward Briceville and keep right on going."

"I need to get to my house on the other side of Coal Creek," Jake said and turned around. The three miners didn't slow down. They looked back at Jake and shook their heads.

Jake headed back to the cuff of Walden's Ridge. He would stay at the edge of the woods until he came into sight of Coal Creek. Then he would go from alley to alley and hide while he made his way safely to his home or Betsy's.

General Carnes sat in one of the passenger cars and took the reports. What were the casualties so far? The Knoxville posse had two of its men killed on Walden's Ridge—Johnny Walthall and Bunch Givens. Several others were injured. He received word that Private Curtis Wood who had been taken from his train after shooting himself had died in Clinton. From Fort Anderson it was reported that two had been killed—one shot by the miners and the other killed in the premature explosion of a shell for one of the field pieces.

"Five dead already!" he shouted to one of the officers. "We'll hang two for each one that was killed. Ten of their leaders will be swinging before the night is through." He looked at his watch. It was past one o'clock. Outside Colonel Sevier was walking toward his car with another message.

"They still can't deliver Anderson. They say they need another six hours to find him."

General Carnes spit onto the crossties. "Take the civilian Chattanooga posse and as many militiamen as you need and start arresting every man in town between the ages of fifteen and seventy-five. Tell the townspeople that I will deal with the prisoners as Colonel Anderson is dealt with."

"Everybody, sir? Arrest everybody?"

"Yes, Colonel Sevier, except for the ones that you can personally vouch for. Bring them here and put them in those boxcars," he said and pointed to five empty boxcars on a side track.

Colonel Sevier's soldiers and the posse began the roundup. Word spread rapidly that all the men of Coal Creek were being arrested. Children wailed when their brothers and fathers were snatched away and pushed toward the boxcars. Women screamed and beat their fists against the soldiers carrying their husbands away until they were pushed down into the dirt streets.

Men darted behind buildings. They stole down to the creek and crawled along the bank, trying to get out of town. Attics were opened and men climbed up to rest with the wasps and spiders amid dusty boards, hiding from the troops who now went from door to door looking for their prey.

Ten soldiers stopped at a grove where boys were throwing a ball. "How old are you?" they asked each boy in turn. Those fifteen and older were dragged off toward the headquarters of General Carnes.

Jake saw some of the activity. What was happening? Why were the women screaming? He made his way through the gap and to the first building in Coal Creek. From there he could look down the railroad track and see the soldiers on the south end of town. He ran to the back of another building. He looked around the corner. Four soldiers marched toward him. They had rifles with bayonets affixed.

Jake ducked back in and shot up the next alley. He had to get to Betsy. He turned the corner and looked back to see a commotion where soldiers were dragging away two men a block away. He headed the other way. He stepped into another alley and caught his breath. Not much farther and he could make a dash for the creek and then on to Betsy's house.

Jake looked back out. Four more soldiers coming from the opposite direction. He ran down the alley and out behind another store. At this exact moment three soldiers stepped out the back door of the store with a prisoner. They were as startled as Jake was. He turned to walk away.

"Halt!" Jake heard the click of the rifles and glanced back over his shoulder. All three were aiming at his head.

He held his hands up. "I surrender."

They took his jacket off and looked for any gun. They turned him about and kicked him toward the railroad tracks. "You're a miner, aren't you? How'd your face and arms get so scratched up? Been on the ridge taking pot shots at our soldiers?" They kicked him with each question. He didn't answer. He kept his hands up and walked in the direction they pushed.

Dick Drummond stayed on the ridge after the skirmish. Later he walked down toward where General Carnes had halted his train. He stayed in the forest and watched until the train and troops pulled out toward Coal Creek. He then crossed the tracks and headed for the Clinch River. They would be looking for him. Someone knew he shot the man who was in the posse.

When he reached the river, he took vines and tied together some logs he found from a past timber cutting. He had rafted down the Clinch before, all the way to Chattanooga, with a harvest of lumber. This time he would be alone. He wasn't risking his neck for killing one of the posse. Colonel Anderson would also be able to identify him as one of the men who spirited him away and kept him prisoner.

The mid-afternoon sun beat down on the boxcars. Jake was thrown into the already partly filled car. His head banged against the side of the car with the force of all three soldiers pushing him. Along his hairline blood seeped out. He fell to the floor and rolled over on his side. The door slammed shut. In the dim light, he saw that he was not alone. The car already held twenty or thirty men as prisoners.

His first thought was that he was in Hell. It was tortuously hot, his throat yearned for water, and there were other lost souls populating the place. He rubbed his head and remembered he was still in Coal Creek. He next thought of Betsy. How would she know? Would she think he was dead? He had to get word to Betsy.

He crawled to the door and looked out through a small crack. Soldiers up and down the track. They were bringing other Coal Creek men and boys to the cars. They were arresting the whole town. The only time they opened the car doors was to throw someone else in. He inched back to the far side, opened his shirt up, and began fanning himself with the cloth.

After the posse and soldiers arrested all they could find in Coal Creek they set out in parties to the surrounding areas.

Betsy and Grandma Dolan kept a vigil for Jake on their front porch. Her father and uncle were at the barn, working and talking. A horseman delivered the news. The soldiers had arrived at Coal Creek. The fighting the day before and on into the night had been fierce. Nobody had seen Jake since the morning before.

Betsy cried softly and wiped tears away with another of Jake's kerchiefs.

Grandma Dolan sat beside her with her hand on her head. "He'll be all right, Betsy. Jake is smart and tough. He'll show up. Don't worry yourself."

Betsy said nothing.

Eight soldiers came marching around the bend from Coal Creek.

"What are they doing here?" Grandma Dolan asked.

Betsy looked up. "They've come to tell us that they've killed Jake," Betsy said. She stood up and ran to meet them.

The soldiers stared at her and pushed her away when she asked about Jake Drummond. They turned into the yard.

"Any men here?" one of them asked.

"Yeah, enough to protect us from you'uns," Grandma Dolan said.

"Where are they?"

"They'll be here when we need them," she said.

"Listen, old woman, I want those men out here now or else I'm going to start breaking up your house."

Grandma Dolan started to get up. "Let me get my poker," she said. Betsy rushed to her and tried to calm her grandmother.

Daniel and Will Boyd appeared from the side of the house. All rifles were raised and pointed toward them. "You're under arrest. Get onto the road. Any other men here?"

"No!" Betsy shouted. "Why are you arresting farmers?"

"They look like miners to me," the commanding soldier said. "If they can prove they're farmers and innocent, General Carnes will release them. We have our orders to arrest every man between fifteen and seventy-five."

Rain returned after the few hours of sunshine. It was welcomed by the prisoners in the boxcars. Daniel Boyd and Will Boyd were kicked into a car in front of Jake's.

The rain beat on the top of Jake's car, cooling the air but creating a deafening roar. He sat and waited.

Near dark, Jake and the other prisoners sensed there was a change in the soldiers voices. Jake scooted closer to the door and listened. Colonel Anderson had been returned to General Carnes. There would be no hangings that night.

While he was listening, the soldiers opened the door and pushed two more captives inside. The officer told his men to leave the door open for a while and maintain a guard at that point. "That heat pouring out of there feels like an oven. We're going to have some dead men in there if we don't give them some air."

The two newcomers were no strangers to Jake. Joining him in the boxcar were Commissioner George Ford and Deputy U. S. Marshall Bud Lindsay.

"You work for the governor, and they arrested you?" Jake asked Ford. He looked at Lindsay, the huge, tough lawman who had been sent to Coal Creek to protect railroad property. His fists were twice the size of Jake's. "Bud, why'd they arrest you?"

"Hell, Jake, they want to hang me. I got a little liquored up and said a few things about the officers," Lindsay said. He pointed to Ford. "They took George's notebook. Said he was fomenting a riot. You know how peaceful Ford is. This is crazy. They're bound and determined to kill someone."

For the next hours, as darkness wrapped around the cars and the rain beat down, the governor's cabinet member, the deputy marshall, and the nominee for the state legislature talked. Still there was no food.

Several of the prisoners became so sick during the night that General Carnes gave the order the next day to move all of them to the school house. There, on Saturday morning, Jake, Daniel, and Will Boyd were reunited when they were placed in Betsy's side of the two-room building.

Where forty students had studied, a hundred prisoners lay about on the benches and in the floor. It was better than the boxcars. They had brought some food—hard biscuits, slices of fried pork loin, and even five gallons of coffee. The officers promised that family could visit on Sunday.

Jake walked around the room. He could almost see Betsy there at the front of the class as she taught her pupils. Was that the scent of her perfume he smelled? On the front wall still hung a small note she had written telling the students of their assignments. He took it down, folded it, and placed it in his pocket.

Sunday morning Betsy harnessed Nellie to the farm wagon. The women were going to church and then to visit the men at the school house.

Rain continued to pour. Grandma Dolan would stay at the house with the twins and with Will's and Ollie's three boys. They were all over fifteen. If they didn't stay out of sight, they would be arrested too.

Betsy found a canvas tarp. Under it, she, her mother, her two brothers, and Ollie rode to the church. The preacher had been spared from arrest, but otherwise the congregation was made up entirely of women and children. The preacher announced that the militia would be taking over the church building later in the day as a jail for more prisoners. The school house was too small.

Betsy listened in silence. Her fingers stretched and tore the small white kerchief she held. She gritted her teeth. They had arrested all the men in her family, taken over her school house, and were now going to occupy her church building. She was going to talk with someone!

They let the prisoners out a few at a time. The Boyd women and children waited to see their men. Hundreds of wagons stood in a circle around the school yard. The rain let up to just a drizzle. Wherever the prisoners went, armed soldiers accompanied them. There was little in the way of private conversation.

After an hour, Will and Daniel came out together. Betsy looked for Jake who she had heard was among the prisoners. She ran up and hugged her father and then her uncle. "Is Jake in there?" she asked her father.

Daniel nodded his head. "He's in there all right." He smiled. "He's been telling anybody who would listen that you're the school teacher there. He told them to be careful and not break any of the benches."

Betsy looked toward the school house and smiled. "When will they let him come out?"

"As soon as his mother gets here. Only family can visit."

"I'm almost family," Betsy said and looked around for Jake's mother. "I don't see her. She's not here. I'm going to get her," she said and began unhitching Nellie from the wagon. "Papa, I love you, but I gotta see Jake." She jumped astride Nellie and started down the road toward the Drummond house.

"I understand," Daniel Boyd yelled after her.

In an hour she was back. She on the mule and Jake's mother walking beside her. She announced to one of the guards whom they were there to see.

"Jake, Jake, you are alive!" she screamed when he came out the door. She rushed to him and they embraced.

General Carnes, after reflecting on the matter and conferring with Attorney General Pickle, decided the lawlessness was a civil matter after all and not a military one. He wouldn't hang anyone. Those arrested would have a hearing before a magistrate of Anderson County. "If they prove themselves innocent, they'll be released. If not we'll hold them for trial."

Monday's train from Knoxville brought several lawyers, but there were few men at the depot to meet them. Since Friday, over four hundred men from Coal Creek had been arrested and placed at the school house and the Methodist church.

General Carnes sent the posses home. The regular troops camped in tents just a quarter mile from the depot. Carnes and his officers took up all the rooms of the Arbor Hotel. He had been successful. Only sporadic firing of rifles was heard at night since they had marched into Coal Creek. He thought he had the leaders of the rebellion in custody—Commissioner Ford, Bud Lindsay, George Irish, and D. B. Monroe. He still would like to hang some of them for murdering the soldiers and posse members, but that would have to wait for due process.

"Do you know where Miss Betsy Boyd lives?" the well dressed gentleman asked the depot clerk. He received directions and was pointed on his way.

Betsy didn't want to do it, but she went anyway with Grandma Dolan to the community cemetery that lay on a hillside across the road from their house. Betsy carried one small cedar box and Grandma Dolan the other.

Betsy dug where her grandmother showed her—into the newest grave. "Just a foot or so. Don't go all the way to the coffin," Grandma Dolan said.

"Why are we doing this, Grandma?"

"Just like I told you. First they take the men. Then they come back for the valuables. This silver set may not be worth much, but it's all I have to pass on to you and your mother. The soldiers ain't getting it."

"What makes you think they'll be back?"

"I done went through one war, Betsy. That's how we got the silver through the Civil War. Soldiers are too dumb to dig into a fresh grave. Even they sometimes have a little respect for the dead."

Betsy dug a shallow hole, placed the boxes inside, and shoveled the dirt back over them.

"Good. Pat it down. We need to plant a few flowers. Make it look real natural," Grandma Dolan said and smiled at their work. She looked up the road. "Uh, oh, lets get back to the house. Looks like the soldiers are coming back."

Betsy looked up. The man in the shiny suit looked familiar. She recognized the walk, the way he held his head.

"Grandma, that's Professor Brimer from the university," Betsy said and ran down the road, leaving Grandma Dolan to cross back to the house by herself. Betsy slowed before she reached Professor Brimer. She didn't know whether to hug him or just shake his hand. She put her hand out.

"Professor Brimer, what are you doing here?"

"Came to check on you, Miss Boyd. I knew the situation here had been treacherous. I wanted to be sure you and your family were all right."

They walked down the road toward the Boyd house while Betsy filled him in on all the details since Thursday. He shook his head at each sad account. All the men arrested.

They reached the house and sat on the porch with Grandma Dolan. Betsy's mother and aunt joined them.

"Habeas corpus," Professor Brimer finally said and took a long draw on his pipe.

The women looked at each other. Betsy shook her head. "I don't have my dictionary, Professor Brimer. What does that mean?"

"Bring forth the body. Give an accounting. Why are they holding the bodies of your father and uncle?"

"And my boyfriend Jake?"

"Uh, huh, him too," Professor Brimer said and nodded. "I'm a lawyer, you know. We'll just go into town tomorrow and ask General Carnes to 'bring forth the bodies' of your men."

"Alive," Betsy added.

"Yes, very much so," Professor Brimer said and blew out a cloud of smoke.

Early the next morning, before sunrise, Betsy climbed the ladder in the barn to her secret hiding place. She reached back between the wall and the hay and took out the pouch that contained Jake's red kerchief and, within, the remaining hundred dollars from her trade of the scrip with Mr. Jenkins. Bond money. Professor Brimer had told her that even if they obtained the release of the three men they might have to post a bond to secure their appearing in court at a later date. She counted out the paper currency, folded it back inside the kerchief, and placed it in a pocket on the front of her dress. There was no better use for her money than to redeem her uncle, father, and Jake.

"Who are you asking about?" one of the officers asked, looking at his list of prisoners.

"Will Boyd, Daniel Boyd, and Jake Drummond," Betsy said with Professor Brimer standing next to her.

"Yeah, they're still here. They've been moved to the church house. You'll have to get in line and talk with General Carnes about any release. At the Arbor Hotel."

The line of men and women waiting to talk with the general snaked out the building and through the yard to the store next door. Betsy gave a sigh when she saw the line. "We'll never get in there," she told the professor.

"Wait here, Miss Boyd, I'll see if they'll see those who have lawyers first." He walked to the door and squeezed through the line into the front hall of the hotel. In a few minutes he returned.

"The officer said to go to the church building and wait for the general there. He's going to take up the cases of those who have special needs, like sickness in the family, and those who have lawyers first," Professor Brimer said.

They waited an hour at the church before Carnes arrived.

In another hour they were called in.

"Sir, I met you last year when you were camped on the university grounds in Knoxville," Professor Brimer said and extended his hand.

General Carnes squinted his eyes and looked at the professor. "History professor? Is that correct?"

"Yes, sir. And a lawyer too."

Carnes frowned. "What a pity." He looked up and smiled. "And who's the young lady?"

"She's an employee of mine. Soon to be a student at the university, we hope. Her father and uncle are being held. Will Boyd and Daniel Boyd."

"And my boyfriend, Jake Drummond," Betsy added.

General Carnes looked down his list. "Will Boyd says he's a farmer. Daniel Boyd's a miner but not involved in the recent violence. Is that what you say, Miss Boyd?"

"Yes, sir. I was with both of them."

"All right. I'll release those two under a thousand dollars bond each to return to court for a preliminary hearing when notified. We have over five hundred now. I don't know when we can have hearings for all."

"We'll waive their cases to the grand jury, sir. We don't insist on a preliminary," Professor Brimer said.

"That's fine, Professor. But their bond remains the same," General Carnes responded while he wrote notes beside the names. "Are they property owners? If they are, they can sign their own bonds plus twenty-five dollars cash to secure their appearance. Anything else?"

"Jake Drummond, sir," Betsy said.

The general's fingers moved down the page. A frown enveloped his lips and his forehead drew up into deep furrows. "Is he related to Dick Drummond?"

"Yes, his brother," Betsy answered.

"Dick Drummond was involved in the capture of Colonel Anderson. He's a fugitive. If Jake Drummond will give up his brother, we'll release him. If not, we're holding him for a hearing."

"When can we have a hearing, sir?" Professor Brimer asked.

"We're starting them today. We'll put him down for tomorrow. That's all I can do. Anything else?"

"No, sir," Professor Brimer said.

"Yes, sir," Betsy said. "I have something to ask. I'm the school teacher. You've taken over our building. School starts the first of October. Will you be out? And this is where I go to church. When can we expect that you would also be out of it?"

"It's almost six weeks to the first of October. I believe we'll only need the school for another week. If we can bond everybody out who's being kept here at the church, we should be through with it in another week also. I understand your concern. But we just don't have anywhere else to put all these criminals."

"Accused, sir," Betsy said and turned to go out. She turned back. "Good day, sir, we'll see you tomorrow."

Militia Firing on Adjacent Mountain

Freedom and Death

By Wednesday, Dick Drummond had poled his roughly put together raft down the Clinch River to Kingston to where it met the Tennessee and on to Chattanooga. He left the raft on the bank of the river near Moccasin Bend and went to look for a job in an iron mill, swearing never to return to Coal Creek.

It took a day and a half to produce enough evidence to convince Squire Bernard Kincaid that there was reason to believe D. B. Monroe, who the military thought to be the ring leader of the miners, was guilty of conspiracy to commit murder. He bound him over to the next term of the grand jury.

Jake Drummond's case lingered, along with several hundred others. If each defendant had a day and a half preliminary hearing, Carnes and his troops would be in Coal Creek for the centennial celebration of Tennessee in 1896. Deals were struck—low bonds for those who waived their preliminary hearings and agreed to let their cases go directly to the grand jury.

However, General Carnes wanted to hear a few of the men's stories. What had really happened with Colonel Anderson's capture? Anderson would not testify against Monroe, and said Thomas Hatmaker, who was with Dick Drummond when the colonel walked down to Coal Creek, was actually a friend and peaceful influence.

Late on Wednesday when Jake's case was finally called, everyone was tired. For those who had hearings, the evidence had been repeated again and again. The same guards from the Tennessee Mine or the Knoxville Iron Company would point a finger at the accused and say they remembered him being among the mob on the night when the convicts were released and the Tennessee Mine stockade burned. It was so repetitious and obviously contrived that even General Carnes shook his head and mouthed the words he knew the guards would say.

Professor Brimer stood with Jake when he was finally called.

"Jake Drummond. You're accused of conspiring to burn the stockade of the Tennessee Mine. How do you plead?" Squire Kincaid asked.

"Not guilty," Professor Brimer spoke for his client.

The magistrate nodded toward General Carnes. "There's an interest in the whereabouts of your brother, Dick Drummond. Do you know where he is?"

Jake opened his mouth to speak, but before he could, Professor Brimer spoke for him.

"My client wishes to invoke the privilege of the Fifth Amendment to the Constitution of the United States of America."

"This is Coal Creek. What does the U. S. Constitution have to do with us?" General Carnes asked and stood up. "Besides, he was only asked where his brother was. How would that infringe on your client's rights?"

"This is Coal Creek, sir. But the last time I looked, it was still a part of the United States. And to invoke the words of a famous Biblical figure, 'Am I my brother's keeper?'" Professor Brimer said. A roar of laughter rolled across the room but stopped abruptly when the general looked around.

"I don't know where my brother is," Jake said from his seat. "I don't care where he is! I never want to see him again!"

From her position in the back of the room, Betsy wasn't sure she had heard what Jake said. Then she knew she had heard him. What had happened between Jake and Dick?

General Carnes leaned over and whispered to Squire Kincaid. Then the magistrate looked straight at Jake. "Are you willing to waive your right to a preliminary hearing?"

Professor Brimer bent over and spoke to Jake and then looked at the magistrate. "Yes, with the condition of a low bond."

"Five hundred dollars. Two property owners sign the bond plus fifty dollars cash," Squire Kincaid said and motioned Jake to go to where the clerk was busy at his desk. Betsy rushed up with her last fifty dollars.

Grandma Dolan sat on the front porch and watched while Betsy said goodbye to Professor Brimer the next morning.

They were at the edge of the yard. Betsy reached out to shake the professor's hand. "Thank you for all your help."

"Yes, . . . I must catch my train," he said while his hand lingered, holding hers. "Miss Boyd, you will be back to the university tomorrow, won't you?"

"Yes, sir. I'm sorry I've missed a whole week. I'll make it up." She pulled her hand back. "Tomorrow. I'll be in tomorrow." She turned and walked back to the porch and her grandmother while Professor Brimer walked down the road.

"He likes you," Grandma Dolan said.

Betsy looked at her grandmother and then down the road to where the professor was disappearing around the bend. "What do you mean?"

"He likes you."

"Well, I like him too."

"No. I mean he really likes you. I saw the way he wouldn't turn loose of your hand," Grandma Dolan said.

Betsy blushed. "Oh, Grandma, you don't know what you're talking about. He was just shaking my hand. He has never been anything but proper with me. He always calls me 'Miss Boyd.' He probably has even forgotten that my name is Betsy."

Grandma Dolan began to hum a tune while her hands knitted. She looked at Betsy and smiled.

The train slowly left the depot at Coal Creek. Professor Brimer had a window seat that allowed him a view of the road he had just finished walking. He looked down the lane. "Betsy . . . Betsy . . . Betsy."

The next day Betsy considered what her grandmother had said while on her train ride to Knoxville, all during the day when she typed the papers for Professor Brimer, and on her ride back to Coal Creek. She liked and respected him. He did dress well and was educated. But he was much too old for her. She didn't even know if he was married.

All through the work day she had caught herself glancing over to where he was working behind his desk. There was always the white shirt, tie, vest, and suit coat when he stood. She mostly liked his humor—and his self confidence. And the respect he had for women and their intelligence.

He was funny. She always left the university with a smile on her face. Some joke, some funny story. She thought back to when he stood with Jake and made the whole courtroom laugh. "Biblical figure." He had forgotten to say it was Cain. And Coal Creek was part of the United States. It was just the way he said it.

Grandma Dolan was wrong though. Professor Brimer could not "like" Betsy the way she had said. He was too busy with research and study.

Besides, she loved Jake. It was nice to think that someone else might find her attractive and cared for her, but she loved the cowboy miner who was full of life and could swing onto and off of Charmer just like he was a part of the horse.

The train slowed as it neared Coal Creek. A crowd blocked the track at the depot. Betsy held her head out the window. A group of soldiers was pushing people back. Women were crying. Men were shouting and shaking fists toward the soldiers.

Betsy stepped down from her car fifty yards from where it normally stopped. She started walking toward the depot. There was more cursing. She walked faster. Another group of soldiers rushed up. She broke into a trot.

On the platform the boots of a man lying face up pointed toward the sky. She could only see the legs . . . and the streak of blood trailing off the platform.

"What's happened?" she asked and walked nearer.

A young black woman saw her coming. She was crying. She ran toward Betsy and threw her arms around her.

"What's wrong?" Betsy asked again.

"They shot Jake," the black woman said. "The soldiers shot him in the head. He's dead."

Betsy's knees buckled, the sky began to spin, and darkness took her sight. She fell to the ground at the feet of the young black woman.

Nashville's Company C at Coal Creek

The Leaving

Jake Drummond floated above her when Betsy finally saw through the velvety darkness of her fainting. The young black woman wiped Betsy's face with a cloth soaked in cool water. Betsy saw other faces, but Jake stood out—his ivory skin and radiant blue eyes, bluer now than ever.

"Am I in Heaven?" she asked in a weak and hesitating voice.

"No, just Coal Creek," Jake answered.

"But . . . you're dead." Betsy noticed the young lady who had given her the dreaded news. She pointed. "She told me."

Jake leaned over and kissed Betsy on the lips. He whispered, "I guess if I'm dead, it's not disrespectful to kiss you."

"But . . . what happened?"

"It was Jake Whitsen," Jake told her. "He was waving at some troops on the train. A gun went off. They don't know if it was an accident or on purpose. Jake Whitsen's dead."

Betsy still lay on the ground near the platform. She looked up at Jake. "Yes, yes!"

"Yes, what?" Jake asked.

"That's my answer to the question you asked me on Christmas Eve."

Jake thought back. The cold night. The knife. The mule. The question. His eyes widened. "You'll marry me?"

"Yes. How many times do I have to say it?" Betsy smiled.

Jake bent down and kissed her again.

Over five thousand gathered in Clinton for the funeral of Jake Whitsen two days later. The friendly old black miner had a habit of greeting everyone with a shaking of his fist and a nonsensical question. The soldiers on the train didn't know what to make of the gesture when he shook his fist at the car in which they were riding. An untrained finger on the trigger of a Springfield rifle squeezed, and Jake Whitsen was sent to an early grave.

From Briceville, Coal Creek, and Clinton the mourners came to show their love for Jake Whitsen and to show their solidarity in the face of the occupying military force. The little clapboard church was not nearly large enough to accommodate the crowd, so men and women on horseback and in wagons encircled the building and sang along with the hymns that poured out through the open doors and windows.

Betsy and Jake sat together in her wagon while the rest of the Boyds and Jake's mother gathered beneath a tree.

"This is the largest crowd I've ever seen," Betsy told Jake after looking at the yards and hillsides filled with people.

"If the soldiers hadn't killed him and he just died in a mine accident, there would probably be about a hundred here," Jake said.

"You still haven't heard from Dick?" Betsy asked.

Jake shook his head. "No. I've been back up on Walden's Ridge more than a dozen times looking for him. I thought maybe he got shot and his body was still there. But there's no sign of him. One of the others who was there said he saw him going down the opposite side toward Clinton. Maybe he got away."

"He'll be back," Betsy said.

"I don't know that I want him back," Jake said. "I think he did an awful thing."

"What did he do?" Betsy asked.

Jake looked at her and shook his head. "It's better that you don't know. I have to live with it, but you don't."

Their conversation turned to their marriage and plans for a small wedding at the Methodist church.

"As soon as General Carnes gets the prisoners out, we'll get married," Betsy said and squeezed Jake's hand.

"I'm ready," Jake said.

The singing ended, and through the front doorway of the church came the pallbearers carrying the coffin of Jake Whitsen toward its destination at the hillside cemetery. Behind the coffin walked the widow, supported on both sides by hands of family members who kept her from falling to the ground.

"The soldiers have to go. There'll never be peace as long as they're here," Jake said.

On Saturday, September 10, 1892, two weeks and two days before her nineteenth birthday, Betsy Boyd stood with Jake Drummond in the Methodist Church of Coal Creek ready to declare her wedding vows. Near her stood her best friend from childhood, Sarah Thomas Moore.

Jake, with his father dead and his brother gone, chose Will Boyd, Betsy's uncle, to stand with him.

The two weeks from the time that Betsy had said yes until the wedding day had rushed by. Betsy bought material for her wedding dress in Knoxville. She, her mother, aunt, and grandmother sewed and pieced it together in the evenings after all the other work was done.

While the women were busy getting ready for the wedding, Jake and the men of the community had come together to build a small house for the new couple. On five acres of land that Uncle Will gave them as a wedding present, the plain little three-room house took shape. Unemployed miners sprang to action for Jake and quickly nailed the wood and timbers together while four of the more talented men built back-to-back fireplaces with a stone chimney near the center of the house.

Uncle Will had told Betsy to make a farmer out of Jake and keep him away from mining. To that end, Will and the others also put up a small barn with two stalls for Charmer and Miss Steele, a corn storage ben, and an adjoining pig sty. Betsy's father gave the couple two pigs from the offspring of Bernice-the-sow. Other wedding gifts included six laying hens, a rooster, a pair of ducks, a wagon load of hay, and three quilts.

The little church was filled. For the first time in a year and a half, Grandma Dolan left the Boyd homestead and rode to the church in the farm wagon. She sat beside Belle and Estelle who giggled and pointed to their sister, standing like an angel, resplendent in white.

On the back row sat Professor Robert Brimer and Jim Powell, principal of Knoxville High School. Professor Brimer took a white handkerchief from his pocket and wiped his eyes.

"It's nice to see our student get married, isn't it? And emotional, too," Powell said to his friend.

"Yes, quite," Professor Brimer said.

Betsy looked at Jake while the preacher began to open his Bible. Jake's lips were drawn tightly over his teeth. His eyelashes fluttered, but there were no tears. Betsy had seen tears in her father's eyes when he walked her up the aisle. It was a sight she couldn't remember ever seeing before. For the past year and a half there had been many things that could have brought tears, but none had been shed by her father . . . until today.

The preacher began to speak.

His days filled with work of all kinds as Jake adjusted to married life. A few days of mine work here and a few there were sandwiched between hard days on the farm of Will Boyd, learning the craft of a farmer. He split logs for posts, he repaired fences, he raked the last hay of the season and loaded it onto wagons.

In late afternoon when the chores were done, Jake would take Charmer and ride off one direction one day and another the next. He stopped and pleaded for votes. At miners' cabins he reminded them he was their hope to lead the fight to repeal the lease law and to rid the valley of convicts and militia.

"The convicts were bad enough to have around. But at least we knew where we stood with them. The military is worse. Every action we take is met with a more terrible result. Just get rid of the military and I'll vote for you." Jake heard these words over and over in his talks with miners' families. Their thoughts centered upon the presence of the blue-coated militia more than the competition of the convicts.

"Get rid of the military and I'll vote for you." He mouthed the words over and over. Didn't they know that he couldn't rid the valley of the military until the convicts were gone? And he couldn't do either until after the legislature convened in January. He needed their votes before then.

In Clinton and around the other areas of Anderson County where mining wasn't predominant, Jake found the voters more interested in peace and prosperity than in the convicts and military.

"If you can guarantee peace in the valley, I'll vote for you." This was the plea of the non-miner voter.

Jake rode on every day. He could not reconcile all of the needs and wants of the various groups of voters with his ability to meet them. His only consolation was that he knew his opponents couldn't either.

Betsy, meanwhile, continued her daily trips to Knoxville. Two weeks remained on her work schedule for the year for Professor Brimer and the completion of her eleventh grade studies under Jim Powell. The first week of October she would begin her second year of teaching at Coal Creek.

"I'm almost half way through with typing your papers on President Johnson," Betsy told Professor Brimer after she looked at the neatly stacked piles. They ran in two-foot high heaps all along the base of one wall of his office. "I don't know whether I can get them all done next year."

"You'll have more than what's here by next year. I'll be adding to them over the fall, winter, and spring. I think you shall always have a job typing the papers of Andrew Johnson, Mrs. Drummond," Professor Brimer said.

Betsy stopped. She hadn't heard it before. *Mrs. Drummond.* It had a sound to it. It rang like a silver bell. Everybody at Coal Creek still called her Betsy. But *Mrs. Drummond.* She liked it.

"Would you say that again, Professor Brimer?"

"What?"

"*Mrs. Drummond.* You have such a good voice. That was the first time anyone called me Mrs. Drummond."

Professor Brimer grimaced then smiled. He repeated it for her.

By mid-October, Jake had ridden every lane and cow path he could find asking for support and votes. Many said they would vote for him. A few turned away and said nothing. Hardly anyone said they would vote against him. He wished the women could vote. Everywhere he rode, the female population took to him, smiled more, and nodded their heads when he was asking their men to vote for him. Betsy and Professor Brimer were right about women's suffrage.

He walked Charmer down the main street of Coal Creek late one evening, stopping when he saw a man he hadn't asked before to vote for him. Passing the Arbor Hotel, Jake saw General Carnes sitting in the yard beneath a maple tree whose leaves were just beginning to turn gold and red. The general waved.

Jake waved back, tied Charmer to the fence post in front of the hotel, and walked toward where the general was sitting.

"Don't bother with me. I can't vote here," the general said and remained seated.

Jake took his hat off. "I know, sir. I just wanted to thank you for not holding me under a higher bond than you allowed the magistrate to set back in August."

The general shook his head. "That was the magistrate's decision and not mine."

Jake nodded. "Yes, sir. But I know he wouldn't set the bond that low if he thought you disagreed."

"You seem to be a bright and energetic young man, Mr. Drummond. You could be a steadying influence on the miners here. I want to encourage that. Lord knows, I don't want to spend the winter here."

"Yes, sir. I was going to ask you if you thought you would be leaving anytime soon?"

The general rubbed his beard and smiled. "Would it help

you to win if we left?"

"Yes, sir, it would. And I would give you my word that I would do everything I could to see that there was no more trouble here. I want to work it out through the legislature. The legal way."

The general looked away toward Vowell Mountain and Fort Anderson. The sun was just setting behind them. "I would say that Fort Anderson and Colonel Anderson will remain longer than we do. This is a temporary camp in Coal Creek. Many of our men have already gone. We're down from seven hundred in mid-August to about two hundred fifty now."

"Any sign of withdrawal would be met with good will, sir. I'll put my word, honor, and life on the line for that."

General Carnes stood. He held out his hand. "I think you're right. Tension could be lessened if we withdraw my force. I'll see what I can do. Good luck, Mr. Drummond."

Two weeks later, Betsy stood before the stone fireplace that faced the bedroom of their new house. She sniffed. The scent of the wood remained. It was like living in a sawmill. She liked it. It was a sign of newness, just as her life with Jake was new. The dawning of their relationship was really just beginning. She loved dawns—the promise of a new day. And spring—the hope of a fresh season.

There was a small fire burning. The weather was still delightfully warm. The mornings were cool—just another excuse to cling closely in bed to Jake's back—but the days were bright. Their little cabin squatted beneath great oaks and maples that had over the past few days began to shed gold and crimson leaves.

She bent over, took the poker, and gently prodded the logs. Sparks flew up the chimney as flames licked up around the wood. She smiled. She had succumbed to tradition—their first fire was started with embers that she and Jake carried over from Uncle Will's fireplace. The hundred-year-old fire continued.

Betsy took a cloth and wiped the stone mantel free of dust. She reached down to the table and picked up the wooden mule that

Jake had carved for her and given to her at Christmas. She placed it in the center of the stone ledge. Around it she circled the red and white kerchief of his in which she had carried the scrip. A few of the brass tokens remained. She sprinkled them within the circle. A miner's daughter, Jake, and the independent woman. This was her heritage.

She looked at them, pulled up a rocking chair in front of the fireplace, and sat down. Peace.

The sound of pounding hoofs coming from the lane stirred her from her dreams. She recognized them as being those of Charmer.

Jake burst through the door. "Betsy, Betsy, come here! They're leaving. General Carnes and his troops are packing up. They're going. Come with me to the depot."

Jake took her hand and ran back out. He lifted her in one full swing off her feet and onto Charmer. He mounted his horse and they were off. Betsy wrapped her arms around his waist and leaned into his back. Jake was a much better horseman than she, but she held on while Jake spurred his heels into Charmer on the mad dash to the depot.

He pulled up to a trot and then to a walk when the depot came into sight. The troops lined the three sets of tracks. Others were finishing loading the tents and other camp supplies into the freight cars. A crowd was gathering to witness the departure of Carnes and the militia. It was smaller than the one that met him in August, but no one would be arrested on his departure as they had been on his arrival.

Within an hour, the train was loaded, troops boarded, and the engine began the slow chugging as steam pressure built. Without fanfare, without great speeches, and without the hostile sound of gunfire, General Carnes and the Tennessee National Guard began their journey homeward toward Nashville and Memphis.

Betsy pointed to the last car of the train. General Carnes stood at the entrance. He looked in their direction and touched his hand to his hat. Jake did the same. It was in his hands now. A week before the election Coal Creek was free of the occupying force. Only Colonel Anderson and his men at the fort on Vowell Mountain remained. They would stay to guard the convicts in the mine below, but the great plague of blue-coats was gone.

Some of the miners and townspeople gathered around Jake. "You did it, Jake," one of them said and others nodded their heads. "The general told someone you had talked him into leaving. He said you guaranteed peace. We're with you, boy. We'll give the legislature a chance in January to do something about the rest of them up on the ridge—and the convicts."

Jake had to hold tightly to the reins of Charmer. They all crowded around, wanting to shake his hand. He shook his head and looked after the train that was disappearing around the bend toward Clinton. What burden had the general left with him?

In Chattanooga the next day, Dick Drummond learned that General Carnes and the troops from Coal Creek would be passing through. He had to see for himself. He walked to the Read House and then over to the depot. In another hour the train arrived from Knoxville. The Chattanooga militiamen were reunited with their families. From beneath the canopy of the station, Dick Drummond watched as the train pulled back out, headed for Nashville and Memphis. It was time for him to return to Coal Creek.

On Tuesday, November 8, 1892, Grover Cleveland was elected President of the United States over Benjamin Harrison. In Tennessee, Peter Turney was elected governor with John Buchanan finishing a distant third. Buchanan garnered only twelve per cent of the vote—less than ten in Knox and Anderson Counties.

In Anderson County, Jake Drummond won his bid for state representative by a mere one hundred fifty vote margin. That night in a silent prayer he thanked God—and General Carnes for leaving the valley the week before.

Jake To Nashville

With a new governor and a new legislature, the citizens of Coal Creek and Briceville had their spirits revived for what they believed would be a bright 1893. General Carnes and his men were gone, but high on Vowell Mountain, Fort Anderson remained with a hundred fifty militiamen.

Jake Drummond would be the miners' voice in Nashville in January. Any hopes they had of dislodging the garrison from the hill and the convicts from the Knoxville Iron Company mine lay with the young miner-turned-legislator and the sentiment and public opinion of the citizens of Tennessee.

The cost of the insurrection was mounting. At an average of over seven thousand dollars per month, the state's military fund was depleted, and the general assembly would be asked for more money.

Among the requests that had not been paid late into 1892 were two, one from an undertaker and one from a soldier.

Coal Creek, Tennessee

To: H. H. Norman, Adjutant General
Nashville, Tennessee

Dear Sir:

Enclosed please find account against the state for two coffins furnished for the burial of your soldier boys.

Please send check for same as I am needing the money. I spoke to Col. Anderson about the matter, and he advised me to send bill to you.

Hoping to receive your favor at an early day, I am

Yours truly.
R. M. Edwards
Undertaker

Nashville, Tennessee

To: Colonel R. L. Watkins

Kind Sir,

I was in Company C of the Chattanooga Volunteers under Lieutenant Bonham when called out for our trip to Coal Creek. I received a Marlin 16 shot 32 cal. and delivered same to Sheriff Skillern.

I was one of the tallest men in the company, and consequently, I got my share of holding the tongue of the rear gun. Colonel, who will I get to give me a voucher for what is coming to me? Can I get one of the guns we carried and what will it cost? My right arm and shoulder have hurt me ever since that trip.

Next time we are called to go, I hope it will not rain more than half the time.

Yours respectfully,
W. Noyes Carr Jr.
910 S. High St.,
Nashville, Tennessee

A deep snow fell in the valley of Coal Creek on December 20, coating the trees, ground, houses and barns in a white meringue. Cold, battering winds swept in the next day, leaving a pristine, sparkling white cast against the clear, azure sky.

Betsy looked out on the scene on the morning of Christmas Eve from the kitchen of their little home. In the distance a slender plume of smoke spiraled above the trees marking the home of the Boyds. The grip of cold had remained so strong that the snow had hardly melted any at all.

It was beautiful but impractical. Snow meant more hay had to be fed to the livestock. School turned out early for the Christmas recess. And to the miners, it only made it more difficult walking or riding to the mines. Once inside the shafts, the world returned to blackness and the ever constant temperature of a cave.

Jake had one more week of work in the Shamrock Mine before boarding a train for Nashville. All miners would have Christmas off this year—Sunday—but Jake also took Christmas Eve. He was in the barn feeding Charmer, Miss Steele, and the three head of cattle they had accumulated since their marriage. Breakfast was about ready, and afterwards they would visit Jake's mother and then go to Betsy's family's home for part of the afternoon and evening. Jake had built a wood sled and rigged a harness for Miss Steele to pull them in the deep snow.

It sounded like fun to Betsy. The little girl in her still wanted to run outside and play—to build sculptured men of snow or to roll it into small hard balls and have a feigned fight with Jake.

Just two days before she had made her train trip to Knoxville and bought hard candy, fruit, and a small gift for each of her family and for Jake's mother. For Jake she had arranged for a tailor to make him a suit that would match those of the sharpest dressers in Nashville. She had picked the cloth and the style—Jake would have no taste in that area. She had even taken his measurements, giving him the excuse that she wanted to practice sewing. It was to be delivered to the Coal Creek depot today.

"Where are we going first?" Jake asked. He finished the

last bite of a slice of ham and sopped up gravy from his plate with half a biscuit. "You're really a good cook, Betsy."

Betsy looked at him and smiled. "Not all that good. I just watched you for a year at my folks. I know what you like. Basic and simple. Ham, gravy, biscuits, and eggs for breakfast. Fried chicken or beef for dinner when you're here and not in the mine. Or the same for supper when you've worked in the mine all day. The more fancy things, I still have a hard time with."

"I don't really want to go to my mother's if Dick's there. You know that, don't you?"

"Why? I know you've had a falling out—something you won't talk about. But it's Christmas. Can't you make up with your own brother?"

Jake swallowed the last bite of biscuit. "Not for what he did. He runs away. All of the rest of us get arrested. But he doesn't."

"Is that what you're mad about? You got arrested and he didn't?"

"No. But he's one of the ones who should've been."

Gray clouds rolled in across the mountains and snow began to fall again before Jake harnessed Miss Steele and brought her to the side of the house. Betsy could not remember a previous Christmas when they had snow in the valley although she had dreamed about it. She grabbed two quilts, bundled her coat around her, and stepped into the cold, but refreshing, air. Jake stood while she sat facing backwards on a board that spanned the width of the sled. She watched their house and barn recede behind her and listened to the crunching snow beneath the runners of the sled.

Jake's mother came to the porch and waved when the mule-drawn rig arrived. Betsy looked around and didn't see anyone other than Mrs. Drummond. She waved.

"Come in, come in. It's a bit warmer in the house, but not much."

Jake busied himself with doing things—bringing more wood and coal inside, checking the barn and animals, and looking into the spring house for what was cooling there. The two Mrs. Drummonds sat beside the stove and talked.

"Now, Betsy, I want you to come stay over here with me when Jake's away in Nashville. I don't feel right about you being over there by yourself."

"Oh, I'll be all right. I have school to teach by day, and there'll still be chores to do with the animals and all by evening. I feel safe enough."

The two women began cooking dinner together. Jake stayed outside. He found things in the barn to mend, hay to be turned, and corn to be shucked.

"What is it between Jake and Dick?" Betsy asked.

"What do you mean?"

"Something's happened. Jake won't say, but I know something bad happened between them."

Jake's mother shook her head. "I don't know. Neither one will talk about it. They just avoid each other. What can I do?" A tear slid down her cheek. "I want my children to get along. I don't have much left but them."

Betsy looked out the window. Dick Drummond walked on the snow-covered path toward the barn. Jake came to the barn's door. Dick walked to within an arm's length. He began to point his finger at Jake and then shake it toward his face. Jake slapped it away, grabbed his brother by his coat, and pinned him to the outside wall of the barn.

Betsy ran to the door. "You all stop that, right now!" she shouted. "Your poor mother's in here trying to get dinner ready. It's about Christmas. Now both of you calm down and come in."

Jake turned his brother loose. Dick stepped inside the barn just long enough to retrieve a bottle from behind a post and then walked back down the road toward Coal Creek.

At the Boyds things were quieter and calmer when the sled bearing Betsy and Jake pulled into the yard. The new snow covered the ruts worn in the old by travelers before them and lapped off the roof of the house like icing off the top of a cake.

Faint amber light shone through the windows from the fireplace and oil lanterns. Dusk was coming earlier with the falling snow. Jake took Miss Steele to the barn while Betsy joined the rest of her family.

Betsy eased to the parlor's entrance before anyone knew she was there carrying gifts, fruit, and candy in one of her quilts and the package she had retrieved from the depot for Jake. Grandma Dolan sat in front of the fireplace. Estelle and Belle sat in front of her. For what must have been the millionth time in her memory, Betsy listened to Grandma Dolan recite the twins' favorite rhyme and watched the stiff fingers of her grandmother dance atop those of her sisters.

"William-a-William a Trimbletoes,
He's a good fisherman,
Catches hens, puts them in a pen,
Some lay eggs, some none,
Wire, briar, limberlock,
Ten geese in a flock,
Clock falls down,
Mouse runs out,
'O' 'U' 'T'
Spells out goes he."

The twins laughed and so did Grandma Dolan.

Jake had hardly eaten anything at his mother's and sat through Christmas Eve supper at Betsy's folks the same way. Betsy looked at him, determined that she wouldn't let his mood ruin their first Christmas together as husband and wife.

With the carols sung and old tales revisited and embellished, one by one the children began to ease away to bed. Jake, Will, and Daniel sat in one corner and talked about mining and farming. The women sat around the table in the kitchen and planned the Christmas meal.

A half hour before midnight, Betsy, a quilt draped across her shoulders, came through the kitchen door into the parlor and took Jake by the hand. She leaned down and whispered. "Let's go to the loft of the barn. Like last year. See if the animals talk at midnight."

The snow was deeper yet. Jake lifted Betsy into his arms and carried her to the barn. Betsy looked into his eyes, while snowflakes dusted his lashes, and wondered what deep sadness and rift separated her husband and his brother.

She climbed the ladder and went to the exact spot where they had sat the year before when Jake had asked her to marry him. He swung the hay loft door open to the outside where the deep snow muted all sound. From the house the slight trace of orange light flickered across the snow and showed it still slanting in peppering sheets from the dark sky.

Betsy reached into the crevice between the hay and barn wall and retrieved her only possession still there—the guitar. She sat down and scooted back into Jake's arms and began to strum the strings. Jake wrapped the quilt around them, making allowance for the guitar, and began to kiss his wife's neck.

Jake boarded the train the next Saturday. He carried his new suit, packed lovingly by Betsy, and awaited the following Monday to don it for the first time at the swearing in of the Forty-eighth General Assembly in Nashville.

Betsy stood on the platform of the depot at Coal Creek and waved. She insisted on wearing the new dress that Jake had bought for here. She said it was a special occasion—the seeing off of Anderson County's new representative. No one else seemed to care. They were doubtful things would change whomever they sent to Nashville. Most of the snow was gone, and what was left was dirty and black from the soot of the train engines.

Jake raised the window. "I'll be home as often as possible, Betsy. If you need anything, just come to the depot and send a telegram to the Capitol Building. I'll do the same."

By the time the train reached Knoxville, Jake was having second thoughts. He walked to the caboose and watched the miles retreat. He was exchanging the familiar for the unfamiliar, things he loved for those he didn't, his birthright for elective office. He wanted to jump off and run back down the tracks to Coal Creek and switch places with someone else who could speak more eloquently, write better, and represent more vehemently than he. Why had he sought this office when all he wanted was Betsy Boyd and a coal miner's job?

In a few minutes he walked back to his car, sat down, and took up the book that Betsy had given him, a collection of the writings of Henry David Thoreau and Walt Whitman. He turned to a Whitman poem, "I Hear America Singing" and read of all those who sang while they worked.

> *Those of mechanics—each one singing his, as it should be,*
> *blithe and strong;*
> *The carpenter singing his, as he measures his plank or beam,*
> *The mason singing his, as he makes ready for work, or leaves*
> *off work;*
> *The boatman singing what belongs to him in his boat—the*
> *deckhand singing on the steamboat deck;*

Then he turned to the "Song of the Open Road" and a few lines caught his eye.

> *Henceforth I ask not good-fortune—I myself am good fortune;*
> *Henceforth I whimper no more, postpone no more,*
> *need nothing,*
> *Strong and content, I travel the open road.*

He leaned back and looked out the window. What song did miners sing? He would be strong—whimper no more, nor postpone. Scenes of the Tennessee Valley sped by his window, here and there a patch of crusty snow remained. A child or farmer would wave at the train. He would wave back. Dusk began to settle in while Chattanooga and Nashville beckoned ahead. Jake contented himself with the companionship of Thoreau and Whitman.

Early in the evening of New Year's Day 1893, Jake's train

pulled into Nashville's Union Station. He was truly lost now. His only trips to the capital city had been in the company of more experienced men. He stepped to the platform and a cold wind bit at his face. Inside the building that was like a cathedral the footfalls and voices of the comers and goers echoed like falling water in a great cave. Where were the carriages and the hotels? He looked around. Everyone else seemed to know where they were going.

"Mr. Drummond, are you Jake Drummond?" one of two men approaching him asked. They smiled, took cigars from their mouths, and blew out huge puffs of smoke. They wore fine suits and top hats. A young lady was on the arm of each man.

"Yes . . . I . . . I'm Jake Drummond," Jake said and held out his hand.

"Come along with us. We have you a room waiting in a fine hotel and a carriage to carry us there."

He followed.

Jake lay in his bed after his new friends had left. He looked at the paper they had given him. These were kind people. He held in his hand a pass good for a year on any train. On his table was a voucher that would allow him as many telegrams as he would need while in Nashville. A tailor had been waiting in the lobby and measured him for two new suits. He could eat at the dining room in the hotel at no cost—it was all included in the room that the men also said was free. The young ladies had even said they would check with him later to see if there was anything else he needed.

He went to the lobby to try his new telegraph privileges.

Nashville, Tennessee

To: Betsy Drummond
Coal Creek, Tennessee

Arrived Nashville. Fine folks. Good room, food, and railroad pass. All gifts. Swear in on Monday.

Jake Drummond
State Representative

The next morning when Jake arrived at the Capitol for the swearing-in ceremony a telegram awaited him on his desk.

Coal Creek, Tennessee

To: Jake Drummond
State Representative
State Capitol
Nashville, Tennessee
Deuteronomy 16: 19.
Betsy Drummond
Coal Creek, Tennessee

Jake looked around for a Bible. He asked those nearby. The place was full of activity. The floor of the house chamber was filled with the representatives, family, lobbyists, clerks, reporters, those from Governor Buchanan's staff, and those seeking favor with the governor-elect. Jake was pointed to the speaker's platform where a ceremonial Bible lay in a corner of a massive cherrywood desk. He quickly thumbed through the pages until he found the passage.

Thou shalt not wrest judgment; thou shalt not respect persons, neither take a gift: for a gift doth blind the eyes of the wise, and pervert the words of the righteous.

He laid the Bible back in its place and walked back to his assigned desk. The speaker called the house to order. All stood and were sworn in.

Jake was a one-issue legislator. His job in Nashville was to help end the lease system for convicts and thereby dislodge the soldiers from the ridge behind Coal Creek. To that end he expended his energies the first two weeks. He sought and was given a position on the penitentiary committee of the house. It would make recommendations to the entire legislature. He also was assigned to the committee that oversaw state military expenditures.

While many in Nashville and the state were fretting about the health of governor-elect Peter Turney, who some said lay on his death bed, Jake visited the Nashville prison and spoke with the warden. He looked at the books of expenses for prisons and for the soldiers. There was the key. It would be less expensive to build new prisons than to keep the militia on standby for outbreaks of violence. If nothing else, politicians understood money.

By January 16, Peter Turney had recovered enough to be sworn in as governor at his home in Winchester, thus averting the possibility that John Buchanan would hold over as governor. There was good news for Jake's interests when both the outgoing and incoming governors recommended to the legislature the abolition of the convict lease system and the construction of new prisons.

A bill had already been introduced to purchase at least five thousand acres of undeveloped coal lands and to build a new penitentiary at a cost not to exceed two hundred thousand dollars. Convicts could mine coal—but only for state use. A farm would be located next to it of at least a thousand acres. The prison would be erected between the farm and the coal lands.

An architect suggested that the prison be built of massive stone with the interior, corridors and cells, of steel. It would be built three tiers high according to the latest plans of sanitation and convenience. All convicts would be worked either on the farm or in the mines of the prison property.

On his first trip home after two weeks in Nashville, Jake and Betsy discussed her first telegram to him.

"The railroad lobbyists can't buy me with a hotel room, food, and a rail pass, Betsy. They're just good guys, trying to help out a little."

"They don't want to buy you, Jake. They just want to *rent* you at the proper time."

A three-week recess of the legislature was called after the second week of February to give committees time to work and report back to the whole body and to give those who desired it an opportunity to go to Washington for the inauguration of Grover Cleveland on March 4.

Jake, who now paid for his own hotel room, food, and railroad tickets, and the other members of the penitentiary committee planned visits to all the branch prisons. The Knoxville Iron Company stockade at Coal Creek was included on the itinerary.

During the last week of February, ten members of the committee walked inside the palisaded walls of the stockade at Coal Creek. Jake had ridden past it many times on Charmer and had viewed it from atop Walden's Ridge, but he had never been behind the walls. Rumors abounded about the conditions—beatings, disease, and unmarked graves between the walls and the mine openings—but up until now the concern was only that the convicts were taking the jobs of the miners.

For three hours, Jake and the other men walked among the convicts—deep into the mines and into the huts that were their cells at night. Many of the convicts were practically naked even in the midst of winter. They ate on the run, carrying wet cornbread and pieces of fat pork through the water and dust of the mines. Bed matting was non-existent. The stench of the huts betrayed the unsanitary conditions that left open, running sores on the bodies of over half the convicts. They had no change of clothing, no sheets, no pillows, no socks, or underclothing.

Jake had read the report of the penitentiary committee that visited a year and a half before. The promise that things would be better had not been fulfilled. The local warden explained that they were holding down costs. "We can feed them on three or four cents a day."

The committee made its report to the legislature early after its return from recess. Newspapers across the state picked up on the report and spoke to a shocked public in editorials, typical of which was the Knoxville *Daily Journal*'s words of March 10, 1893:

"Surely Siberia could not excel the branch and main prisons in horror, and physical and mental degradation.

"From the report we learn that from every aspect from whence they may be beheld these prisons are literally hells on earth.

"The mind fails to imagine any situation more awful than that of the poor wretches, miserable outcasts, confined in prison for penitentiary and reformatory reasons. Insufficiently clothed and fed, confined in coal banks by day and pest-holes by night, infected with vermin, days of wretchedness and nights devoid of hope, exposed to deadly and contagious venereal diseases, practicing unutterable abominations upon each other, subject to scourgings for failure to do the daily task or infractions of discipline—what more awful deplorable state of affairs can the human mind imagine?"

The committee's report pushed the momentum forward. And when the figures were finally in for the expense of maintaining all the military to put down the rebellious coal miners, enough votes were found to turn the tide. The state would build a new main prison and a branch prison somewhere in the East Tennessee coal area. The lease system would come to an end—but not until 1896. It would not be renewed, but it would be honored until that time.

Jake Drummond was among the group of legislators who hand-carried the bill to Governor Peter Turney for his signature. Down the sweeping, limestone stairway from the second floor to the first of the Capitol, Jake and the other six walked. The governor greeted them.

"I want to thank each of you and the legislature for working out this thorny problem. It's never easy to vote for money to build a prison when taxes have to support it. This will end many of our problems.

"In future years, the convicts will work on the farm or mine coal for state use. The conditions will be humane, and they won't compete with free men for work," the governor said and shook the hand of each legislator.

When he stepped to Jake, he paused. "Mr. Drummond. I want to commend you. You have worked diligently on this matter. You have been an influence for peace in Coal Creek. I look forward to the day when we can remove the militia and the convicts from your fair town."

Jake looked him in the eye. "Thank you, sir. I ask that you consider removing the soldiers from Fort Anderson immediately. I and the other miners will guarantee the safety of the convicts until their time to leave arrives. It will help to keep tensions from boiling over during the hot months of the summer."

Governor Turney motioned Jake to step away from the other legislators and speak with him more privately. "You may be correct, Representative Drummond. However, if you're incorrect, it would cost the state a great deal more to reestablish the fort than it does to maintain it. I will think it over, but they will probably remain for at least another year to be sure all is peaceful."

Jake gestured toward the window and looked out into the darkness of the night at the sight of Nashville's lights below the Capitol.

"Governor, how would you feel if the militia was camped right outside watching your every move, or in your hometown of Winchester, and they camped on the hill overlooking your farm? And every now and then they aimed a Gatling gun at you and laughed?"

The governor ran his hand through his hair, closed his eyes, and turned around. "I see your point. I'll think on it. But in the meantime, if I can ever be of service to you at Coal Creek, please call on me. We all need to work to keep the peace."

On Monday, April 10, the legislature adjourned. Jake Drummond, a first time legislator, learned to take the half loaf if he couldn't get the whole.

Betsy met Jake at the depot in Coal Creek. She had Miss Steele harnessed to a wagon.

Jake rushed into her arms. They walked around the building. "I'm glad to be home, Betsy. I never want to leave you again."

He kissed her. Then he looked for his horse or her mule. He saw Miss Steele harnessed to the wagon. "Why the wagon?"

Betsy patted her stomach. "I've got to be more careful. I'm about four months along on having a baby."

Jake's bags slipped from his hand and his mouth dropped open. "When are you due?"

"The first of September." They rushed together again.

August 1893

When Betsy arrived at the depot in Coal Creek after a work day at Professor Brimer's office, Jake was there to meet her, as he had been every day during the summer. She was just a month from her delivery date, and Jake wasn't taking any chances. She wouldn't hear of ending her summer job early, but Jake assured her of a safe ride home in the wagon each day.

"Jake, Jake!" Betsy yelled as she stepped from the car to the platform. "Look. It's official. The University of Tennessee will take women, beginning with the fall term. Just six weeks away." She waved a copy of the Knoxville *Daily Journal* which she had opened to an inside page.

She handed it to her husband, and Jake read the advertisement.

University of Tennessee

Academic, Law and Teachers' Departments

Session opens September 14th. Entrance examinations September 11th. All who pass will receive State Scholarships with free tuition. **WOMEN,** 17 years of age, **ADMITTED TO ALL DEPARTMENTS** and privileges on same terms as men.

Expenses very moderate. Write for illustrated announcement.

PRESIDENT UNIVERSITY OF TENNESSEE
KNOXVILLE

Jake reached down and gently patted Betsy on her abdomen which was now greatly enlarged. "I don't believe you'll be able to attend this term. The baby's due about the first of the month."

"I'll make arrangements for that. Nothing's going to stop me now. Mr. Powell says I'll have my diploma by the middle of this month. They'll forward a copy to the university. And Professor Brimer's working with me on taking the entrance exam."

"What about the baby? What'll you do about the baby?"

"We'll make do. The Lord will provide. You have to have faith."

Grandma Dolan had followed Betsy's pregnancy very closely. She had already arranged with one of the midwives of Coal Creek to be present at the birth. Each day when Betsy arrived from Knoxville, Grandma Dolan would have her lie down. Then she would feel her forehead for her temperature and rub her hand along the contour of Betsy's abdomen as though she could feel the child inside.

"Lie down, Betsy," she said as soon as Betsy came through the door. "Let me check you out."

Betsy complied with the routine. Jake sat next to her and held her hand.

"Lawsy, child. You keep getting bigger and bigger. Are you sure it's the first of September that you're due and not the first of August?"

"Yes, Grandma. Another month. The university starts the middle of September. I figure two weeks after giving birth I should be pretty well recovered."

Grandma Dolan shook her head. "You don't need to be thinking about going to the university. This child is going to need you right here."

Dick Drummond reached back and felt of his pockets. He had a flask of whiskey in each—one for him and one for Colonel Anderson. Since arriving back in Coal Creek the first of November, he had only seen the colonel one time, and that had been last week in Coal Creek. Anderson had been very forgiving, considering the abduction incident. Anderson had invited Drummond up to the fort to see him anytime he wanted. "Bring some refreshment when you come," Anderson had told him.

Jake's brother walked through the gap and onto the little winding road that ascended Vowell Mountain. The humid August heat had him taking a white handkerchief from his pocket to wipe the sweat from his forehead. He looked at the fort, now just a hundred yards ahead, and waved the white cloth. There was no need for a jumpy soldier to shoot a miner.

"Halt. Who goes there?" the sentry barked.

"Dick Drummond to see Colonel Anderson."

"Wait there."

Drummond turned and viewed the town of Coal Creek through the gap in the ridge. No wonder the soldiers were able to beat back the attack of the miners last August. Their position was impenetrable.

He sat down on a rock and waited. Shortly, two soldiers approached. "Drummond, what're you doing here?" Lieutenant Perry Fyffe asked and spit at the miner's shoes.

Drummond stood. "I'm here to see Colonel Anderson, Lieutenant."

"He send for you?"

"Not exactly. He told me to come visit him sometime. And I'm here," Drummond said and held out his hands to his side.

Fyffe nodded to the other soldier. The private swung the butt of his rifle into Drummond's stomach. The breath rushed from Drummond, and he sank to his knees with his head thrusting forward into the dirt, unable to say a word. He rolled over, holding his stomach and trying to suck air back into his lungs.

Fyffe laughed. "Good work, Private Laugherty. This is one of those damn miners that captured Colonel Anderson last year. He ought to be shot."

Dick Drummond still lay in the dirt. He looked up into the faces of Fyffe and Laugherty. He would never forget the face of the private. He got to his knees just as Colonel Anderson approached.

"What's going on here, Lieutenant?"

"Drummond, sir. We caught him. He's one of the men who held you captive."

"I know, Fyffe. I was there. They didn't harm me. Leave him be. I told Drummond he could come up here. Now get back to your posts—both of you."

Drummond leaned against the rock. He reached back and took one of the flasks out of his pocket. He unscrewed the cap and took a swig and then handed it to Anderson. Anderson looked over his shoulder toward the fort, sat down beside Drummond, and turned the flask up. He swallowed and then coughed. "Durn good stuff. Homemade or bought?"

"Moonshine, Anderson. I've got another flask for you. You're going to have to tell your soldiers not to be so rough on me. I can barely breathe. I won't forget Lieutenant Fyffe or Private Laugherty."

"Ah, Drummond, those boys were just protecting their commanding officer," Anderson said and turned the flask up again. "They're harmless."

For the next three nights, Dick Drummond lay at the foot of Vowell Mountain where he could see any soldiers who left Fort Anderson. He cradled his Winchester rifle in his arms and waited for either Lieutenant Perry Fyffe or Private William Laugherty to leave the fort alone.

On Monday, August 7, he got his wish. He recognized Private Laugherty, who was with another soldier, sneaking off from the fort at dusk. Drummond lay quietly behind a tree as the two soldiers passed by. He took his Winchester and aimed at the back of the private's head. He pulled the hammer back and put his finger on the trigger. He turned his head and looked up at the fort. He was too close. He slipped the hammer back down and began to follow the soldiers.

They turned toward Briceville. Loud talk and laughter came from the two soldiers. They pointed their fingers and their rifles at miners' houses as they continued down the dusty road.

One would stop, pick up a rock, and throw it toward the creek. Dick Drummond kept a close eye on them while he skirted the road from the fringe of the woods.

An hour later it was completely dark. The two soldiers reached Briceville and turned into the yard of the house where an oil lamp with a red shade sat in a window. Dick Drummond hid behind a fence and watched as the door opened and the men were greeted by the women of the house. He smiled. He had been to the same house before himself. He knew the room to which they would be going. He left his Winchester propped against the gate and went to find a few other young miners.

Inside the house, Private Laugherty and his friend, Bill Irwin, hugged the first two young women who came out to greet them. The madam of the house, Mrs. Parager, looked the soldiers over. "You two boys are getting to be regulars. Do you like what you see here?"

Irwin spoke up. "Yes, ma'am. It sure is lonely up on the hill. Laugherty and I had to do some sneaking to get out tonight."

"Well, we're glad to have you back. Soldiers' money spends just as good as miners'. Remember we don't take scrip," Mrs. Parager said and let out a roar of laughter. "You pays before you takes the girls to the room. Understand?"

The soldiers nodded their acknowledgement. One of the girls brought out a bottle of liquor. They all sat and passed the bottle around. "You've got to pay for the liquor too," Mrs. Parager said and held out her hand.

Laugherty reached into his pocket and tossed her a silver dollar. "That should hold you for a while."

When the first bottle was empty, and the second, the soldiers went into separate rooms with the girls of their choice. Mrs. Parager retired to the kitchen with another bottle. She laid out the silver dollars on the table and counted them.

An hour later, Mrs. Parager was startled from her slumber at the table by the sound of a pounding on the metal roof of the house. The sound continued and became even louder. "It's a hail storm," she said and ran to the window. The sky was clear. The beating on the roof persisted. She looked out and saw pieces of rock sliding off the house. "The mountains are tumbling down!" she screamed and ran to one of the rooms where the soldiers were. "Get out, get out," she yelled.

Both soldiers appeared about the same time from their respective rooms. They dressed hurriedly, pulling up their pants and buttoning their shirts while they tried to get their feet into their boots. "What's happening?" Irwin asked. "What's all the noise?"

"The mountain's falling or the sky's falling," Mrs. Parager said. "I saw pieces of it coming off the roof."

Laugherty stepped to a window and pulled back the curtain. "Hell, there's men across the road throwing rocks at the house," he said and reached for his rifle.

Before he could position his rifle, firing began from outside. A bullet came through the window Laugherty had just looked out and thudded into the opposite wall.

"Put out the lamps!" Irwin yelled and doused the one nearest him. "Stay on the floor," he told the woman and girls.

Glass shattered and rained down on them from the same window. All the lamps were out except the one with the red shade in the far window. Laugherty crawled toward it accompanied by the crackle of rifles. The soldiers had not yet been able to return fire.

Bill Irwin crawled toward the first window. Laugherty squirmed on his belly to the area beneath the lamp and reached up. It was just a bit out of his grasp. He raised up, grabbed the lamp, and snuffed it out. He toppled over just as he blew the flame from the wick.

"Laugherty, Laugherty, you all right?" Irwin asked when he saw his friend fall over. No reply. Irwin crawled toward his friend amid the constant firing. The lamp had lodged beneath Laugherty. Irwin turned him over. Again, no response. In the darkness he could see nothing, but he felt a warm liquid flowing from Laugherty's head. He hoped it was the coal oil from the lamp. He brought his hand up and smelled the fluid.

"Laugherty's shot!" he yelled to the women. Irwin scrambled to the back door, scooted out, and rolled to the creek beyond.

When he reached the bank on the far side, he ran.

An honor guard accompanied the body of Private William Laugherty to Knoxville the next day in a special car of the regular train. A floral arrangement made up to look like the United States flag was readied in Knoxville.

In Colonel Anderson's tent, Lieutenant Fyffe stormed about and cursed. One of his men had been "assassinated" and he would have his vengeance. Anderson was equally concerned but cautioned his men to let the civil authorities handle it.

"Colonel, a local jury's not going to convict a miner for killing a soldier. We'll get no justice in Anderson County," Fyffe said. "We should round up all the suspects and put the culprit before a firing squad or hang him."

"What were the men doing down there in the first place?" Anderson asked. "There's orders not to go out alone. They were away without leave. You're asking for trouble if you go into the miners' towns without a company of soldiers or a . . ."

"An escort, sir? Like you have with Dick Drummond?"

Colonel Anderson's face reddened. He stood up and pointed to Fyffe. "That's enough of that, Lieutenant. Calm down and let the civil authorities do their work."

"I bet Dick Drummond is involved in this, Colonel. You remember Laugherty was the one who hit Drummond with his rifle."

"Yes, and you're the one who put him up to it, Lieutenant!"

Fyffe turned and walked quickly from the tent.

The next day while Colonel Anderson was away for the funeral of Laugherty in Knoxville, Fyffe gathered a group of younger soldiers around him.

"I'll be the officer on duty tonight. Some of you may want to go into Briceville. Dick Drummond is boarding at the house of a Mr. Landrum. Drummond is the one I believe is responsible for the death of Private Laugherty.

"I want him. Alive or dead. There can be extra leave time

for you if you're successful. Remember, if anybody ever asks you, this is not an order and . . . nobody ever left the fort tonight," Fyffe said and winked at the soldiers.

An hour before midnight Colonel Anderson retired to his bed and did not see the twenty soldiers walk down the mountain and take the road to Briceville. Lieutenant Fyffe watched until they disappeared along the dark road.

In Briceville W. R. Landrum talked with his wife and boarders, Dick Drummond and Robert Peek, until nearly eleven. Then the boarders went to their rooms on the second floor and the Landrums retired to their bedroom.

Only the sound of the gurgling creek and the raspy music of crickets came through the Landrums' open window until an hour past midnight.

Then a voice rang out. "Surround the house!" Landrum sat up and looked out the window. In the pale moonlight, he saw men in uniforms crouching and moving about in his yard with bayonets affixed to their rifles.

Then someone began to beat on the front door. Landrum's wife awoke and asked her husband what was happening. "I don't know. There's men outside. Looks like the militia."

The banging at the door became louder, and there were shouts. "Open up! Open up! Or we'll break the door down!"

Landrum looked at his wife and then made his way to the door. He answered through the closed door, "What do you want?"

"Drummond!" came the answer. "Open up or we'll burn your house down."

Robert Peek joined Landrum at the door. "Who is it? What do they want?"

Landrum looked toward the stairway. "They say they want Drummond . . . soldiers I believe."

Upstairs Dick Drummond heard the commotion and reached for his Winchester. He dressed in an instant and looked out from the second story window. Soldiers had the house surrounded.

There was no escape. He slipped down the back stairway and into the kitchen. He pushed a table against the door leading to the front and propped a chair against the back door. He lay down in the floor. His hands were wet and his heart pounded in his chest. They would not take him alive. He would get as many of them as he could.

The soldiers rushed in past Landrum and Peek. "Where's Drummond?" they asked.

Landrum pointed to the stairway. "Why do you want Drummond? What are you going to do with him?"

The soldiers didn't answer but rushed up the stairway. One kicked the door open. Five rushed in with their rifles leveled. They overturned the bed and kicked a wardrobe onto its side. They came back out. "Nobody's up here."

One soldier pointed to the door leading to the kitchen. He leaned into it. It wouldn't open. "You in there, Drummond?"

Dick Drummond looked up from the floor to the crack of light coming around the door. "Yeah! Who wants to know? I'll get at least one of you if you come through that door."

"Come out, Drummond. We're just here to arrest you. We'll take you back up to the fort."

"Arrest me for what? I haven't done anything."

"If you haven't, you have nothing to worry about."

"What if I don't come out?"

"We'll come in shooting. You'll be dead, and these innocent folks might get hurt. You don't want that, do you?"

Drummond rolled over and scooted to the back door. He raised up and looked out. More soldiers were there. He looked back toward the hallway and the light. "Is Colonel Anderson at the fort?"

"Yes."

"You'll take me to Colonel Anderson?"

"Sure. That's right."

Dick Drummond sat up. A shoot-out meant certain death. Colonel Anderson would get him out of this jam. He laid the

Winchester down. "I'm coming. My hands are up. Don't hurt the Landrums."

He walked into the hallway. Two soldiers grabbed him and tied his hands behind his back. Another one rammed the stock of his rifle into Drummond's stomach. He fell over but they caught him before he hit the floor. He looked up into the face of the one who had hit him with the rifle. He would remember the face the rest of his life.

The soldier dragged him out and away from the Landrum house. The Landrums sat up the remainder of the night. They would go to the fort in the morning and complain to Colonel Anderson about the way the soldiers arrested Dick Drummond.

At daybreak, Landrum's son ran up the creek toward the fort to see if he could find any trace of the soldiers still around. He returned in less than a half hour.

"Pa, Pa! They hung Dick Drummond. Down by the creek."

Landrum followed behind his son as fast as he could run. Just over three hundred yards from his house, the train track crossed over the creek. From the trestle, the body of Dick Drummond swayed gently in the morning breeze, his feet barely touching the water.

Death and Birth

The sun had not fully ascended over the eastern ridges when the horseman rode through Coal Creek and on to the lane where the Boyd home was with the news of Dick Drummond's death. To every house where he knew a miner lived, he galloped, stopped briefly to yell the news to those who were just having breakfast, and then was off again on down the road.

Only Grandma Dolan sat on the porch at the Boyds when the rider turned into the yard. Will, Daniel, Sally, Ollie, and even the children were at the barn or in the fields already. The newsbearer came as close to the porch as he could but didn't dismount. Grandma Dolan cupped her hand to her ear as he shouted the news.

"The soldiers hung Drummond!"

"What's that?" she asked.

"The soldiers done hung Drummond."

"Who? Drummond?"

"Drummond. The miner." He reined his horse around and galloped away.

Grandma Dolan rose from her chair, stumbled, and grabbed at her head before falling. Slowly, she struggled to her knees and crawled through the doorway. She reached her chair in front of the fireplace and pulled herself up. She took her poker and weakly jabbed at the smoldering wood.

"Betsy . . . Betsy . . . what will Betsy do without Jake?" she asked softly before her head drooped over.

After Betsy heard the news of Dick Drummond's death,

she walked as fast as her condition would allow to Jake's mother's house. Jake was in Knoxville on legislative and mine business. Betsy had to telegraph him as soon as she could, but Jake's mother needed someone first.

"Yes, I know," his mother said. "They've killed Dick." She sat rocking in a chair on the porch of the house. There were no tears. Her eyes barely blinked, and her face was drawn and white.

For a half hour Betsy sat next to her and just held her hand. She knew of no words that would bring real comfort to a mother who had just lost a son to what had been described already around Coal Creek as a "mob of soldiers."

"Betsy, you should to go on and find Jake. He'll need to be here."

Betsy walked to the depot. Already a crowd of angry miners was gathering and pointing toward the ridge where Fort Anderson's white tents still sparkled in the morning sunlight. She pushed her way through to the office where the telegraph was. How do you tell your husband that his brother has been killed? And in a telegram?

She just went ahead and said it.

Come home. Your brother is dead. I am with your mother.

She waited for a while to see if there would be a reply. Would they be able to find him and give him the dreadful message? An answer came.

Will come at once. Train not available. Will ride bicycle. Stay at mother's.

Betsy turned and walked back through the ever increasing crowd. A shot rang out. She fell to the platform. A hand helped her up. Someone was just shooting into the air. She walked slowly back down the lane.

When Jake received word of his brother's death, there was no scheduled train back to Coal Creek from Knoxville until evening. He had only ridden a bicycle a half dozen times in his life, but he borrowed one and followed the railroad track out of Knoxville toward Clinton. He would ride, then walk, then ride some more. Push, coast, and pedal onward. At the Clinch River, he had to cross on the railroad trestle. He put his ear to the rail, listened, and then ran across carrying the bicycle.

Betsy's mother discovered Grandma Dolan's lifeless body in the chair when she came in from the barn to begin preparing dinner for the family. Grandma Dolan often fell asleep in the same chair and her appearance was no different than that. But when Sally Boyd tried to rouse her mother, Grandma Dolan's body toppled over onto the floor.

Before the children came in, Will and Daniel carried the frail remains to a bed and closed the door.

"Who'll go tell Betsy?" Sally asked. "She was an old woman, but no one was expecting this." When no one volunteered, Sally said she would go. "Daniel, hitch up the wagon. I can ride with you to Betsy's, and you can go on to the undertaker's and make the arrangements."

At Jake's mother's house, Betsy began cooking dinner. Family and friends would soon come, and there had to be food.

When the wagon bearing Daniel and Sally Boyd reached the Drummond house, Sally looked over and waved at Jake's mother on the porch but drew no response. "That's strange. She acted like she didn't see me."

Daniel and Sally found no one at home at Betsy's and returned to Jake's mother's. "I'll stay here and see if she knows where Betsy is. You go on to town," Sally told her husband.

From the kitchen, Betsy looked out and saw the wagon. Her mother was walking toward the house, and her father was riding toward Coal Creek. She smiled. They were coming to add their words of comfort for Jake's mother. She finished peeling the last potato and dropped it into the pot.

"Thank you for coming, Sally," Jake's mother said.

"What?"

"I appreciate friends in time of mourning."

Sally Boyd stared at Jake's mother. What was she talking about?

Betsy walked onto the porch. "Mother, thank you for coming by. Mrs. Drummond appreciates it. Jake's on his way from Knoxville. It's bad to get news of your brother's death by telegram."

Sally's mouth dropped open. "Brother's death? Who died?"

"You don't know?" Betsy asked. "The soldiers hung Dick last night. A miner on horseback rode up and down the lane telling everybody. Where were you when he rode by?"

"I don't know, Betsy. I don't know. At the barn I guess." Sally Boyd sat down and dabbed her eyes with a handkerchief. She looked at Betsy. "Sit down. There's more."

Betsy grabbed at her abdomen when she heard the dark news. "I wish I had been there at her last moments. She was eighty-seven, but she so wanted to see this baby born. Just two more weeks and she could have seen her great-grandchild. I've got to go inside and lie down."

Jake rode for five hours between Knoxville and Coal Creek. Sweat from the exhausting ride soaked his clothes. He looked at the crowd of miners at the depot and began to ask about his brother. What happened? Where? Why? They thought Dick had shot Private Laugherty?

They closed in around him. "We're ready to go, Jake. Let's go to the fort and pull those lynchers out and give them a taste of their own medicine," someone said, and there were shouts of agreement.

Jake leaned against the wall of the depot and struggled to

remain standing. He began to speak in low tones to those around him and, as he did, the other miners pressed closer to hear. Quiet enveloped them. What would the brother of the slain miner say? When would they attack?

"I just want to go to my mother's and find my wife. My brother's dead. Nothing we do will bring him back. I have to see that he's properly buried. If the soldiers did this, they need to pay for it . . . ." Voices joined in shouts of revenge. "But they need to pay legally. We have to be a people of laws and not of mob rule. It works both ways. Give me time. Let me bury Dick. Let me talk with the governor. No shooting, please. Go to your homes. No one else need give his life."

Jake slumped over and slid onto the floor of the platform. They revived him with a wet cloth and loaded him into a wagon. Two miners drove him toward his mother's, and the crowd began to disperse. If Dick Drummond's brother could wait for the law to take its course, the other miners could too. "Give the representative time to talk with the governor," someone said as the depot area returned to normal.

Betsy was determined to go and say her farewell to Grandma Dolan before the body was taken to the undertaker's. Jake tried to dissuade her.

He sat beside her on the bed. "Betsy, you're in no condition to go down there. Wait until tomorrow. You've had too much stress for today."

"Just hitch Miss Steele to the wagon. I've got to go."

In the bedroom where Grandma Dolan's body lay as though only asleep, Betsy leaned over and stroked the silvery hair and spoke into ears that no longer could hear her voice. "I loved you, Grandma. I always loved you." Then she sat beside her grandmother for one last visit and talked.

A half hour later she stepped from the bedroom half bent over. "It's time! It's time! The baby's coming!" she shouted to

Jake.

Aunt Ollie gathered Betsy into the other room that had a large bed. "Jake go get the midwife—Mrs. McGhee. Bring Sally back too. Hurry now!"

Jake knew exactly where the midwife lived—Betsy had pointed out the house everytime they had passed through Coal Creek for the last four months. He snapped the reins over the back of Miss Steele and got her into a trot toward town.

In a half hour he was back with the midwife and Betsy's mother.

"You men just wait in the kitchen. Keep the children quiet. The women will take care of the birthing," Mrs. McGhee told Jake, Daniel, and Will. "Just bring us some clean towels and sheets. This may take some time. It's her first."

Every few minutes, Jake asked Will to check his watch. He paced about the kitchen while the two older men played cards. He walked to the barn and checked on Miss Steele. He came back. Still there was no birth. "How long's it been?" Jake asked Will.

"Just an hour, boy. Settle down."

Jake walked to the porch, back to the kitchen, and then sat down at the table. "How long does this take?"

Daniel looked up from his cards. "There's three things you can't hurry up: A man making whiskey, a woman birthing a child, and a sow feeding its young. The baby will get here when it's supposed to."

Jake looked up. "It wasn't supposed to for two more weeks. Something may be wrong."

"It's in the Lord's hands," Will Boyd said.

"And the midwife's," Daniel added.

An hour passed and then another. Sally came out and drew some cool water. She shook her head when she was asked if the baby was there yet.

The sun set with the shadows of the mountains creeping over the valley and closing it in darkness. Ollie came from the room to retrieve more lamps.

"What's happening?" Jake asked.

"It's just taking a while. You men are going to have to get

your own supper. It may be morning before this baby decides to be born."

An hour later Jake heard Betsy cry out. "Why is she hollering?" he asked Daniel.

"Having a baby ain't easy," Daniel said and laid down his hand of cards. "Let's see if there's anything we can fix to eat."

"I'm not hungry," Jake said.

Jake walked out and sat on the porch. He bowed his head. "Oh, Lord, I know you may not know the sound of my voice as I haven't spoken to you in a while. But I have one thing to ask. Please don't let nothing happen to my Betsy and give us a healthy baby—if it be Your will. Amen."

He looked up the road to where he knew his mother must be sitting alone or with the body of his brother. He would go, but his place now was here. A horse and wagon with a lantern appeared around the bend. The undertaker coming for Grandma Dolan. He would get no more business from this house.

Then there was a cry—different from Betsy's—from a young throat. Jake rushed back inside but the door to the room remained closed.

"I heard it!" Jake shouted to Betsy's father. "The baby's here. Why won't they open up?"

By now the undertaker was to the door and knocking. Daniel and Will showed him to the room where Grandma Dolan lay.

Betsy's door opened. The midwife motioned for Jake to come near. She finally smiled. "You have a healthy daughter. A little small, but I believe she's going to be all right. She certainly has healthy lungs."

The undertaker and his assistant carried the body of Grandma Dolan out on a canvas stretcher. Just as they reached the door with their load, the infant cried out again.

Jake smiled. "How is Betsy?"

"She's fine. It'll take a while for—"

"Mrs. McGhee, hurry here!" Sally yelled, "She's having another one." In less than an hour this time, the other twin was born—a boy.

When he was finally allowed in, Jake held Betsy's hand. She was asleep—exhausted. The women watched. One baby lay on one side of Betsy and one on the other.

"We should have known there were twins," Sally said. "I had twins. My Aunt Ella had twins. Betsy was so big. We should have known."

By dawn Betsy stirred from her sleep. Jake was beside her. The women were in the kitchen.

"Twins," she said softly and looked at each child. "A boy and a girl, right?" she asked. Jake nodded.

"I want to name the girl for Grandma Dolan. Is that all right?"

Again he nodded. "And for you, Betsy."

Betsy thought. "Well, how about Elizabeth Dolan Drummond. We could call her Dolly."

"And the boy?"

"For you, Jake. Jacob Drummond Jr."

"No, Betsy. How about . . . Richard Jacob Drummond—for my brother too?"

Betsy nodded her approval. "And we'll call him . . .?"

"Richard." Jake leaned over and kissed Betsy on her forehead.

Jake placed pillows behind Betsy's back so she could sit up and handed both babes to her.

Betsy looked at them and smiled. Softly she began, *"William-a-William a Trimbletoes, he's a good fisherman . . . ."*

Autumn Peace

The steps to the governor's office on the first floor of the Capitol seemed steeper and more numerous to Jake when he climbed them a week after his children's birth. He found it difficult to focus all his energies on his appointment with Governor Turney when Betsy was still recovering in Coal Creek. At least the governor was true to his word in granting him an audience.

Governor Turney moved around his desk and held out his hand to Jake. "Representative Drummond. Please accept my regrets on the death of your brother."

Jake nodded. "Yes, sir. Thank you."

"And my congratulations on your becoming a father . . . of twins—is that right?"

"Yes, sir. They're doing fine."

The governor took Jake to a chair near a window overlooking a growing Nashville. They both sat and exchanged pleasantries for a few minutes.

Jake glanced at the clock standing against a far wall and thought of his family. He needed to be home.

"Governor, it's about the soldiers—"

"We'll prosecute the ones responsible for your brother's death, Jake, if we can identify them . . . and if proof shows they were involved."

"Thank you, sir. But I'm more concerned about the future than I am the past. If Fort Anderson and its soldiers remain there looking down on Coal Creek, there's going to be more trouble."

"What do you suggest?"

"Sir, as soon as possible, they need to be removed. And I will guarantee—"

"The safety of the stockade and convicts?"

"Yes, sir."

The governor stood and walked to another window. "I've been thinking, Jake, about what you said when I signed that bill. You pointed out this window and asked how I would feel with soldiers camped on the Capitol grounds or at my farm in Winchester. Now, I see that you were right. The soldiers need to be removed. I should have done it before. It could have saved the lives of Laugherty and your brother.

"I am working on a proclamation which I will issue tomorrow. And I will come to Coal Creek before the end of the month to announce that the soldiers will be removed—no later than the first week of September. I'm sorry your brother had to die."

Jake stood and stepped toward the governor. He reached out to shake his hand, then stepped closer and embraced him.

"Thank you, sir. You won't regret it. My brother . . . my brother may have died for a purpose. Some accomplish more in their dying than they do in their living."

Late the next evening when Jake arrived at the depot at Coal Creek, tired from his trip, he looked out the window of his coach and saw a crowd with several people waving copies of newspapers in the air. As soon as he stepped down, he was surrounded by miners, miners' wives, and children.

"You did it, Jake. The governor said they're going," someone shouted and shoved a Knoxville *Daily Journal* into his hands. He read the full proclamation of the governor and his eyes latched onto the words for which he was looking.

It is my purpose, as soon as the necessary arrangements which are in progress can be perfected, to remove the soldiers from the mining prison camps. I think this can be done at an early date.

Jake pushed through the crowd, waving to acknowledge the cheers and congratulations of the people. Betsy had to know. It was over—at least the soldiers would be gone.

Governor Peter Turney came to Coal Creek on Wednesday, August 30, and spoke to miners and citizens at the depot from the rear of the train.

"The troops will be gone within ten days. I trust that they will never have to be sent here again. I have the assurance of the good miners of this area that all will be peaceful. I, like you, anticipate the day when the convicts will no longer compete with the working men of this valley and you shall be able to toil with the assurance that the labor of your body will be rewarded and you may reside in this serene valley with your families in tranquility."

Jake stood nearby on the platform and thought of all that had occurred during the past two and a half years. Lives lost. Property destroyed. And then the coming together of the miners for peace. His brother dying, his children born. He looked up to the point that they now called *Militia Hill* with the white tents still flapping, but now they were more like the flags of surrender.

Betsy, with her twins, and the entire Boyd family joined Jake and all of Coal Creek and Briceville at the depot on Thursday, September 7, to view in silence the loading and leaving of the remaining militia. Eight cars carried the troops and two boxcars contained their tents and armaments when the engineer sounded the whistle and the locomotive's wheels finally caught the track. The train slowly moved out of the valley of the miners and toward Clinton. There the militia would camp until the civil authorities considered the cases against the fifteen soldiers charged with the hanging of Dick Drummond.

Colonel Keller Anderson came to the rear of the caboose and silently saluted the people of Coal Creek. His gesture was not returned.

Professor Brimer stood behind the table and watched as the registrar took the information from Betsy Drummond. He turned to Jim Powell and shook his hand. "She did it, Jim, and you helped. Our Betsy is the first woman to register on a full and equal basis with men at the University of Tennessee."

"Robert, you were the one with the idea. But Betsy made it happen." They both looked back at Betsy and smiled.

Betsy was not alone. Thirty other women began classes on September 14, 1893, at the University of Tennessee in Knoxville. All the women had exceeded the average score of men on the entrance exam—and Betsy Drummond was highest among the women. They came from all over East Tennessee and beyond to attend the university. The school president, in his opening remarks, spoke on the "Mission of the Educated Woman."

When the speechmaking and registration were through, Jake and Betsy followed Professor Brimer and Jim Powell back to the science building and down into the professor's office. On his desk sat a cake and a bowl of punch.

And in the corner where Betsy had typed for the past three summers, the machine had been removed to another place, and there instead sat twin cradles holding month-old Dolly and Richard.

The women in the building volunteered to watch the babies during the time Betsy was in class. The walls had been repainted to a soothing yellow, and from the ceiling Professor Brimer had hung cut-out wood figures of birds on string for the children to watch.

Betsy took a Bible and opened to a passage in Ecclesiastes. Everyone looked toward Betsy. "This is a time for celebration but also for remembrance." She read aloud:

To every thing there is a season, and a time to every purpose under heaven: a time to be born, and a time to die; . . . a time to kill, and a time to heal; . . . a time to weep, and a time to laugh; . . . a time to love, and a time to hate; a time of war, and a time of peace.

Epilogue

Later in 1893, all the soldiers charged with hanging Dick Drummond were acquitted by a court in Anderson County. The militia left, never to return. Of the miners, only D. B. Monroe, a native of Ohio, served any prison time—just over a year.

In 1896, the convicts were taken from Coal Creek to either the new prison at Nashville or to a prison stockade on state-owned coal land in Morgan County which later became Brushy Mountain State Penitentiary. Convict labor in competition with free men came to an end some twenty to thirty years earlier in Tennessee than in other Southern states because of the efforts of the miners at Coal Creek, Briceville, Inman, and Tracy City.

Gene Merrill, the early leader of the miners, fled the area during the military crackdown and was never arrested. He later returned, continued his labor organizing, and opened a photograph enlarging shop in Knoxville.

George Ford, who zealously chronicled the mining troubles for Governor Buchanan as his Secretary of Labor, relocated to Knoxville where he founded the Knoxville *Independent* on Labor Day, 1894, and remained active in progressive labor matters until his death in 1945 at the age of ninety.

Governor John Price Buchanan retired to his farm in Murfreesboro where he died on May 11, 1930, at the age of eighty-two. At the time of his death, he was the last surviving Confederate soldier to have served as governor.

Betsy Drummond graduated among the top ten in her class in 1897 and returned to Coal Creek as principal of the school. In 1898 and 1899 she gave birth to two more sons and took time off to be with them.

Jake Drummond did not run for reelection to the legislature but returned to the mines, to the job he loved. He, Betsy's father,

Daniel, and 182 other miners were killed in the Fratersville Mine explosion in 1902. He lived long enough to leave Betsy a note. "I love you. Take care of the children. Tell them not to be miners." He was buried near Betsy's grandmother in the community cemetery.

Betsy Drummond moved to Knoxville where she became a principal of one of the high schools. In 1905, she married Professor Robert Brimer. They had one child.

In 1910, Betsy Brimer was promoted into school administration in the Knoxville system, and she also returned to the University of Tennessee for an advanced degree. She was the first woman in her neighborhood to register to vote after women's suffrage was passed in 1920.

Betsy continued to climb the ladder in her profession until she was assistant superintendent of schools, where she stayed until her retirement. Robert Brimer died in 1947.

On July 14, 1966, Betsy Boyd Drummond Brimer died at her little home in Knoxville at the age of ninety-two. It was the seventy-fifth anniversary of the first storming of the stockades by the miners in Briceville and Coal Creek. It was her last wish to be taken back to Coal Creek (now Lake City) to be buried between Grandma Dolan and Jake Drummond.

In removing Betsy's personal items from her house, her granddaughter went to the mantel and gazed at an odd assortment of keepsakes—Betsy's first brass school bell with the wood handle, a few brass tokens encircled by a red kerchief, and a small hand-carved wooden mule.

Today, the brilliant white Chumbley house is only a memory. The openings to the Knoxville Iron Company mine are overgrown with vines. But on Militia Hill, less than three miles from busy Interstate 75, a person can walk and still see the earthen embankments of Fort Anderson, and when the breeze is just right, smell the acrid aroma of burnt gunpowder from the Coal Creek War.

Acknowledgments

First and foremost, I greatly appreciate the efforts of my fine editor, Gaynell Seale, in making this a much better and more readable book than it would have been without her. Once again her masterful touch is evident throughout.

In a time where a book is sometimes judged by its cover, I thank Usha Rao for creating an artistic cover which captures the essence of the book. I'm deeply grateful for having her talent displayed.

To my wife, Sara, I say thanks for taking the time to read the manuscript and comment on it.

John Rice Irwin, founder and director of the Museum of Appalachia at Norris, encouraged me when I first wrote some newspaper articles about the Coal Creek War a few years ago. He has invited me to the Homecoming at the Museum each October to sign copies of the book.

Although this is a fiction-enhanced story of real events, I have tried to be as accurate with the actual happenings of the Coal Creek War as possible. Eugene Merrill, George Ford, Governor John Buchanan, Governor Peter Turney, D. B. Monroe, George Irish, Dick Drummond, Johnny Walthall, Colonel Granville Sevier, Colonel Keller Anderson, General S. T. Carnes, John Chumbley, Henry Gibson, Rufus Rutherford, E. P. Wade, Adjutant General H. H. Norman, John Goodwin, B. A. Jenkins, Bud Lindsay, and others mentioned in this story were actual people. The dates and times of the events are as accurate as I could place them from actual documents of that time. The letters and telegrams between the governor and his officials were taken word for word from papers in the archives of the state library. Speeches were quoted from newspaper accounts.

There should be a monument somewhere to George W. Ford for preserving his account of the happenings of 1891-92 in his reports to the governor. I also drew on the reports of the adjutant general to the governor for the viewpoint of the military.

The photos in the book are from *Harper's Weekly* or from a souvenir booklet that Company C from Nashville had printed with photos made by W. E. Singleton of Knoxville.

Others whose writings or help I have used in researching material for the book include: Pete Daniel, James Dombrowski, Andrew C. Hutson Jr., Marshall McGhee, R. Clifford Seeber, Snyder Roberts, Archie Green, Charles "Boomer" Winfrey, and Fred Wyatt.

Publications read and borrowed from include: the Knoxville *Sentinel*, the Knoxville *Daily Journal*, *Harper's Weekly*, *Tennessee Historical Quarterly*, the *United Mine Workers' Journal*, the *East Tennessee Historical Society's Publications*, reports of the adjutant general in Governor Buchanan's papers at the State Library and Archives, and the report of George Ford to the governor.

State records reflect that over a hundred convicts died while in confinement at the Knoxville Iron Company mine at Coal Creek. Most of them were buried there in graves still unmarked to this day.

Many thanks also to the unnamed newspaper reporters who descended upon Coal Creek in 1891-92 and wrote the stories about this unusual event in American and Tennessee history.

In this book, I sought to tell the story of those times so that we might know and remember the struggles that they went through to insure the present generation a more peaceful and safer work environment and society. It is now our job to bear the torch in this generation.